Coping With Yarn

Also by Jean Shelby

Welcome to Garden Valley

Winter in July (FREE to my email subscribers)

Coming soon!

From A to Z (to be released January, 2025)

Coping With Yarn

Garden Valley Series

BY JEAN SHELBY

JEAN BOOKS, LLC

This book is dedicated to the person who inspired it, Lisa. May you continue to bring a sparkle of light to every room you enter. I can't wait to see how far your YouTube channel goes. Keep crocheting your amazing masterpieces!

Chapter 1 Lisa

Wanna Be YouTuber

"Hi, I'm Lisa with Coping With Yarn, and today I'm going to slow crochet you… what? Darn it." I push the stop button, delete the video, and start again. "Hi, I'm Lisa from the channel Coping With Yarn, and I'm Lisa… ugh! Okay, time to take five."

It's my fifth introduction that I've thrown in the digital trash can. Chuggers, my pudgy pug, snores softly on my lap, completely unbothered by my mouth fumbles. I give him a scratch behind the ears. "Why am I nervous when it's just you and me in here?" I glance around the guest room, packed to the brim with yarn in every color and texture imaginable. This is supposed to be my happy place, where I share my crochet projects with the world. Yet today, I'm tripping over words like I'm walking in high heels for the first time.

With just a dozen videos uploaded, I'm still finding my footing in this YouTube world. It's funny how a fun hobby can quickly turn into an adrenaline sport when a camera's involved. Still, I've come a long way from those shaky, cringeworthy, out-of-focus videos. At least now it doesn't take me two weeks to upload a video.

"Remember when I couldn't bring myself to push record?" I say aloud, trying to hype myself up. My phone is propped on a wobbly stack of books on an old TV tray. One day, I'll have a real camera and maybe even a ring light. There's always room to grow. For now, it's just me, my phone, and top-notch determination to share something meaningful. The dream of reaching more people and making an impact keeps me going.

I'm far from making any money, but at least I'm not just talking to my friends about this stuff anymore. I even have a few loyal fans who regularly comment. Seeing my subscriber count inch up bit by bit is thrilling, even if I'm lightyears away from the four thousand watch hours and one thousand subscribers needed for YouTube monetization. I'm here for the joy of creating and the tiny moments of connection.

My channel might bounce between different topics, but the core is about offering mental health tips. I lighten the topic by sprinkling in my obsession: crocheting a cozy blanket, a cute pillow, or an adorable animal.

The idea is simple: finding something to ease our mental struggles. It's the perfect complement to a hobby that became my passion twenty-five years ago when I was just ten. I've made hundreds of critters, and my fingers are nowhere near tired of weaving the soft texture of colorful yarn. Good thing, too, because I'm practically swimming in skeins!

"I think I could fill a pool with all these," I say. This hobby is the perfect way for me to cope with life's pressures. I know firsthand how it can clear a cluttered mind. When I start feeling frazzled, I know that if I don't slow down, depression is bound to follow. That's when I let my fingers work their magic, weaving my worries into a colorful masterpiece.

I swish my black mop of hair away with irritation. "Darn, these curls." I'd have the ease of a pixy cut if it was up to me, but my husband Patrick would leave me. Well, not really, but isn't that what people say? In all honesty, my thick hair would puff up like a poodle's if I chopped it.

It has become my morning routine to shut myself in the guest room. My silly antics are kept secret behind this door, well, until I click the upload button. It's not like I have a ton of options where I can film. While we're comfortable in our dainty fifteen hundred square feet, my mother dramatically disapproves. Ours could fit five times in her monstrous house.

"It's not about her right now," I scold for bringing her up. "Okay, time to get it together." I play around with the height of my phone, adding another thick book under the two already on the TV tray. With my first videos, I learned the hard way that the view from down below the chin is less than flattering. "I don't need to put a spotlight on this," I say, flicking the waddle of skin under my chin.

While I'm setting up, a text message from my mother pops on the screen. It's another link to an exercise video with a 'helpful' statement.

I just did this workout. Maybe you can, too!

"Subtle, mom," I grumble. Her messages remind me about how I will never rise to her impossibly high standards. If she knew I was posting videos about mental health and crocheting, she'd have a conniption! My dad and my sister are what they call 'real doctors' and do general surgery. My mom is the office manager of their operation, pun intended since they are super successful. It puts my dinky job at the clinic to shame. The kind of content I create on YouTube is unheard of in their world.

But these videos help people—and they help me too. Sharing my passion for crochet and sprinkling in a bit of advice is my way of spreading some joy in the world.

My time is dwindling, and I only have an hour before I need drop Adrienne off at school and get to work. "Let's do this!" I rotate my topics between crochet lessons, mental health advice, or a video about me. Today is a video with some simple tips. "Okay, let's try this again. Record."

I tap the record button and pause for a few beats before speaking. After a deep breath, I try again.

"Hey, everyone, it's Lisa with Coping With Yarn, and today I want to talk about tackling that pesky to-do list that seems to multiply like rabbits instead of shrinking." I hold up my latest project—a soft, pink crocheted pig. "I'm working on this little guy today. Probably destined to join the pile of critters in my closet, but hey, I'm hooked!" I giggle. At least my corny jokes make me laugh. "I'll link the pattern I'm using down below. It's a pretty simple one."

"The topic for today's video was inspired by a little meltdown I had earlier this week." I keep my voice upbeat, even as I share a glimpse into my own struggles. "Yes, I have a degree in mental health, but that doesn't mean I'm not a little crazy myself!" I laugh again, pausing to show the yarn twisting around my fingers. "I get to diagnose myself with all sorts of things. Wouldn't life be boring if we had nothing to work on?"

I think of my mother, who would totally agree that I need to work on myself but has a set of goals for me that are the opposite of my own. I shake my head slightly to throw this thought aside.

"Anyway, I was fretting about getting everything done in the day. I'm sure many of you can relate. My plate is full between working, taking my daughter to all her extracurricular activities, grocery shopping, making dinner, cleaning my house… you name it, it was on the list! I was at work when my mind started stewing more than tonight's dinner. Everything became overwhelming. I took a break, went to my car, picked up my yarn and hook, and only focused on the project for a few minutes."

I pause for about twenty seconds, holding my project off Chuggers, who's now snuggled deep on my lap, his favorite spot when I'm crocheting. Hopefully, my viewers will feel this activity's relaxing benefits as the yarn gathers into more lines that round out my piggy. "I like to think I'm weaving through my struggles just as my hands are weaving through this yarn. You can do this with anything that relaxes you: walking, playing the piano, coloring. I don't suggest watching TV. This switches us to zombie mode, and we ignore our problems too much."

I chuckle yet again. I can't help it; my silly jokes tickle my funny bone.

"After a few minutes of relaxing into my project, I thought about the list nagging at me like a mama hen fretting about her nest. I put a spin on it and instead thought: 'There isn't anything on my list that is different than any other day.' And instead of fretting about getting everything done A.S.A.P, I put a spin on it."

"You can only do one thing at a time, and that's okay. That's how we're designed. Most people brag about multitasking, but sometimes it's too much for our brains. Focus on task number one, see it through, praise yourself for doing your best, and then move to the next if you have the time and energy."

I wrap up with a few more tips on handling stress, making sure to keep it lighthearted. My goal isn't to be some serious self-help guru; it's to help people find little pockets of peace amongst their daily chaos.

I blab on about my project and add a few more tips about not being too hard on yourself. If I could only take my own advice…

"That's it for today!" I say, holding up the half-finished pig. "I'll finish this little guy later. Thanks for watching, and remember to find time for a little 'you' time today."

I hit the stop button and sink into my favorite grey cushy chair. "What do you think, Chuggers? Did we nail it?" I glance through my footage and listen to make sure my audio didn't cut out or anything dumb like that. Everything that could go wrong with a video has gone wrong for me. It's a raw video of me talking. Nothing fancy but it's one-hundred percent me. I've only been doing this for a few weeks and haven't had the time to learn anything extra as far as adding special noises or pictures.

I post two videos per week, usually on Monday and Thursday. "Looks like the next one will be a 'Mental Health Monday.'" Adding this hobby to my already busy life is a lot. I've been bitten by the addiction bug. All I want to do is film videos and crochet!

With a satisfied smile, I upload the video. It's not perfect, but it's real, and that's what matters. I'm here to connect, to share, and maybe to offer a little light in someone's day. I don't have tons of views, but it's all part of the journey. Even if it's a slow climb to YouTube stardom, I'll keep on going— one stitch at a time.

I open Adrienne's door to wake her up for the day. I

tiptoe to her bed, taking a few moments to watch her sleep. She's a beautiful sight, lying on her back with her hands on her stomach. She's a mini, much cuter version of me. Her black hair is fanned out on her pillow, making her creamy olive skin pop.

Her hazel eyes flutter open and focus on me. These, she got from Patrick. "Hi, Mommy." This happens a lot for us. We are so in sync that even my presence in her room wakes her.

"Morning, beautiful. Time to wake up." I brush her soft face with my finger, cherishing this time with her in a way I doubt my mother ever did.

"Okay," she says, shifting to her left side and pulling the blankets over her head.

"I'll be back in a few minutes, and then Ms. Tickles will visit!" Adrienne giggles and wiggles under the covers. "Or, maybe she's here now. Yup, she just walked in." I dance the tips of my fingers over her back up to her neck. The sound of her laughter makes me smile. "It's Thursday, and it's raining. You have PE today. Last week, you didn't like wearing a dress during P.E., so keep that in mind when you get ready, okay?"

"Okay," her tiny voice says from under the covers.

"I'll check on you in a few minutes." I get up to leave and hear her covers rustle. I turn and see her holding her arms out for a hug. This is a greeting I'll never turn down. I have my hobbies and goals, but she is the joy that keeps me going, even when I'm hit by the blues. I'm grateful that today isn't one of those days so far.

I head to my bedroom, glancing outside at our lush, green backyard full of trees that are getting a shower. The soft glow of the morning gives light to the birds hopping around my feeders. I feel the pull to sit in my round chair and crochet while Adrienne plays with her stuffed animals in the living room. That darn thing called work puts a stop to my hobbies. And I'm one of the lucky ones and like my job. I couldn't imagine dreading the workday. Patrick has to be outside in the rain. That would *not* be kind to my curly hair.

Patrick is barely awake, snuggled deep in our covers. I jump on the bed with the high I get after completing a video. "Got another video done, huh?" he mumbles, opening one eye.

"Yup. I love it! My last video has fifty views! It's small beans compared to those big channels with hundreds or thousands, but watching my numbers climb is fun."

"I'm glad you're doing something you like, especially since it's free." He reaches over and threads a chunk of my hair around his finger.

"You'd be a natural at crocheting," I say, indicating my black ringlet wrapped around his index finger. "Aren't construction guys supposed to be early risers?"

"We can't work until the sun comes up, babe." He lifts the covers and shuffles to the bathroom. He looks at his phone on the way, for sure seeing the notification of my new video.

"The sun has been up for ten minutes now, lazy bones."

"I don't know how you're so chipper at six-fifteen."

"It's just me doing what I've been able to do since I was one: talk." It's about as much praise as he gives me in my activities. Patrick doesn't care one bit about social media, nor does he watch my videos. It's fine with me. My projects keep me happy, and that's what's important.

I change into my dark blue short-sleeved scrubs, praising my warm body for not needing many layers, even with the chilly fall air. Let's face it, the layer of extra fluff is what's really keeping me from freezing.

I trade places with Patrick in the bathroom when he's done. I block his way out of the bathroom and tackle him with a hug. "Gotcha!" I say before releasing him.

"Ooh, be careful there, hon," he says, squeezing his neck muscle. I take over for him with a sympathetic expression.

"Still sore, huh?"

"*Always* sore," he corrects.

"You've gotta do your yoga, Pat," I say while swiping foundation on my skin. "I promise not to post a video of you in spandex."

"That might be your most popular video!"

I laugh and open the bathroom window. The fresh September air makes me forget how small this off-white master bathroom is. The scent and tinkling sound of rain only add joy to my morning routine.

My phone dings with a notice that I have a comment! "Already?" I grab my phone, and see it was from my friend, Joanie. "Awe," I say with a sag of my shoulders. A comment is a comment in the world of YouTube algorithms, but it would have been nice to have more newbies send a message.

My videos usually only get a dozen or so views in the first twenty-four hours of being posted. My goal isn't to have thousands of views, though that would be glorious. These subscribers are faceless and nameless, but I know I'm helping them. Even if I help someone make a better decision, brighten a day, or encourage another to take control of their life, my mission will be complete.

My videos are fun to make, but there are other reasons I spend my mornings on them. No, this isn't what I went to school for, to talk into a camera to an audience I can't see. Something inside of me is pulling me to do this. It's a bit too early to call this my destiny, but the need is just as strong. It makes me feel good to meld my knowledge, experience, and quirky ways of dealing with mental struggles. I just know that someone out there is getting something from my advice.

Chapter 2 Ariel

Daydreams are a Lie

I love to daydream about sneaking out of this town. It's the end of the day after making deliveries for the dads. The summer after my senior year of high school has been the worst yet. Now that I'm out of school, they've filled my days with their dirty work.

"Got a light?" Charlotte holds her cigarette between her two fingers, looking less than cool.

I reach out and flick my lighter to ignite her smoke. I light my own and lean back on the tree that has been our meeting place for the last four years. We meet up here just about every night after I get off 'work.'

"How was your day?" She has no idea I'm delivering drugs, and I'll keep it that way. "Still wanting to leave your 'horrible life'?" she mocks with her fingers in air quotes.

"Always," I say with seriousness.

"There's nothing out there for you, Ariel. You know that, right? This town doesn't have anything good up its sleeve for any of us." Nice. Another great pep talk from my friend. She's the best one I've been able to gather. If it was up to me, I wouldn't have any, but it's nice to have someone, even if I do keep her at arm's length. There's less chance of someone figuring out what happens at my home that way.

We shoot the breeze, loitering in different shades of black outfits. For most kids my age, it's a goth fashion statement. I adopted the dark, baggy look at twelve, cigarette in hand, as my way to disappear. These clothes cover my ultra-thin frame while I hope to remain monochromatically boring. Even my hair matches the dark clothes that cover me. Hopefully, if I go 'missing,' it will be difficult to describe what I actually look like under all this fabric and makeup. Like anyone would notice if I was gone. I fit in less with this town than I do at home, and that's saying something.

My phone dings, reminding me it's time for my next chore.

"Ariel, you going to the grocery store today?" Charlotte asks with a lighter tone. Charlotte sticks around for one reason, for me to pick up the tab.

"I already went," I lie. All she wants to do is bum a twenty off me or have me buy her a bag of chips or smokes. I don't need someone to steal my 'allowance.' It's my ticket out of here.

"Maybe tomorrow," she says with a shrug. "I'm heading to Hunter's tonight for a movie if you want to come."

"Maybe," I say, knowing the dads won't let me out of the house once I get home. "See ya."

I take the same route to the store for the same ingredients I've used for dinner for the last five years. I'd fill our freezer with meat and those freezer pizzas, but the dads don't want this. It's one of my sole purposes in life to make dinner for my useless dads—and to get their beer, of course. I'm only eighteen, but I have a source.

It's not as bad as it sounds. While there isn't much effort

involved in scratching a box of Hamburger Helper open, it does allow me to measure, mix, and stir the ingredients together. There's something about cooking that I actually like.

I turn the car off after the front bumper bounces off the light post. I'm mildly glad the fender held on by bungee cords and duct tape doesn't fall off. I rush inside to beat the clock that's edging toward my curfew. My biggest goal is to avoid a lecture from the dads after a hot, sweaty day.

That's right, 'dads' is plural, though it hasn't always been that way. My mom left back when my hair was still its natural honey-brown instead of the jet-black 'Nice'n Easy' color. The next day, my 'uncle' moved in to work on the family business. Even at five years old, I knew they were up to no good.

I've had to push myself to grow up faster than most so I can keep up with the bullshit home life I've been dealt. Now that I'm out of school, I've been adopted into their business by doing their drug runs full-time. Yippee.

I throw the usual ingredients in the cart, add a few things for myself, and rush through the checkout line. It's Tuesday, so the food I bought on Friday has already run out. I'm not really complaining. This is a big source of my income. The dads rarely ask for their money back and have no idea how much anything costs. The extra change adds to my hefty 'bank account' stashed in the wall in my closet.

I check out, use my scrawny arms to load everything in the crappy car, and stop by the back of the store. I crack open my latest book while waiting for Mike to add the two cases of beer to the trunk. This is the only thing I look forward to during the day, escaping into a world of fantasy that takes me from my own. I know now it can never happen, but when I was younger I used to wave my hands around, trying to whisk myself away from here.

"My rates are about to go up, Air-Re-Ull," my beer supplier says, enunciating my name. "This is getting risky, with you being a minor and all."

"Same shit as always, Mike," I drawl, forcing a bored tone, which isn't far from the truth. "Just take your fifty bucks for ten seconds of work and stuff it." I speed off, brushing the right side of the car on a pallet, nearly sending it toppling over. Oh well.

The scenery shifts from grimy storefronts and loiterers to my neighborhood, where rusted cars lurk behind weeds tall enough to brush against my knees. These used to be fun when I was a little girl and I played in them with the neighborhood kids. Those kids have since moved away, a theme that has followed me. You make friends with someone, and they move away, probably because their families have literally found that the grass is greener somewhere else.

We blend in with the ambiance of our neighborhood with the broken refrigerator in the driveway, chipped house paint, and soiled couch on the front porch. If there's anything to be grateful for, it's that our secrets stay behind the screen door that has been ripped to shreds for years. That's all I needed growing up was for everyone at school to know that the marijuana problem in this town comes from my dining room.

But I'm not in school anymore. I no longer have to worry about the other kids finding out. I'm done with the pettiness of high school, where the girls were preoccupied with which shade of pink they would wear to the prom. Now, I can focus on the plan I've been perfecting for the last five years.

I step through the front door into what always feels like another world, where the dark clouds are constantly overhead. The drapes haven't been thrown open since my mom left over a decade ago. The same brown, dust-filled furniture remains untouched in the sunk-in living room. The cloudy air is filled with the pungent smell of weed, which is why my bedroom door is permanently closed.

My mood drops to the level of darkness this house holds. I have no good memories here.

I drop my mini black backpack and a small bag of groceries in my bedroom, the first door on the left. The dads have a room on the other side of the front door, but they usually conk out in front of the TV in a beer-induced stupor. I have no idea their romantic relationship or if there is one. Like I care. The one and only thing the dads provide me with is the stack of weekly cash they give me for groceries.

I make one more trip to the car and fill my arms with grocery bags. I find the dads in their place: the covered porch off the dining room they've converted to do their 'work.' They created this space to keep their toxic smell out of the house, but it doesn't do much good. I've suspected their business has branched into the harder stuff, but what I don't know literally keeps me safer.

As usual, Phil has a cigarette hanging from his mouth while my real dad bundles dried bushes.

"About frickin' time," Gary grumbles when I drop the bags off in the kitchen. "We're starving and thirsty."

And apparently, completely unable to fix food for yourself.

"Look, the little mermaid's home." Phil laughs in response to his daily greeting. At least they know my name, which is more than ninety-nine point nine percent of the people in this town. They aren't that bad of guys, except for making and dealing drugs and all. Marijuana has been legalized in this state in low doses. The way the dads grow, bundle, and ship it out of this stinky-ass house, we could probably supply the whole state's legal limit for a couple of years.

For a profitable yet illegal business, they are frugal with their money. And they look it, too. Gary wears a dirty grey shirt with holes in it day in and day out. Phil rarely changes his jeans and gets his hair cut maybe once a year. Honestly, they hardly ever venture from this cramped space in the house. I've never understood their drive for this type of work other than it allowing them to drink themselves into a deep sleep every night. I guess when that's what you want to do with your life…

And I don't.

"We have guys coming over tonight," Gary informs, barely flicking his eyes at me.

"We're picking up pizza," Phil says, letting me know I'm off the hook for dinner prep tonight.

"You'll need to get out of here," Gary says.

I perk up at this news. "You mean I can go to Charlotte's? A couple of her friends are getting together, and…"

"No. You'll be in your room." I'm used to these commands and barely-there glances. Gary flip flops between giving a shit and completely forgetting I exist. Apparently tonight it one of those 'caring' times.

Do I want out? Of course! I have a full-fledged plan in case I get enough balls to live out the running away dream. I've gone over it twenty times a day for years now, tweaking it to perfection.

Problem one: the dads seldom leave. And problem two: they have this weird radar on me and know when I've been gone too long. Their stomach grumblings for their next meal probably is what rats me out.

My phone vibrates as I slump to my room, wondering when this will all end. I've kept this secret device silent and out of sight.

Your change of name has been approved. Please drop by at your convenience to pick up your papers.

I check the time, seeing that the records department will close in less than an hour. I tuck my phone away and return to the kitchen. I lean against the counter and pick at my nails, developing a lie so I can leave the house again. "Hey, um, I forgot something at the store. Can I… can I go back?"

Gary shifts only his eyes to me. "Make it quick," he says through his cigarette.

"Yup." I speed-walk to the car, scraping the driver's side of the car on the stupid rock next to the driveway when I back out. "Oops," I say without worry.

I race across town to the records department with excitement filling my stomach. I finally took the first step to freedom and filed to change my name months ago when I turned eighteen. It seems like a miracle has happened for this to have gone through.

I park, scraping my tires against the curb. "Guess that means I'm here," I say with a shrug.

Thirty minutes later, I'm back in the car with the envelope containing my new identity. I've never been so excited in my entire life! Since my birthday last November, I've been waiting to take this first step toward my dream of running away.

I bring up the number for the DMV and hit the call button. I switch lanes, and a honk rings out after cutting someone off. "Deal with it, dickhead! No, I'm not talking to you," I tell the guy who answers. "How long does switching my license to my new name take? I have the papers and everything."

"You'll have to make an appointment. We have a

cancellation tomorrow at ten. We give you a temporary sticker to cover your current license until we mail the new one out in about a week," the man says with a dull voice.

"I'll take it!" It's like time has sped up with the oversight of a guardian angel waving his hand over these prospects to ensure they go through. It's all I've been doing, waiting for these years to go by so I can be in this very position.

Maybe this daydream of starting a new life isn't so far-fetched after all.

***

I escape to the serenity of my room the second I get home. I grab my bag of chips and California rolls that I stashed in the bedroom fridge and plop myself on the oversized pillow I use as a chair.

The dads never come into my room. Ever. I lock it up tight, even though I know they're too focused on their 'business' to come in here. I can't afford them finding my money stacks.

I snuck in a college class this summer, signing up while still in high school. I got most of my high school credits out of the way by my junior year, and I jumped on the offering of taking college classes for nearly free. As of now, I'm almost done with my first year of prerequisites. I have no idea what I want to be, but anything would win first place against the 'family business.'

I used my fake name for college when I signed up for the online classes. Luckily, they didn't require any ID or the signature of a parent. A few fifties thrown at Mike from the grocery store did the trick of changing my name. I look at my new name, thanking my earlier self for following through with this quest. I don't have superpowers other than the grit and determination it has taken to not run away sooner.

What has been a swirl of fantasy over the years is finally taking shape. These loose ends have formed together to build somewhat of a rope for me to escape. It might be flimsy, but I'll grasp it and use whatever strength these scrawny arms have to pull me from an inevitable fate of illegal drugs and destruction.

Drunken laughter from the 'party' the dads are throwing rings out. I know this is one way the dads drum up business. They invite new people over to get shitty-ass drunk and high before passing out all over the house. Luckily, I'm so far from their minds that they don't mention they have a teenage daughter in the house.

I stick the wedge under my door, pulling the knob with my foot jammed into the piece of wood. It adds another layer of protection to the three locks I've installed. I sneak into my closet, take off the fake panel behind my clothes, and pull out the small safe I found in the garage when I was ten. Even back then, I realized that wasting the extra cash the dads didn't ask for after my grocery store runs was idiotic. Yes, I started going to the grocery store for them at that age, walking or using a crappy bike as transportation.

I unfold the thirty bucks in my pocket and add it to the stack of cash I've been saving. I average about a hundred dollars a week. Even more is added depending on how drunk the dads get. I know all the hiding places, sometimes sneaking out at night after they've passed out. Still, I'm careful to peel only a twenty off to add to my escape plan, hoping they'll never figure this out. So far, I've gone unnoticed.

I've splurged a few times on clothes, the small refrigerator in my room, and going out to eat here and there, but other than that, I've been able to put away quite a bit.

After prepping my sushi roll, I bring up YouTube. My shoulders sink with relief upon seeing her. "Ahh, Lisa," I say with a smile. I start up my dinosaur of a computer, something I snagged from school one year when I found out it was doomed for the dumpster. I listen to the woman I've begun to idolize over the last couple of weeks while I struggle through a math assignment from my college course.

Lisa's giggles come through my earbuds, igniting my own smile. The small snippets of her town in her videos have me fantasizing about living there one day. Before watching her channel, I had planned every detail of leaving, except for which town I'd run to.

I've learned from Lisa that just because I've had a shitty life so far doesn't mean I can't start down a different path. If I can make it out of this town, I can start over in Garden Valley.

Chapter 3 Lisa

Embracing the Unknown

I love my clients at the clinic where I work. Much to my family's disappointment, I'm not a surgeon or even a medical doctor, but I still classify myself in their field. My degree allows me to counsel people who I classify as having 'regular problems.' Basically, I listen to their problems and offer pieces of advice to help with their struggles.

"Thank you, Lisa," Renee says with a pat on my hand as she leaves. "It's so nice to blurt everything out and not have someone tell me I'm making all this stuff up."

"No problem, Renee. It's what I'm here for."

"My last doctor just threw pills at me and showed me the door. I know some people need that, but I feel much lighter after talking and having someone understand what I'm going through."

"I completely agree!" And I do because I've been there myself Don't get me wrong. I'm all for mental health medications, but I've found some tricks to get my through my depressive episodes.

I offer a warm smile as I walk her out, having her stop by the desk to make another appointment.

I've been at this clinic for almost three years. I was a stay-at-home mom until Adrienne started Kindergarten three years ago. I've been back in the workforce since, even though it was like a jolt of lightning not to be home all day. Being home was bliss like none other, but I'm glad I can now contribute to the family. Cooking and cleaning contribute, but Patrick didn't count that nearly as important as bringing in money. I only work until three o'clock, but my paycheck has eased Patrick's financial stress that crept up during my five-year hiatus.

I'm thrilled when the receptionist tells me my next patient has canceled. During these times, I can hole up and satisfy my YouTube obsession. I kick my feet on the ground with a silent fist pump when I see that I've added five subscribers to my community since this morning's video!

I lounge on the couch in the room where I see patients and type out responses to a couple of comments. It's a bit of a downer that I've only gotten fifteen views, but I have those new subscribers to help balance out my disappointment. My mind spins, wondering what more I can do to get my desired views. Maybe my videos are boring, or I'm unlikable.

I slow my spinning mind, reminding myself to enjoy the journey, especially since this is a hobby. It's not like I'm relying on YouTube to pay my bills.

"Hey, Lisa… what's going on?" My boss, James, comes in, pausing when he sees me on the couch with my phone.

Busted!

"Oh, hi, James." I sit up straight and try to hide my phone under my leg, feeling like I've been caught watching a naughty movie. "My patient for this spot canceled, so I'm just taking a break."

"Lisa, you know you're supposed to help out with rooming patients when there's a cancellation."

"Yes, sir. I'm happy to help," I say, popping off the

couch. James raises his eyebrows.

"Okay, well, let's see it." He's not meaning to be a jerk. James is the boss, and I'm the first to admit that I've been a difficult employee. This isn't the first time I've been caught on my phone. It's because of me that James has come up with the no cell phone policy in the office.

I tuck my phone away, counting my lucky stars to be working here. My degree in psychology aligns well with this job. We are a primary care office offering light therapy sessions for patients who need a compassionate ear. I had to barter not to be full-time since I don't have after-school care for Adrienne. I choose to make it a priority to pick her up right after school. As a trade-off, I work one Saturday a month to catch the office up on paperwork.

I room a few patients, clean rooms, and offer to fill in for the receptionist when she goes to lunch. It's a quiet phone day, so I pull up my YouTube account on the computer after glancing over my shoulder to ensure James doesn't catch me again.

I pound out a notification about my next video and hit send. I read yet another suggestion from a viewer to open an Etsy shop to sell my finished crocheted products. This piques my curiosity, but I haven't had time to research it yet. I peek around again and am thankful I'm alone. I pull up Etsy and go to the Q&A page. The suggestion is to open LLC if I want to sell my stuff. Of course, I'll need to connect my Etsy shop to our banking account for deposits. Patrick sure won't be thrilled about that. I sink down, this budding idea being smashed before it can even think of blooming.

"Lisa, can you… what are you doing?" It's James, catching me goofing off yet again. Between work, cooking, cleaning, and Adrienne's ballet and piano lessons, I'm busy nearly every minute at home. I don't have enough time to spend on this hobby that's been calling to me. James straightens and peers down at me. "Lisa, we need to talk before you leave today. Come to my office at two, please."

I spend the next hour ruminating about the hand slap I'm about to get. I'd like to have the defense of working extra hours or through my lunches and breaks, but it's not true. Every spare second I get to myself, I sneak around, check my account, or write a script for my next video. It's like this at home, too. You'd be surprised how much can get done during a two-minute bathroom break. I'm lucky I've found an app to keep up with my talking and transcribe my words into notes.

My jittery legs carry me to James' office near the end of the day, and suddenly, I feel like Alice after nibbling the shrinking mushroom. The towering office furniture looms over me, everything twice as big, making me feel tiny. James and the office manager peer down like curious characters from Wonderland as I clamber onto the oversized chair, half-expecting a Cheshire cat to pop out of nowhere.

James greets me with a face as stern as the Queen of Hearts. Our office manager, Melanie, sits in one of the two colorful chairs across from the main desk. The paper resting on the desk practically glows in a spotlight. The setup sends a jolt through my stomach as I brace for what this might mean.

"I haven't been that bad, have I?" I ask with a high voice that makes me sound like a little girl.

"Sit down, Lisa. We've needed to have this talk for some time now. Remember how, at your review in June, I said your phone use was excessive? I saw you on it three times today, and you were on your YouTube account at the front desk computer."

"I still get my work done…"

"It just doesn't seem like you have the dedication we're looking for." James is a nice man and I'd probably do the same thing if I was in his position. I can see by the sadness on his face that this is as hard of a discussion for him to give as it is for me to hear. Patrick will be so mad at me if it's what I think it is!

"I can put in another Saturday a month," I plead, scooting to the edge of my seat, pleading for mercy. My voice borders desperation, knowing my mother will have another item to add to her long list of disappointments in me.

"I'm sorry. This summer, it was difficult to work around your schedule. I know your daughter was home from school, but we're a doctor's office. We can't be flexible with our office hours. And it's not just that. I've watched a few of your videos. They're great, but I'm afraid it adds to your demerits. It's a conflict of interest to have you give advice like that. What if our patients watch and think it all applies to them?"

I cock my head in confusion, my defensive side waking up. Out of all his criticisms, this one hits home the most. "My advice does apply to them and is similar to what I say here to my clients in person. My videos are really general. All the advice I give surrounds being happy and going for your dreams. I don't see how that…"

"I'm sorry, Lisa. We need a team player, and we'd like your position to be full-time. You've made it clear that you're not willing to work that much. We're going to have to let you go."

Melanie hands me the envelope with an expression filled with sorrow. "This is your final check. There's another check in here with two months' severance pay, and you can file for unemployment benefits. I know it's not much, but…" I slowly take the envelope, looking from one face to another.

"I'm sorry, I'll need you to sign this paper for your file."

I grab the pen with shaky fingers. A tear falls from my eye and splatters on the desk in clear view of my audience. I had better be careful, or I'll soon be swimming in a river of tears, just as Alice did. I wipe my face in embarrassment. "Sorry, this is such a shock," I blurt with a loud sniff. "I really like it here." It shouldn't be a shock. As they've spelled out on this paper, I've been taking advantage, selfishly doing my side hustle in the corners with every free minute. Good going, Lisa.

Twenty minutes later, after I've endured my walk of shame through the office, I trudge to my car with the stereotypical cardboard box of crap. I still have a half hour until Adrienne is out of school. I don't know what to do with these thirty minutes. What in the heck will I do all day without a job? I stayed home for five years but had Adrienne to care for. We did everything together.

I drive to the school in a daze, replaying the meeting. "What a frickin failure!" I yell in my car. I pass a store with Christmas decorations in the window. "It's only September!" I cry behind my closed window, wishing my windows were tinted the darkest shade of black. The red and green decorations in the store fuel my tears further. It seems like Christmas is always coming.

"More like looming." I sink when reminded that I'll face this upcoming season again without my grandma. "Oh, Nana," I sob. I can see her now in my blurred vision, wearing only red and green from October first until the end of the year. What would she say about me losing my job? "Probably that I now have more time to decorate for Christmas." My laugh comes through sobs, sparking even more of a crying spell that I allow myself to get out.

I turn down a deserted dirt road and pull over next to an

alfalfa field. The fields beyond my windshield glow a vibrant green from today's fallen rain. A small rainbow shines to the left, though I barely see it. None of the beauty of my town is enjoyed by me right now.

I grab a napkin from my console and cover my face to let it out. A haunting question floats in the background about how my future mood will handle this blow. Even worse is that I have the break the news of my firing to my husband. Will I embrace this unexpected time off, or will I wilt away in bed? One would think I have the power to decide, but it doesn't always work this way.

After a few minutes, I reach for my phone to warn Patrick I have bad news. I've learned that he handles disruptions to his life better if he has time to process them. My husband has many great qualities, but flexibility isn't one of them.

I only wish my mother were like this. She's more like concrete than clay when shifting her opinion. How on earth am I going to tell her I've been fired? Telling her will be even scarier than telling Patrick!

This will be another disappointment from the daughter she already sees as sub-par. It's a bit backward to be in my mid-thirties and still worrying about my parents' judgment, but that's my life. I moved out of their house and away from their town years ago, but their critical voices still reach me.

It was my sister, Diane, who got all the praise. With fair skin and lighter hair, Diane resembled nothing of our dad's Indian heritage. I doubt this was why she was the favorite daughter. Still, it was easier to believe that my hair color was the reason instead of something internally wrong with me that repelled my parents.

These hiccups in life have always happened to me

regarding work. I had a great job when I was pregnant with Adrienne, but they went under. Another place I worked at burned to the ground, and yet another endured a flood. "I guess I'm the gem of bad luck."

I sigh, knowing this isn't true. I put my hands up as if shielding myself from the negativity that wants to take hold. What I need is some reframing. I can't think of a better way to get through this then to practice what I've said to my patients and my handful of subscribers.

I start my car, willing my chin to stay high. "I am not a bad person," I say out loud, repeating this phrase until I get to Adrienne's school.

Now more than ever, I'll need crocheting to get through this heaviness. I still have twenty minutes before school lets out, so I park and swing my blue bag onto the passenger seat. I've always got my trusty crochet bag by my side, and just like that—bam!—a fun idea for a quick video pops into my head!

I hold my phone at arm's length and hit the record button with my thumb before I give it a second thought. I taught myself how to upload a short, YouTube's answer to reels on other platforms. It's all pretty easy to get a hang of.

"You never know what's going to happen and when you'll have extra time," I say through gritted teeth, holding my bag up. "I have twenty minutes to kill, and I don't want to waste one of them! Let me know if you always carry a crochet bag like this one. I'll share more about why I have this unexpected time in another video later, so stay tuned." I end with an unsure smile staring back at me.

My mind is spinning as much as the ball of yarn from which I'm now pulling thread. How am I going to deal with this? Maybe it's my mom's fault. Her criticisms have a way of coming true. Lord knows she's always hated me working at the clinic. The laugh that follows is precisely what I need at this moment. When in doubt, blame mom for all my problems.

I concentrate on my project, only allowing myself to acknowledge my senses. The color and feel of my yarn are soothing. I use my voice to count my rows. Each knot grounds me to only think about my current task. I pretend I'm crocheting pieces of my journey, each row adding a layer of hope to my future. Right now, with my hands busy and the open window allowing the smell of freshly cut grass to flow in, I'm okay.

"Maybe this was supposed to happen." With this slight shift, a different thought comes: I have two months of severance pay. This will help with the urgency of finding a job. I'll have time to make videos and crochet!

"That's ridiculous! Patrick will make me find a job right away," I utter to my yarn.

The high pitch of children's voices snaps me out of my trance a few minutes later. I tuck my farm project into my blue bag and walk to the pick-up area. Adrienne's smiling face, with her bouncy black curls flowing behind her, grounds me to my happy place. I think her hair makes up a quarter of her weight.

"Mommy!" she says with a hug before pulling away. "Can we have Brian over sometime?"

A little boy walks alongside Adrienne. It's funny to see him with his grass-stained and tousled hair next to Adrienne in her fluffy light-pink dress she couldn't part with, even though it's P.E. day. She's a mixture of playing with the boys while keeping her girlish ways.

The boy peels off to hug his mom as they are joined by other kids, who I assume are his brothers. I don't know Cinda well, but she's always happy to pick her boys up. She hugs him back and asks him about his day. Her round face and smile are welcoming enough, but I don't have the social energy to give her right now.

"Maybe," I answer, unable to thoroughly consider Adrienne's request. Unfortunately, I've kept my eyes on the woman with the black curls too long. She looks my way, and we make eye contact. Darn.

"Our kids are becoming good friends this year," Cinda says, joining us. "I volunteered in class today, and they were partners during science. Adrienne was such a good girl." I listen with envy, always having wanted to volunteer in Adrienne's class. Maybe I can for the next couple of weeks in between jobs!

"That's nice." I wonder if she's coupling my forced smile with my red, puffy eyes. It's something I can spot, but most people don't study others as I do.

"Adrienne told me you have a YouTube channel about yarn?" Cinda says with a cute voice that matches her short stature like mine.

"Yeah, it's just a silly thing I do," I answer. My confidence has vanished, stripping me bare and defenseless. Even the tiniest of negativity could crumble me to the ground.

I turn away from Cinda with my arm around Adrienne, wanting to dash to the safety of our car. "I'll have to check it out. I've always wanted to learn how to crochet. Or is it knitting? I don't even know the difference!"

"Yeah, that's pretty common. Crocheting is with one hook, and knitting is with two needles," I answer automatically. "I have some tutorial videos about getting started if you're interested." It's subtle, but there's something magical about how this topic gently pulls me out of my funk. Like a ray of sunshine, it melts through the icy grip of my mood that wants to curl up and drown in tears.

"I should try that. What's your channel called?"

"Coping With Yarn." Saying the name of my hobby usually lights me up. Right now, it feels like a sucker punch with gravity already dragging me down.

Cinda waits a second and starts laughing with a hand on my forearm. Great, now I'm getting laughed at. "I get it! Using crocheting to cope with life, right?" I nod, expecting her to poke more fun at the name I'm proud of. "That's so clever!" I study her face, looking for an ounce of 'Regina George' sarcasm, but I don't see or hear any in her tone.

"Well, thanks. I'm into the psychology thing," or I used to be up until an hour ago, "and crocheting is my jam," I say quickly to keep with this vibe.

"You should see how much yarn she has!" Adrienne says to Brian.

"That's funny," Cinda says. "Are you a health coach?"

"No," I bark as if this is an absurd idea. I just got fired from my job. Why would anyone want to hire me to help with their life when mine is crumbling like a cookie left out on a hot day?

"The health coach thing is all the rage right now. I doubt anyone has eaten up the market in Garden Valley. Anyway, it was nice to meet you officially. It's funny how we've both been in this town forever, but we're just now talking. It's bound to happen when your kids are in the same class. I'm going to head home and listen to your videos while I make dinner."

"Thank you, that's nice." I allow her interest to brighten my day just as the sun illuminates the hill next to the school. I hold Adrienne's hand on our way to the car with a new outlook on this horrible day. I might have just gotten a new subscriber!

***

Cinda's interest in my channel gave me the boost I needed to keep the slumps away for now. As much as I'd love to entertain the idea, there's no way Patrick will agree with me staying home solely to build my YouTube channel. On the flip side, it's not like I'll be able to spend my entire day looking for a job. This is Garden Valley, for crying out loud. The want ads take up a quarter of a page in the newspaper.

My nerves grow with every minute as I await Patrick's arrival. Adrienne and I stopped by the butcher shop after her ballet class for their delicious stew meat. I made Patrick's favorite beef stroganoff in the Instant Pot and am coupling it with parmesan cheese bread and salad, loading his greens full of extra goodies such as chopped carrots, cheese, and sunflower seeds.

"Those onions need some deodorant," Adrienne says, plugging her nose. I laugh, thankful that she's given me a reason to unwind my shoulders that are tighter than my slip knots. "Hey, Mommy?"

"Yes?" I ask with a smile, knowing that an intriguing question always follows these two words.

"Why do we have eyelashes?"

"They protect your eyes from things getting in them," I answer, adding more vegetables to our salads.

"Like what?" she asks with a scrunched-up face. "Like birds? Why would a bird get in my eye?" She covers her mouth as she giggles, an innocent gesture that only adds to my adoration of her.

"Do you know why we have eyebrows?" I ask, bending to be at her level. Honestly, it doesn't take much of a bend at my height. Adrienne shakes her head with wide eyes in anticipation. "They help shade your eyes." Adrienne thinks about this briefly, looks up at the light, and blinks several times.

"Mine don't work."

It's the first time I've had a real laugh all day. Maybe even all week. It works to clear out some of the heightened worries about spilling my lousy news to Patrick.

I got fired! Me!

"Daddy's home!" Adrienne screams, running from the kitchen to the front door in seconds. My stomach jolts in butterflies, hating that we'll soon talk about how I botched my job. I've failed at one of the most basic adult responsibilities.

"Hey, hey! How's my little girl?" He picks Adrienne up with his left arm, keeping his lunch pail in his right. He's thrilled to hold her, even with a slight limp on his left leg today.

"Good. We're having strog-noff."

"Stroganoff, huh? Sounds delicious. Hey, babe." Patrick drops his things and gives me a peck on the cheek. His happy mood makes me wonder if he even saw my warning text.

"Hey! How was your day?" My voice is overly high as a greeting. He tilts his head slightly, looking at me through squinted brown eyes. After being together for almost twelve years, Patrick knows all of my quirky signals.

"It was good. Stroganoff, huh? What, did you get a speeding ticket or something?" He stretches his calves as he laughs. "Be right back," he says, hand on his left leg as he hobbles to our bedroom to clean up. Nope, he definitely hasn't seen my text.

I watch after him, enjoying the view of his round butt. I never thought I'd be married to someone who weighed less than me, but here we are. I've broken that unspoken agreement to stay the same size as when we were married. My life has been too full of piano lessons, ballet, work, meals, and keeping the house to prioritize exercise.

I pick up his lunch pail and jacket from the floor, busying myself to keep the anxiety from taking over. It's a usual dinner of Adrienne laughing at her dad's immature noises and jokes. I'm stewing harder than the stroganoff did, bracing for a fight. After we're done with dinner, Adrienne runs off to her room to play, leaving us alone. Great.

"So, um, I have bad news." No point in beating around the bush.

"So, there *was* a reason for my favorite dinner." He gives me that playful grin that wiggles his brown hairline. It's something I know is short-lived, and I hate it. I follow him to the kitchen to help clean up.

"Yeah." I nod and slump down, feeling the tears well up again. I search the ground for unfound comfort. This feeling right now, this hopelessness that I'm ashamed to admit overcomes me from time to time, confirms the plunge in energy that's about to come.

"Hey, what's going on? Is everyone okay?" Patrick sets the dishes in the sink and leans against the counter to pull me in for a hug. I let him, needing this calm moment before everything erupts in chaos.

Enough stalling. It's only been a couple of hours, and the secret is already burning a hole in my stomach. I take a deep breath and look him in the face. His tan skin shows the hours of labor he spends outside at the job he's managed to keep for fifteen years. An unmistakable stubble gives him that rustic, lumberjack look I fall for nearly every time I look at him. Yet, I know things are about to turn. I'll soon see the side of him I dislike the most.

"I'm not happy about this, just so you know." My voice is unlike its usual tone, dropping an octave and escaping in barely a whisper. "I don't have a job anymore."

Patrick's arms tense around me as he stands straight. "You what?" he asks incredulously. I link his initial reaction to one of blame. "What happened? I thought things were good at the clinic."

"I did too," I say, swiping at a tear. He releases me from his arms, sending me into solitude. I wonder how much I should tell him. I don't need him to add to the guilt of this being one hundred percent my fault. Patrick isn't exactly one to hold back when it comes to blame. "They said they need someone to work full-time."

"Then you need to work full-time!" he spats, spreading his hands wide as if this is a simple solution I should have thought of.

"I can't work full-time. I need to pick Adrienne up from school."

"They have an after-school program, Lisa," he says bluntly as if it's this easy. This wouldn't be the end of the world, but I know first-hand how long those days were as a kid. I remember vividly staring at the clock, wondering when someone would pick me up. Needless to say, my parents were overly dedicated to their doctor statuses.

"So, what, you want her to be stuck at school for nine hours a day?" We've had this argument multiple times, and I'll never back down on it. "It's not like I'd make that much more by working two more hours a day, Patrick. And I don't want to be one of those families who come home, shove a fast-food meal down, and then rush off to bed. Isn't it nice that you have dinner and a clean house to come home to?"

"You call this clean?"

This comment fuels my fiery side. "Do you know how much time I spend cleaning this house? I spend hours and hours a week cleaning up, and…"

"Don't act like you're doing it for me," he retorts. He looks away and shakes his head. "I'll just put in extra hours since we'll only have one paycheck coming in."

"Patrick, I'll look for another job. You don't even know the details…"

"It's fine, Lisa. We'll go back to scraping by like we did when you decided to stay home with Adrienne." His voice lowers as he stomps by, not realizing how much this whole ordeal is ripping through my insides. "I'm going to get ready for my early morning. You did say I was up after the sun, after all."

I stay in the kitchen, bracing myself against the counter as tears wrack my body. Patrick's disapproval adds to my parents' deep well of disappointment. His words drive straight to the core, crushing me in the moment. It doesn't matter that he'll apologize later; it hurts now.

No, my house is not spotless. I've never made as much money as him. But… what is my but here? Maybe I need to step up and take on more responsibility since, apparently, taking care of our house and our daughter and cooking all the meals doesn't cut it in his book.

I stare into the two acres of land surrounding our home, knowing this isn't the solution. I'm not about to take just any job out there if it means taking me from spending precious time with Adrienne. I can barely make everything work as it is.

My eyes clear with this stern decision, illuminating my surroundings. Nearly every wall needs a fresh coat of paint, and the screen door that fell off during the summer still rests against the house. The warm days are still popping up here and there, giving our grass an unseasonable growth spurt.

My eyes drift to my favorite chair in the corner of the dining room, currently covered in a pile of unfolded laundry. Next to it, another pile of unopened mail lies on the cabinet my parents gave us to 'spruce up the place.'

And with that, I have my solution. I now have the gift of time. Suppose Patrick can realize that my being here is just as important as bringing in a paycheck. In that case, my firing can be turned into something positive. Even with tears pounding down my door, I'm starting to see that this may be the missing link I need.

Chapter 4 Ariel

A Shift in the Pattern

The future has always been an empty abyss, a dark void that effortlessly swallows my hopes and dreams. My plan to leave is far-fetched, but it gives a glimmer of light where all has been black.

"Ariel, listen up," my dad says when I come in the kitchen to make tonight's dinner. It's Gary, my biological father. He stays hunkered over the bundle he's packaging, never looking at me. "Phil and I are going to a convention. You'll need to manage a few pick-ups here at home."

A convention? They're leaving! "Sure!" I say, doing my best to keep my enthusiasm under control.

"No drunken parties, you hear?" Phil jokes.

Do you mean like the one you threw last weekend?

"So, um, how long will you be gone?" I ask, leaning against the counter to appear uninterested when my insides scream happily.

"We'll leave Thursday afternoon and will be gone a week. It's not far from here, in the heart of Vegas. If all goes well, I might be able to talk your dad into taking a few days off," Phil answers. He's filled with many more words than Gary. He hasn't been the worst 'fake' parent over the years. At least I've 'only' been neglected and not physically abused… or worse.

"I'll be fine," I say with sass. I leave the kitchen for my room, willing my twiggy legs to stay under control. I mentally hold the screech from escaping my lips. I shut the door, run to my bathroom, and hold a thick towel over my mouth. "Ahhhhh!" It's happening! I never thought I'd be given this opportunity.

I flee to my closet to check on my money. I glance at the wedge under my door, my safeguard. I'd be devastated if the dads took what I've saved these last eight years. This cash gives me the potential for a new life. I'm a bud that's been waiting in the dark for years. Now, the light is shining, finally giving me the opportunity to bloom.

I have only two days to flesh out my plan before they leave. I've thought about taking the beater Honda, but I barely trust it to take me to the store and back. Plus, it would be ultra-easy for them to find me. A bus ticket out of here is the best bet. The only problem is that the bus station is half an hour away, and it would be a dead giveaway if I left the Honda there or had the trail of a cab.

I tap out a message to Charlotte, figuring she won't be busy. I've toyed with not telling her at all, but I think it'd be pretty crappy for me not to at least let her know I'm leaving.

Are you busy Thursday afternoon? Ariel

Nope! Want to go shopping? Charlotte

No, but can you come over? I need a small favor. Ariel

Yup. Charlotte

I hate relying on her, but it's the one detail of my plan I hadn't ironed out yet. I hope Charlotte won't have loose lips about me leaving. The less details she knows, the better.

This time, nothing's holding me back. My dreams, once hidden away, are finally beginning to take shape. It's time to throw the doors open and breathe life into these long-dormant ambitions.

I lay back with my eyes closed, allowing the daydream to fully play out. I don't have a superpower, but I've got guts. The dads are planning a trip. Well, so am I.

***

I've been waiting for this moment for years, yet Thursday can't come fast enough. I've spent the last few days sneaking around the house late at night to gather forgotten bags and suitcases. Everything I own in this world is behind my bedroom door. I don't have much, but I'm bringing everything except the bed, dresser, small fridge, and what is nailed to the walls.

I look over my driver's license, loving my new name. It's a clever one, too. I pulled my hair into a ponytail for my picture, something completely different than the usual shagginess that falls in my face. I'll change the black and all the darkness it brings as soon as I get to Garden Valley. This has been part of the plan, too. I've been dying my hair black for so long that I'm positive the dads have no idea what my natural color is.

My shoulders flinch when Phil's voice calls out that they're leaving. I scramble for the door, wanting to be at their beck and call, even for this last time. This one last time will show my feigned dedication to them before cutting the ties for good.

"Maybe you can get something other than black to wear while we're gone," Phil says, tugging at my oversized sweatshirt.

"She's going to stay here," my dad commands. It's the

last time I'll be suffocated like this. I absorb his response, knowing I'll soon be free.

"I've left your delivery list on the counter. Make sure you get them all done," Phil orders, as usual.

I lean against the doorway to watch them leave, crossing my arms to keep the sentiment out. This could very well be the last time I see them. I don't feel an ounce of sadness. Why would I? Gary's growl to stay home and Phil's off and on sentiment sums up most of my existence.

Not anymore!

I will myself to count to twenty slowly after they pull away from the driveway. I shut the door and peek out of the dusty curtains to ensure they are down the street. "Bye-bye," I say without one string of attachment.

I fling the brown curtains and whip into action. I run to my room, throw the overstuffed bags over my shoulders, and drop them in the foyer before going back for more. My bus leaves in two hours and I'll be dammed if I'm late. Charlotte pulls in not long after the dads have gone.

"Charlotte, you aren't supposed to be here for another fifteen minutes," I say with long fingers wrapped around my bony hips.

"Sue me," she throws back, getting out of the car and flicking her short cigarette in the driveway.

Nice.

"I have my stuff all ready to go."

"Where are you going?" she asks with a slight chuckle of disbelief. She follows me inside to my room. "Man, it stinks like skunk supreme in here." I've only allowed her beyond our front door once, afraid that she'd blab about my living conditions. I no longer care about this; my mind is focused on leaving as quickly as possible.

"Away." I sling the last heavy bag over my shoulder. It's my one whole bag of books I couldn't part with. "I'm visiting my aunt."

Charlotte's look shows that she sees right through my lies. "With *all* your stuff?"

I sigh, figuring it's not the end of the world if *one person* knows I'm leaving. "I'm getting out of here. I'm leaving, for good."

"You're what?" she barks, looking down at me as if not believing me.

"I'm getting out of this hellhole. I'm done."

"Bullshit. You can't do that. Where will you go? Where will you live, and how will you pay for everything?"

Charlotte hasn't been shy about bumming money from me, but she knows nothing of the wads of cash in the backpack around my shoulder. The money will stay on me at all times during this trip.

I pause at my bedroom door, grab the wooden wedge I've used as an extra lock, and toss it in the same compartment as my current book. I stuff my things into the trunk, and hurry back for the last load.

Charlotte's on my heels the whole time. "Ariel, I thought we would stay miserable in this town together." I can't tell if she's joking. I don't answer. I can't afford a spat with her right now.

"I just have to try," I say with defeat. I'm over the part of trying to explain myself. I'm the one who has had to endure eighteen years in this prison of a home. "You're taking me to the bus station," I inform.

"For a small fee." She smiles, and at this moment, we share that feeling of warmth that the inside joke gives.

"Sure, why would a friend do something for another

friend otherwise?" I smirk back at her. I almost didn't call upon her, but she's the one person I want to say goodbye to.

Charlotte backs out of the cracked driveway with the potholes and weeds. It's my final look at the house I grew up in. "Good riddance," I say without emotion.

My goodbye to Charlotte holds only a smidgen of sentiment. She hasn't always been there for me, but that's more of my doing than hers. The list of people I trust in this world is entirely blank and on purpose. I've kept everyone at arm's length to make ties easy to sever. No friends mean there will be no snail trail behind me for the dads to follow.

Charlotte thinks she's conning me out of a hundred dollars for the drive. I double it to keep her quiet about my secret. I eagerly wait for her to leave the bus station before I buy my ticket. I don't want to chance her seeing my name change or my destination.

I push my cart full of bags and purchase a ticket for the first leg of my trip. It's the first time using my license with my new name. I hold my breath when I hand it over, but the guy barely glances at it before taking my money. Why wouldn't he? I legally changed my name. I'm no longer Ariel, the weird bookworm who wears all black and lives in that creepy dark house with the curtains permanently drawn. I'm still the girl in black from head to toe, but that will sure as shit be one of the first things I change once I'm settled.

I check my bags, firmly holding my backpack full of money around my shoulder. I find my seat next to an older, plump woman already sleeping, and anxiously wait for the bus to pull away. This is it! Once that bus starts moving, I'm never turning back.

Every mile that goes by allows me to leave a part of the blackness of my existence with it. I'm shedding this color and all it has soaked up as if taking a cloak off my shoulders. I'm finally ready to allow it to fly in the wind.

I've had nothing but time to plan this move. Is it considered running away when I'm eighteen? It's been an inner knowing I'm made for something other than cooking, cleaning, and peddling drugs for the dads.

I overheard some kids in class complaining about college. After living my life cooped up, I know it's a gift to have this type of opportunity. College is what I'm the most excited about, especially since watching Lisa's videos about mental health. Her expertise in this area has ignited my interest.

Garden Valley has a state college right in town with plenty of majors to explore. For me, deciding what to do next doesn't feel daunting. I'm ready to figure things out for myself. It's a small town, not some big city to disappear into, and when the dads come looking, it'll be hard for them to hide.

I don't focus on that. Right now, I know each stripe on the road signifies that I'm leaving my old life behind. The most critical step has finally been crossed off: leaving.

Chapter 5 Lisa

New Beginnings

After folding three loads of laundry, prepping dinner, and mowing the lawn, I feel accomplished enough to relinquish to the call of making a video. No matter how much I've ignored it, I've fallen in love with this hobby. It fills me with joy to have coupled my crocheting with staying mentally healthy. I get to share my tips on both topics with the world!

"Or, at least with the *two* people who watch my videos." I roll my eyes. "Easy, Lisa. That's not true." Keeping the negativity away has been an extra chore, something I've had to put boxing gloves on to actively fight throughout the day.

My new morning routine is spending an hour or so looking for new jobs after I've taken Adrienne to school, and then I'm free the rest of the day! Well, unless pessimism takes over.

The mean side wants to taunt and poke until I've become deflated. It wants me to feel sorry for myself and wallow in self-pity. The educated part knows this is a chemical imbalance. The altering minds duke it out in an epic battle that leaves me exhausted with a pounding headache. I'll likely have to deal with this for the rest of my life—this up-and-down see-saw of emotions that leaves me dizzy.

I mentally reach into my toolbelt for a string of optimism to pull. Today, I'm intending to make use of my extra time and do what I love: making videos. Giving these videos my all is enticing and scary at the same time. What if I throw everything I've got at this and ultimately fail? What if my number of subscribers stalls even with extra effort?

I click through my phone to indulge in checking my subscriber count. "Eighty-five!" I'm thrilled, but it's an achievement that's always short-lived. As always, I want to reach the next milestone. What would it take to get to the one-thousand mark? It isn't like I can do a YouTube video every day.

Or can I?

I've been daydreaming about making this my job, but it's crazy talk to be uploading videos full-time. Isn't it? Don't I need to work at an 'actual job,' as Patrick puts it? I wouldn't run out of video ideas; I have a massive list of ideas. Today I have a challenging topic I need to address. I have to do it, or I'll be one of those fake people who smile and make everything look like everything is perfect when the room is burning down around them.

"One impromptu video coming up." I sit on the floor this time, crossing my legs and getting comfy with the view of my light green couch behind me. As always, Chuggers promptly sits in my lap. "Stop it," I say, gently moving his face out of range of licking his butt. He stretches up to kiss my chin, but I luckily dodge his tainted tongue. "Okay, time to do it." I take a breath and hit record.

"Hi, I'm Lisa with Coping With Yarn, helping you untangle the issues of your life one mental health tip at a time. Today, I need to be real about something. Okay, so here goes: I got fired." I take a deep breath and nod into these words, somewhat for effect but also to gather my next words.

"It's hard when things don't go our way. I loved that job. I could practice what I went to school for. Well, for the most part. I was doing my best, and…" Uh oh, waterworks. Isn't it ironic how the harder you try not to cry, the more the tears want to come out? "I don't mean to cry," I say with my voice raising in that high-pitched sort of way where anyone would know that you're crying even if they didn't see you. "It's just when these things happen, it does more than put a damper on your finances. I know I'm not alone when I say that I have to deal with the mental aftermath of failing."

I take a moment to breathe into this, knowing that I'm not going to edit this out.

"I kind of messed up. I mean, my boss did say that they want something else, but I wasn't exactly a stellar employee." I haven't let Patrick know this, but he doesn't watch my videos. "I'm saying this because we all make mistakes and endure tough times. I don't want to come on here with a smile and portray that my life is perfect. This is a mental health channel, and I'm working through my challenges. I was pretty down last night. I cleaned up dinner, read a book to my daughter, and fell asleep on the couch two hours later after staring numbly at the wall."

Now, *this* territory is new for me to talk about. My depression is a part of me that I've guarded against the world. This happens more often than I'd like to admit. Usually, when people describe me, they talk about how upbeat and positive I am. Only Patrick and Adrienne have seen me when I'm down.

"Except for last night, I've been able to keep the unwanted depression from settling in. The bad part tells me I'm a failure. I allowed it to take over, believing the ugly words that were pelting me."

"This morning was better. I got my daughter ready for school with a hug and a promise that I'll be there to pick her up at the end of the day. This is one way I get out of the depression funk, knowing that I have responsibilities to my family. Yes, I put my emotions aside to take care of someone else. Being depressed…" I pause, for the weight of that word is heavy on my lips, "is a serious issue, and it's real. The more attention I give it, the worse it gets. So, step one!" I hold my index finger up to the camera, giving that extra flare that has worked its way into me.

"I ask myself if what I'm upset about is all that bad. The answer is always a big yeppers for me!" I say with a laugh. "But once I think about it, this question gets simpler. I'm not hurting physically; I'm not dying. I'm alive, and I'm thankful for that. Then, I ask what needs to be done. As in, I wake up and think of all the places I'm needed other than my bed." I wipe the remaining wetness of my tears, feeling like I'm over the hump, at least for now.

"You've probably heard these other tips, but I'll list them out anyway because they work for me. If you're feeling down, get up and move around. And that rhymes, so you'll remember it. When I get like this, it helps to go for a walk."

"Another tip is to not drive yourself crazy." I laugh out loud again, the pep talk working wonders. "Here I am, needing a job, but there are only so many in my area. I put in a good effort every morning and move on." I swish my hands past me as if imitating a drift of wind. "Surround yourself with cute, cuddly pets like this one." Chuggers sticks his tongue out and pants as I lift him up, ever the willing participant. "At least he's cute when he's not licking his butt."

"Ultimately…" I pause, wondering if I should veer into

this part of a hot social media topic. "I don't want to be toxically positive. You see me on here, and I'm almost always positive. That is real. But the toxic part would come in if I wasn't coming clean about my depression. I don't want to come on here and say that you shouldn't feel your emotions, that you should push through with a smile and 'everything is going to be okay' attitude all the time. Sit with your feelings. Breathe into them and ask why you're feeling that way. Then, like I did today, try and move on from them."

I conclude the video by wishing everyone the best with their struggles. A few minutes later, I bite the bullet and tap the upload button. Yes, people are going to see this vulnerable side of me. Yes, this could lead to my sister and parents knowing that I have depression and have been fired. But I feel like I owe this to my audience. I want to help anyone out there who is struggling with the same thing. If one person gets one good tip from this video, it's a success.

I spy the incoming clouds from my sliding glass door. Once again, sadness makes its way into my heart. This is a different kind that doesn't have to do with putting on boxing gloves to beat myself up for failing. This is grief. No matter the name, it doesn't feel much better than the depression I felt last night.

My Nana loved this time of the year when the leaves changed. She would wear matching sweatsuit outfits. She loved everything to do with the fall, winter, and Christmas. She would bake almost every day, decorate every inch of my house and her cozy apartment in the back garage, and go to every activity in town.

A memory of Nana comes to me. I allow it to play out instead of shoving it down, as I've done dozens of times since she's passed.

"Lisa, it's okay to cry, but it's not like I'm spanking your butt over burning the banana bread."

"But I put so much time into it!" my ten-year-old self cried.

"I don't think that's what's wrong," I remember looking up at Nana. *"I think you just wanted a way to get the butter into your mouth,"* she said, thrusting her chin in the air to teasingly challenge me.

I smile and looked down, still wanting to live in the disappointment of the burnt bread.

"We can make those rolls in the freezer, and you can put half a stick of butter on them." She laughed as she worked her hands into the burnt bread, breaking it into smaller pieces.

"What are you doing, Nana?" I asked with surprise.

"I'm breaking this up to mix into the garden. Works great as a fertilizer."

To this day, I still don't know if this is true. I remember digging a hole with Nana and happily sprinkling in my charred bread, thinking it would help her garden grow. I can hear the exact pitch of her laugh. I smile as I hold the blanket we crocheted together to my cheek. It's funny; I've been pushing the memory of Nana away. This one, however, felt good to relive.

I've mostly abstained from holiday activities the last two years since she passed. I realize this has deprived my family of thoroughly enjoying the holiday season, but darn it, it hurts to have Nana gone. She was everything to me that my mother wasn't.

I sigh. Christmas is coming whether I want it to or not. The weather is getting colder. The sun goes to bed earlier. And, as I saw the other day, the stores are already outfitting themselves in green and red. I shake my head from the idea of fully diving into the festivities this year. That decision has yet to be made.

A hummingbird rests on the red feeder in front of the window, drinking the fresh sugar water I made yesterday. This was Nana's favorite animal, the hummingbird. Sometimes, I wonder if one of them who comes by here is her spirit saying hello. Another hummingbird comes to the feeder. The two chase each other around the yard. Even from inside, I can hear their chirping. "Hey, stop that." They need so much energy to keep those tiny wings going and I hate how they waste it to fight each other.

The thought correlates to my situation in a roundabout way. Another step comes to me that I would have liked to have added to the video I just uploaded. I hold my phone up to record a 'short' before I lose my nerve.

"One way to combat depression or feeling down is to realize how precious your energy is. This is easier said than done, but you've been given this day, this time to be here. You shouldn't waste it in bed or feel sorry for yourself. Yes, that's tough love, but someone's gotta say it!" I allow my signature laugh to shine through. "So, get up! Write a list for yourself and get to work!"

I upload this video, wondering if it will be received as insensitive by whoever views it. I type the title of the video: 'Some toughness, with much love.'

I take my own advice, jotting down the goals I've been harboring in my mind. It could be a month from now or next week that I find my next job. I will not waste this time of solitude, a rare gift to be in charge of my own schedule.

One thing has been stopping me from starting a business: filing for an LLC. It gives me yet another idea for a short video. I hold my camera up again, hitting record. "Here is some advice if you have a long list like I do: tackle the hardest, scariest item on your list. Do it first! This way, the rest of the items will seem like a breeze, and you will get the biggest nag off your back."

I save this video and scribble a reminder to upload it tomorrow. "People are going to think I'm nuts!" I shout at Chuggers. "Which one is scarier: researching how to start an LLC or learning how to edit videos? What about learning how to do one of those fancy intros to a video? Gosh, I have a lot to do! First, I need my triple 'C' to keep me going!"

Yes, I've gone through some disappointment, but my coffee with caramel creamer, A.K.A., 'the triple C combo,' hasn't let me down yet.

I've decided to research how to start an LLC in Oregon. I simply type this into my search window and get a website. An hour later, I'm finishing a call with someone from the Secretary of State's office to help finish filling out my forms.

"You'll get your paperwork in just a few days. I can't wait to check out your channel, Lisa," the lady on the phone says with genuine excitement. "I've always wanted to learn how to crochet. Do you have a playlist on YouTube for beginners?"

"Not yet. I don't really know how to do that," I answer sheepishly. Darn it, Lisa, you're going to lose a subscriber because you've been too afraid to tackle this one.

"My brother has a YouTube channel. He says it's easier to get on a computer and do that sort of thing instead of using his phone."

The information perks me up better than my triple C combo. "I'll have to try that out. Thank you so much for your help, Vicki!"

"It was a pleasure working with you."

Well, that was easy. I sit with my thoughts for a minute, trying to allow the goodness of this call and completed task to feel good. Why haven't I filed for an LLC sooner? I could have been so much farther along than this stage of starting from scratch right now.

"Don't go down that rocky road," I chide, instead allowing to give myself praise for getting it done. "Bonus!" I bark, startling Chuggers. "Sorry, boy. Every goal I meet takes me a step closer to proving myself. And I finally have the time now," I say simply, sitting up straight to combat the dumpy feeling. I open my computer and look at the clock in the lower corner. There's plenty of time to continue on to the next item on my list before I need to pick Adrienne up.

I type in my username and password to YouTube and watch as the wheel spins. "I'm in!" I yell in surprise. Is it just me, or is there a password elf in the computer that tries to jumble our passwords all the time?

"I'm doing this right now! Playlists!" I pound my feet beneath me when I see the heading on my YouTube channel. A few clicks later, I've figured it out. "I've… created… playlists." I sit back, allowing this victory to sink in.

I've conquered some easy tasks today that I previously labeled impossible. Maybe it wasn't the right time then. I need another month of this type of productivity to get this dream rolling. "You never know; it could happen," I say out loud. Speaking this into existence makes me feel like this dream just might become my reality.

Chapter 6 Ariel

A Warm Welcome

It took fifteen hours and three bus changes to put enough pavement behind me to get to Garden Valley. Now that my feet rest on the sidewalk, I know every minute of that long-ass trip was worth it. I got through two books as the miles ticked away. I took a nap, allowing a daydream of a new life to lull me to sleep. I keep reminding myself that every mile behind me means it will be that much harder for the dads to find me.

And I know they will try.

Gary has never been able to accept when someone goes against his rules. I remember one time when he hunted someone down for not paying him. It took him a week, but he finally found the guy. He made sure I stayed home, but his bloody shirt and knuckles were enough evidence that he is not one to cross. It's another reason why I didn't tell anyone about my plan. He can add pressure to get information, but no one can give in if no one knows anything about me.

So, here I stand on Maple Street, surrounded by all my things. "You're frickin' kidding me?" It's like a screen projecting a perfect town setting before me. The morning sun peeks above a mountain in the distance, spreading its rays overhead, lighting miles and miles of farmland. And I'm here! I've never seen open land like this, except for our backyard, covered in tents full of weed.

I stand with that awkward out of place feeling. I've never been good at standing still. It's one reason, probably the only one, why I took up smoking. With my cigarette, I have something to do instead of crossing my arms like the helpless runaway I am.

Luckily, the bus station allowed me to rent a cart to carry all my stuff. First, I need to find where I'm staying tonight.

I push my cart with my mismatched bags down the cobblestone sidewalks, the wheels clanking loudly with each step as if announcing my arrival. It's an attractive town with historical-looking buildings occupying several street blocks. To the back of me is a low-rising hill with two-story brick buildings. This is the college, making itself known with a perfect aesthetic. It's nice to have the visual since the college was the other driving factor for me to come here.

Each of the box-like storefronts takes on a specific color or theme. One is dark purple with majestic-looking crystals and trinkets inside. A pink boutique passes by next with expensive-looking clothing. I discretely look in the windows of the shops. I come up with the definite opinion that this is the happiest-looking town I've ever been in.

The sun is barely up today, and early birds are making what looks like their regular rounds. Closed signs are being turned to open, people are eating their pink pastries and doughnuts, and laughter is shared among friends. My eyes drift down the street and land on the swirly sign of the most welcomed sight: a salon. I sure as hell will be visiting there to get rid of this old identity.

I'm young, but I know enough that my dark-colored

clothes don't fit in. I've never been more aware of my goth-like state than now. Back home, no, that's not what I want to call it anymore. That was most definitely not my home! Somehow, I'll have to expunge those memories from my mind. For now, I'll refer to it as 'back then.'

Back then, I dressed in all black, painted my eyes and lips black, and matched it with my hair. I wanted to do the opposite of sticking out.

Just as I'm sticking out now.

The streets are far from crowded, but those who are here definitely know I've arrived. Eyes follow my every footstep. Whispered words are shared behind hands. I even saw a woman hold her coffee to her stomach as I walked by. I can't tell if this is all in my imagination or real. Either way, I feel like the grim-frickin-reaper.

Even after I toss my cigarette and sweep the dark hair from my face, I stick out like a black crayon amongst a carton of pastels. I'm the one dirtying up the sidewalks of the otherwise squeaky-clean streets.

This is why I'm here, though, right? So, I don't go down the same path as the dads and get accustomed to a life of crime and the dirtiness that comes with it. So I don't shut myself up in my house twenty-four hours a day and become an instigator of the bad neighborhoods in the world by dealing drugs.

Even with all my reasons to be here I fight the urge to leave as quickly as I came. Wouldn't it be easier to settle back in with the dads instead of starting every piece of my life over? At this point, they don't even know I've left.

I will myself to push my things toward the inn I've booked a room at. I find the building easy enough since it takes up the whole end of a cul-de-sac down one of the only roads in town. My doubts flee the second I see the beautiful white and green three-story building. I'm excited as hell to hole up in the building decorated with vines.

The road appears to have been built solely to lead to the grand building. Large trees line the streets and surround the building. Planter boxes greet me out front as I slowly make my way inside. Pushing my cart full of bags along the cobblestone sidewalks is challenging, but I manage to activate my puny muscles. So much for super strength powers.

I feel like royalty when I walk on the ruby-red rug leading through the double doors to the lobby. I'm hardly accustomed to this luxury. I allow myself to gawk as I take in the large floral arrangements and high chandelier. I finally have the chance to write my own book and even make it the genre of my choosing. This is *my* adventure now.

The girl at the front desk flashes her rosy cheeks, which go well with her light brown, bouncy hair. Oh, if I could be that bright and cheery! She seems to be only a couple years older than me and is worlds happier. I can't imagine working in such a place would bring joy, but maybe she's as free as I am.

"Hello and welcome to Garden Valley Inn. Do you have a reservation?"

I hand over my papers without a peep. Printed on her name tag is 'Amber.' She's as vibrant as her name, shining her light in this world. As for me, I've trained myself to be quiet, to barely be a nightlight in the corner of a forgotten room.

"I see you right here," she says to her monitor. "You're in room 18B, right up those stairs and down the hall on the left. Will you need help with your things?" She glances down at the pile of mismatched bags. Her smile remains, masking what I assume is ill judgment of me.

"No, thanks," I say quietly. I push the cart towards the elevator, craving the cleanliness of a shower more than a big meal.

"We have a limited menu, but we do offer room service," she says, reading my mind. Her gleaming white teeth shine as she hands me my welcome packet. Her head tilts as if in sympathy as she takes in my clothes. Or probably, how I don't fill them out. I'm wearing an outfit that is at least two sizes too big but still in the single digits. I've never been much of an eater, allowing my picky ways to ax out most food choices.

One glance down Amber's body reveals a dream physique. It is to me, at least. Next to her curves, I look like a little kid. Her salmon-colored vest and black pants aren't flashy, but one glimpse shows an hourglass figure I'm guessing any man would love.

I inwardly roll my eyes at the thought. As if I need a boyfriend right now!

I take the papers and head to the elevator, passing a display of pamphlets about Garden Valley and the surrounding area. I do my best to play it cool, ignoring the sudden urge to take each one. I quickly take a few of the information leaflets, pausing at the one about the college in town.

"I'm taking some classes there," Amber says, suddenly by my side, filling empty slots in the display. "There are a lot of good programs. The most popular majors are computer technology, psychology, and dental hygiene."

"Yuck, I almost hate cleaning my own teeth," I mutter without thinking first to keep my words in.

Amber laughs in response. She's a bundle of cheer compared to Charlotte with her red Kool-Aid-stained hair and ripped fishnet stockings. I doubt Amber wouldn't even wear

Charlotte's look for Halloween.

"I'm still getting through my prerequisites. It's taking me forever since I work here most days. But my manager says I can study when it's slow. I'm thinking of getting into something with science. Or I hear their culinary program is good, too." She laughs again, resting her hand on my shoulder for a moment. "Maybe I'll be examining my food under a microscope."

I force myself to smile at her 'joke' when my mind is stuck on her touch. It's been years since someone has touched me… I don't like it. The dads were the opposite of anything found in a parenting book. They didn't even held my hand as a child. As such, I've never been an affectionate person.

"Thanks again." When I glance at the menu, the word 'omelet' jumps out at me, and my stomach grumbles as if begging me to order the entire right side.

She tilts her head again and gives me a sympathetic smile with a nod. "We'll whip something up for you as soon as you give us a call."

I clutch the pamphlets and push my cart into the elevator. This place is nice, but my expectation of the room resembles my dingy old living room. My living room from 'back then,' when I could barely leave the house.

I count the numbers up to eighteen as anticipation builds with each step. I've booked my room for a few days. After that, who knows? I have plenty of money, but I know it'll stretch further if I can find an apartment or a place to rent.

"A good old-fashioned key," I say, fitting the key in the hole. I push the door open to reveal brightness beyond. Large windows across the room show trees beyond. Leaves dance in a light breeze. I push my heavy load into the room before allowing myself to be fully hypnotized by the soothing effects of the view.

The room's grey, white, and blue decorations are clean and inviting. It's one thing I hated about my house. The dark brown furniture, drapes, and carpet always looked dirty. They smelled it, too.

The door swings shut, leaving me to myself. I was alone most of the time in my room 'back then,' but this offers none of the loneliness I've endured. I grab the wooden wedge from my bag and push it under the door. I don't know this town well enough to grant it a wedge-free door. Yes, it provides a barrier between me and the unknown world behind it, but it also gives me the feeling of safety.

Standing at the hotel room window, I gaze out at the streets of my dream town. The soft hum of life below is like a song I've been waiting my whole life to hear. For the first time, everything feels right—like I'm exactly where I'm meant to be. The weight I've carried for so long has lifted, replaced by a lightness I can hardly believe. This is my new beginning. I can't help but smile, my heart swelling with a sense of hope I never knew was possible.

Chapter 7 Ariel

Ariel Becomes...

I wolf down the entire breakfast menu of a filled omelet, French toast, and oatmeal with a cup of brown sugar. I sit back in the plush chair with my hand over the slight bump in my stomach. With any luck, my body will transition into a shape that doesn't resemble a stick.

This suite is typical, with a queen-sized bed, an adjoined bathroom, and the round table I'm relaxing at. A plush, flowery lounge rests under the window, inviting me to relax in the air that isn't cloudy with the stench of weed. With freedom now a part of my present, I could easily live in a place like this.

I'm quickly lulled into a nap, my body needing rest after spending the night on the bus. I'm awakened by a knocking noise two hours later, frozen by fear in the lounge chair. My first instinct is that the dads have found me. It's over. I won't be able to live even a day in my new life. The knocking rings through the room again, but it's not from the door; it's from outside.

"What is that?" I peer out the window, searching for what's making the noise. To the right is a red-headed bird with white and black coloring on its back. "Aren't you a troublemaker?" It's funny. This is how I was described in school by the teachers who liked to punish me based on my appearance.

I wasn't been the best kid out there, but I wasn't *that* bad. I wasn't a rebel beyond the black clothes and cigarettes. All of it has been a façade to cover up the real me. But how do I even know? In the back of my mind, I've wondered if I'm even a good person. So what if I've gotten good grades? Whoopee. School wasn't exactly hard. It's not like I had much to do besides delivering drugs and doing homework.

I take my time in the shower, scrubbing my hair as if the layers of black dye will magically wash away. I watch the clear water wash down the drain, wishing it could take my past with it. It doesn't work like this. I've removed myself from the dire situation, but it'll take much more effort to remove the memories from me.

I toss on an oversized long-sleeved shirt that blends perfectly with the rest of my dark, monochromatic wardrobe. With all this cash on hand, I could probably afford to add a few more colors to the mix.

I thread my skinny legs in baggy jeans, wanting to trade these out for something that fits. Wearing baggy clothes has shielded my true form from the world. It has also kept me from getting noticed at school. The skinny girls with crop tops got the most attention from the popular guys. This is one skinny girl who still doesn't want any part in that.

It's gone along with my plan to have this look. I've envisioned being the girl who wore black from her hair color down to her shoes, one day emerging and debuting myself to the world in color.

"Starting with my hair."

I tuck my current book in my mini backpack, the room

key in my pocket, and ensure my door closes tightly behind me. I keep my head down when passing Amber in the lobby, hoping to go unnoticed.

"If you're going around town, there's a map right here," Amber says, handing me a map when I pass her desk.

"Uh, thanks," I say quietly, taking it from her.

"It's small, but this shows all the fun shops. Have a great time!"

I give a nod before leaving. I already know where I'm going, and I hope I don't need an appointment.

I'm sure-footed as I walk to the salon, even though I turn down the wrong street. I don't let this deter me. This is the plan, and I'm sticking to it.

A breeze rustles the leaves above me, bringing the sweet scent of Garden Valley to my nose. I've never known a town that didn't hold the stench of marijuana growing. I look out over the valley and can see for miles. There isn't a haze about this town, offering me a fresh look at where my future lies.

Even with unsure glances, everyone wears a smile as big as Amber's. I answer with a look to the ground but no longer shake my hair in my face. It's been my usual to hide, and I'm ready to take the invisibility cloak off.

With laser focus I approach the swirling sign with *Clippers Salon and Day Spa* written in cursive. The jingling door is to be expected in this small town. It's funny that noise can be a cliché. Even so, I like it. The windows lining the salon allow plenty of natural light. The chandeliers overhead aren't necessarily needed, but they add a fancy element to the place. Soft greys, blues, and greens decorate the walls in a classy way. The cozy feel is inviting, even for me.

"Come on in," a younger woman shouts across the salon. I want this makeover, but with each step she takes to approach me, I fight the urge to recoil and run like a scared cat. She slows as she approaches, her expression taking on a softness. "I'm Bailey," she says with her hand on her chest. "Would you like to make an appointment?" I hesitate, looking away from her and around the waiting area. "I have an opening right now if you'd like to…"

"I'll take it!" I blurt. Bailey giggles and waves me over to her station. I follow, feeling more than ready to shed this look.

"What are you after today?" Bailey asks with a hop of excitement. "Do you want just a trim or a color?"

"I want it light brown," I answer. "My natural hair is this brown color up here." I tilt my head towards the mirror with my fingers in my roots. "I hate this black!" Bailey laughs slightly, which I'm assuming is due to my forwardness. "Is that rude?"

"Not to me," Bailey says with confidence. "I like it when I don't have to guess what to do for a client. What about the length? You have such beautiful…"

"I want it off!" I blurt, covering my mouth. Bailey answers with a smile, so I continue. "I'd like it up to here," I say more politely with my hand at my shoulders. "And I like your bangs, but I'd have no idea how to do them."

Bailey isn't surprised at all by my forwardness. She puts her hands in my hair and fluffs it up while looking in the mirror. It reminds me of those clips on YouTube of professional hair stylists working their masterpieces on the women in the chair. Bailey doesn't seem that much older than me. And yet, here she is, playing the part of the expert as if she's been doing this for decades.

"Mine takes thirty seconds flat. I use a curly brush and hairspray. There's really nothing to it."

Bailey shows me the binder filled with different bundles

of hair colors. We go through and land on a honey tint. "I'll mix this up and be back in a few minutes."

I nod, and she bounces off with the color book. I take my book out of my bag and scan a few paragraphs while waiting. A book has always been my way out of worry. Whether it's an adventure, fantasy, or focused on the main character discovering her powers, I'm hooked. I'm sure there isn't anything to worry about here. Bailey seems perfectly capable of doing my hair, which is odd since she doesn't look that much older than me.

She comes back with a black cup and paintbrush resting in it. It's all new to me, having not gone through this experience before. I haven't touched scissors to my hair in years.

"Let's get you set up." She wafts a light pink cape over my shoulders. I pretend it's a shield of resilience, giving me my own powers to continue with this transition. "I like to start with the blunt cut first. Working on a shorter cut with color is always easier, so…" Bailey forms my hair into a ponytail and holds it down at the base of my neck. She grabs a pair of long scissors and holds them over my head. "Ready?" she asks without a hint of hesitation.

I nod in response, afraid of what might come out if I try and speak. It's not the cutting of the hair that I'm scared of. This is a big step in my transformation, changing my look. With this shedding of my long hair and change of color, I'm getting rid of Ariel. I'm getting rid of the old me who conformed to everything the dads requested. I'm collapsing the tunnel leading to a life of unmet inner expectations and desires. It's a makeover that will open me up to the potential I know I have.

Bailey squeezes her scissors through my hair again and

again until it separates entirely from my head. She holds up the glob of long hair cut from my head.

"Here it is!" Bailey says, flopping the severed hair in the air.

My hands fly to my mouth to cover the gasp that escapes. "It's always been long," I say as a cover-up.

"I'm sure it's quite a shock," Bailey responds, brushing through the rest of my hair resting on my shoulders. "I just cut off a good six inches! I've never been able to leave my hair alone for long enough to allow it to grow to that length. That must have taken some dedication."

"It sure did," I say, feeling the double meaning throughout my body.

It's the thing that is expected not only in this intimate one-on-one setting but in the world itself: conversation. Still, I'm not about to explain the volumes of books it would take to describe the true meaning of my response.

It's a pampering treatment I've never experienced, with Bailey's hands running the show. She chatters on about everything from the weather to the harvest festival that's coming up in town. I take it all in, not only the topic but the pampering treatment and graciousness of this woman.

"And there I was, trying to strap these babies down to stop the milk from leaking all over him." She arches her back, thrusting her chest out with a laugh. I can't help but chuckle at her story of rekindling her romance with her baby's dad. I don't know how we got on the topic, but her secret baby story that's fit for the screen. It seems like Garden Valley isn't immune to some spicy drama.

"You have so much hair here to work with," Bailey says with exasperation. She has kept my back to the mirror to surprise me when she's all done. "It's some of the thickest hair

I've had the pleasure of putting my hands in."

"What's going on, ladies?" A tall woman saunters in with a fashion bag dangling from her left forearm. Her presence takes me back, but not because of her beauty. It's because I've seen her before.

Her name is Monica. I met her at a makeup conference that she attended in Vegas. I was there as a tag-along with the dads at one of their stupid events. I remember how kind she was in helping match me with a cleanser for my blemishes. She's as upbeat as she was then, a perfect match for Bailey and this salon. This town has already proven to be a good choice for me, even if the flowery charm is the opposite of my persona. I'm smart enough to know I can't live in a cave of gloom forever.

Monica adds music to the salon, amping up my mini-makeover experience. I'm not expecting a miracle here. I have no idea what I'll look like after the whole roll of foil on my head comes off. As long as my hair doesn't have a drop of black in it, I'll be happy.

"That needs to sit for about a half hour." Bailey pats my shoulders before joining Monica in the back office. Luckily, Monica went straight back to her office, barely even taking a peek at me.

"Eight weddings down, one to go." Monica pulls out a box full of pieces of fabric and starts filling it with candy. She hands the first one to Bailey, who ties a pink bow around the top.

"Did you call to make sure the cake is on schedule?" Bailey asks.

"Gloria says she is getting through it, but she was clear that this is her last cake. It was a side hobby, and she says our wedding gigs have been too stressful."

"Ugh," Bailey moans, allowing her arms to dangle by her sides. "If someone would just move next door with some baking skills, we would give them so much business."

My eyes are pointed towards my book, but my ears stay fixed on their conversation. It's something I haven't been around; successful women running their own business. My eyes stare blankly at the words, with new thoughts dancing in my mind. The possibilities in this town are endless. It's a weird feeling that has joined me in this chair. Monica and Bailey are proof that I can do this adult thing. I haven't done it before, and I would bet they didn't have the shitty upbringing I had. None of that matters, though. I'm here now and am ready to tackle anything that comes my way.

"Okay, let's get you washed out." Bailey leads me to the washing station and places a folded towel under my neck. "Let me know if this is too hot or cold for you." It's weird to have someone else wash my hair. My mother barely did this for me when she was in the picture.

"It's fine," I say before she continues to talk. She massages my scalp and explains their dabbling in the wedding planning business.

"It's been keeping us busy, that's for sure."

"How did you know you could do that?" It's a question I've always wanted to ask successful people. How do they know they aren't going to fail once they took the first step toward their goal?

"Well, none of us can predict the future. I've always wanted to do hair, so I went for it. Monica was on the makeup side of things and she has an eye for planning and decorating. We put our two passions together, and voila! The wedding business was born."

I stay quiet, despite my barely having a clue about what

to do with my life. Bailey guides me back to the chair, dabbing my wet hair with a fluffy light green towel.

"I put myself through college almost three years ago now. That was when my son, Sammy, was a baby. Gosh, it wasn't easy. But I got through it. No peeking." She turns the chair, so I'm facing her and away from the mirror. "Are you going to the college in town?" Bailey asks with a perk to her voice. I shake my head slightly, not knowing how to answer. What in the heck am I doing here? Why do I think I can make it when I have none of the skills these very adult women have.

"I hear they have great programs," Monica chimes as she cleans the lobby. "The next term is starting in a week or so. The campus is just down the street if you're interested." She shares a look with Bailey that shows they'll be talking about me when I leave.

Bailey turns on the blow dryer and yells over the sound. "I just need it a little dryer before I can start shaping the cut. Do you have anything specific you want me to do?" I shrug, having no idea what look would be good for me. "A blank palette, I love it! I know just the look for your petite features!"

She grabs her sheers and gets to work. No doubt she'll leave me looking better than when I came in. Bailey talks the whole time while she snips my hair. She bends in front of me to ensure my left and right sides are equal. I'm being fussed over for the first time, and it feels good.

"Bangs?"

"Yup," I say defiantly with a nod.

She partitions a section of hair by my forehead, holds it down, and snips it right in front of my eyes. The action brings a smile to my face. Snip it all away! I keep to myself as I watch my hair fall to the ground, pretending it's my past. I'm sure glad I didn't have this thought earlier. I might have done something much more drastic, like buzzing it all off.

Bailey throws my hair in the air and snips at it on its way down. It's wispy, light, and showy, and I love it.

Twenty minutes later, after a blowout and straightening session, Bailey is done and ready for my big reveal. "Are we ready to see this beautiful masterpiece?" She spins me around. It's my second gasp of the day once I see my reflection. I stand and step to the mirror to get a closer look. I hold my hands over my mouth to keep the squeal in.

Gone is the dingy black I've lived in for years. My reflection glows back. My new hair color and fresh cut have me looking bright, clean, and ready to take on the world.

"Thank you, Bailey!"

"This is one of our best transformations if I can toot my own horn."

"Toot away, darlin'; she looks great! Wait until those boys see you in college," Monica says, hand on hip while leaning against the front counter.

"I'm not interested in that at all." I do something I've never done before: I put my hand on my hip and give them a look of defiance. The women laugh at my firm stance. I do something else I've never done before: I laugh with them. No spandex suit required for this super power—just a fierce attitude and the will to keep going when life gets tough.

***

I've watched those makeover shows before, where the ugly duckling goes into the salon and comes out a swan. The woman has all the confidence and can conquer the world! Yes, I've seen these, but I have never felt the effects of such a thing—until now.

I walk down the street, feeling my bouncy hair rise and fall with every step. My chin isn't as high as it should be, but it isn't an inch from my chest either.

On my way back to the inn I walk by a sign announcing that the community college is up ahead. It's more than intriguing. It pulls me in, making me wonder if I can trespass on the property to take a peek. I've always wanted to attend a real college, not just take classes online. Now's my chance.

"Damn these things," I say, stomping my cigarette in the dirt after my last drag. I wave the smoke around me, hoping it hasn't stuck to my clothes too much.

The campus emits a fresh grass smell instead of the stale skunk stench that made my nose curl 'back then.' I'm immediately intimidated by the large, two-story brick buildings and the open campus layout. I get stares from the other kids. At first, I feel like they're looking down on me before I remember my makeover. These people are the same age as me. At eighteen, I'm almost an adult. 'Almost' because they want my vote but hardly offer more privileges. I realize these aren't stares. The kids are my age. They're taking a glance as ordinary people do when they walk by someone.

"Do you need some help?" The friendly voice comes as a surprise. I look up into his face. Like, way up. He seems to be about my age, but his height resembles more of a man than a teenager. He absently cleans his glasses on his shirt as he looks over the campus. I'm glad since it gives me a chance to look him over, assuming he can't see me since his 'eyes' are in his hands. He's all goofy, from his big nose and ears that stick out to his arms that look as long as my legs. Everything on him is oversized compared to me.

"Are you lost?" he asks with a smile. That's mega-sized, too!

I look down to hide my flushed cheeks, which are a dead giveaway to what I'm thinking. I know he doesn't know *exactly* what I'm thinking, but I'm sure the red on my skin simplistically shows I think he's cute. Even with this new hairdo, I'm sure he doesn't feel the same about me.

But he did ask me a question. I'm no longer invisible, which will take some getting used to. Behind these baggy clothes is someone I'm waiting to discover. That's why I'm here, to uncover this person. She's here and pure, waiting to find her way.

"Uh, I'm looking for where I can sign in or sign up, something along those lines." I have no idea if I'm using the correct language here. My classes were a 'point and click' process on the computer.

"The registrar's office is that way," he says while wiping his glasses on his shirt. He threads them over his years, raises his bushy brown eyebrows, and smiles. I'm going to melt on the spot. Why can't an ugly boy be helping me right now?

The brick building is within sight, so I nod thanks.

"I'm actually heading there myself," he says with a tilt of his chin. He heads off that way, not waiting for me. I look to my left and right before I realize I need to follow his long strides.

He walks away, giving me more time to inspect him. I urge myself to not stare at his butt. I always saw myself ending up with one of those bad boys with dark hair, dark eyes, and that stubble look. This guy is the opposite and would fit in on a beach somewhere with his light hair. He's a beaming ray of sunshine. His squeaky-clean look is a stark difference from the roughness of the dads, and I like it.

I glance around the campus as I follow. Its beauty matches the rest of the town. There's more green on this campus than in my old town combined. Buildings sit atop rolling hills full of grass, bushes, and flowers. An expansive hill to my left is dedicated to a flower display of petunias spelled out in the college's name: Garden Valley State. Banners hang from old-fashioned iron lamp posts with the college logo and colors of purple and gold.

"It's right in here," he says, opening the door for me and sweeping his hand forward. His isn't a deep voice, but one that gleams a light into the innocence surrounding him. He has 'small-town farm boy' written all over him. I hesitate before leading the way into the building. I had hoped to tuck a class catalog under my arm and leave. But now the cute guy is here, hindering my plan.

"I actually work here a few hours a week," he says, going behind the desk.

Of course you do.

"So, how can I help?"

He leans against the counter and still towers over me. The smile that takes over most of his face probably works to get all the girls, but it makes me want to tuck into my shell. My vision of having a little old lady help me register has flown out the window.

"I just need a list of classes or something."

"Obviously, you want to enroll, right? You've already seen first-hand how nice the students are." He holds his hands wide to comically refer to himself. I do my best to hold my smile down by tugging my lip down with my teeth. I shift my weight, having no idea how to respond. "Here you go," he says quickly, handing me a thick grey booklet. "This is a list of all the classes. They start a week from Monday. Don't worry, we're not at max capacity, so you still have plenty of time to register. Do you have any credits to transfer?" I nod, which, thankfully, is enough to keep him going. "Great. First, you'll need to apply, which you can do here. Don't worry; they accept everyone," he whispers behind his hand.

He leads me to a computer where I can apply and get the ball rolling. Thankfully, I've kept my transcripts in my bag, which he scurries off to scan into the system.

"I'm Jordan, by the way," he says when he returns.

I sit with my bag slung over my right shoulder, clutching it with both hands. His long torso is bent right next to me while his right arm is stretched to use the mouse. I can't help but stare at his arm, which is covered with soft-looking blonde hair. A clean soap scent floats in the air. It mulls together with his looks, intoxicating my senses.

"You can log in here and sign up for classes if you want." He adds to the bank of smiles I've received today. I have no idea if this is the road I will take. College is on my list of priorities, but that feels jumbled and upside-down at the moment. All this is far-fetched. It's a dream.

And yet… here I am.

I raise my hands to the keyboard, pausing between all my movements, hoping for a moment of solitude to sort through my thoughts. But the cute guy stays put. I move my bag, and he's there. I shift a few times, and yup, still there. Okay, here we go. I type in the name that matches my new license.

"Hey, how do you pronounce your name?"

It's an innocent question. One that I've only been asked a few times in life. It's an old life where I used to answer by a different name. It was a life that had been sheltered. A life that kept me from regular human interaction and activities.

I look down and around before looking him in the eye. I cross yet another barrier today and give a small smile back. "Leira. My name is Leira."

Chapter 8 Lisa

Crossing Paths

It's been six days since I was fired. Six days and barely anything to show for it. I have all the time in the world to scrub the corners and dust even the high shelves. This hardly feels like a win. Having a clean house while working nearly full-time, now there's an achievement. A clean house and a freezer full of dinners is an accomplishment. It means I'm winning at this game that doesn't keep score, but I don't feel that way.

I've been awake for two hours. I've laid in bed, allowing the negative voice to eat at me. My to-do list is normally my number one combat to depression, but today my mood is circling down the drain and is taking me with it.

"Honey, I'm going to take Adrienne to school. Are you going to get up soon?" It's Patrick, peeking his head into my view from under the covers, his finger twirling a locket of my hair.

"Can you send her in for a hug, please?" Adrienne comes in a minute later with her bag around her shoulders. "Have a good day, sweetie. I'll pick you up, okay?" Somehow.

"Okay. I hope you feel better, Mommy." Her petite arms feel good around me. I try to hold it in, but a tear escapes through my closed eyelids. I wipe at it behind her back before we pull away.

"See you soon." I keep my voice light with a smile. I know I'd cry harder if I saw my sad reflection. Once I hear Patrick's truck pull out of the driveway, I let the emotions loose, sobbing into my pillow. It's not an act of feeling sorry for myself. I can't even explain all that I'm sad about. So, I lost my job, big deal!

I am not my job!

It's difficult to control my lows when they hit me this hard. I turn on my side, and my shirt gets bunched behind my back. I move again, and the bottom of my sweats goes up to my knees. "Ugh, I hate that!" I reach under the covers to yank them down, suddenly repulsed by my mood. I slam my fist into my pillow and turn my cries into a scream. "I hate being like this!"

It's one technique I've used with mild success: jolting my mood by screaming. "I have to go to the bathroom, and if you don't like it then tough titties," I snarl, arguing with my depression.

I pull my bottom sheet off the mattress, throw my blankets on my bed, and knock my pillow to the floor to deter myself from crawling back in. "I have better things to do today. I'm an important person with many tasks to complete. Let's see, I have to finish the cow I started yesterday. After I finish him, I'll make a couple of horses, and my farm collection will be complete. Of course, I'll need to film all this and upload the videos. People are waiting to see them."

I like this shift, aiming to drag my mood up with me. I've been determined not to use pills to push the depression away, wanting to conquer those feelings by pulling every tool out of my belt if need be. I pushed hard in glorious happiness for a few days after I lost my job, trying to prove to myself and my husband that being at home can be as productive as a day at the clinic. I've scrubbed the house, attempted to organize my hundreds of skeins of yarn, repainted the living room and guest room, re-decorated the guest bathroom, and cleaned the garage. This was on top of my regular chores of taking Adrienne to ballet, spending time playing with her, cooking dinner, and cleaning up.

But that sneaky shadow of depression was always lurking, waiting for my energy to dip. You'd think I'd have learned by now—pushing myself always ends in a crash, complete with a side of negative self-talk.

A text dings in from my mom. "Ugh," I say, looking up at the ceiling. "What now?"

Let's go shopping to buy you some nice clothes. Mom

From the surface, this gesture seems nice, except I know the missing part of the sentence: 'So you can look nice for a change.'

I have no desire to text her back. I'm too busy acting like going to the bathroom is the most important thing to do right now.

My phone jingles again with the familiar sound of gaining a new subscriber. "Yippee, skippie, new subscribers!" I say to Chuggers, who jumped off the bed to join me. I quickly wash my hands and face, the action pulling me further from the dark hole that nearly sucked me in for the day. I trot to my phone to view the YouTube message. "Seven new subscribers since last night!" This is pure success! People like my videos! I'm building my community!

I get dressed and leave my bedroom for good. I saunter down the hall and pop two pieces of bread in the toaster. "One triple C combination coming right up," I say, forcing the blues away. While the weather matches my mood in bed, I'm now greeting the clouds with my own sunshine.

"Maybe I'll start with a walk." I gaze outside with the mug warming my hands. I close my eyes, picturing this warmth running through my body, pushing all my negativity away.

"It's not bad to be sad," Nana used to say. She like to speak in rhymes, usually reciting sayings about Christmas.

My smile makes me wonder if a person can be contently depressed? "I guess we'll see," I say, feeling that this is a great way to explain my feelings.

I allow myself the luxury of swiping through videos on YouTube as I nibble my avocado toast. A video suggestion comes up about editing videos from the phone. "Yeah, right, like I'll be able to learn how to edit a video in 7 minutes." A thought comes to mind: I can watch this video if I want to. I don't have to duck into a room and hide to watch it. I can watch videos all day because I don't have a boss who will tell me not to. "Sorry, Patrick, you're not my boss!"

I click on the video and the guy with the English accent appears briefly before quickly cutting away to his computer screen. I have no idea how people do this, clicking around on their computer while adding a professionally-sounding voice-over. I switch to watching the video on my laptop so I can tap around on my phone.

One video leads to another, and soon enough, I'm testing my newfound knowledge of the footage I recorded yesterday. There was a part where I blabbed on and on about a crocheting technique. I quickly cut some of this out, smoothing the video into the next topic. This task alone sends a jolt of triumph through me. "That was easy," I mumble.

So why haven't I done this yet? My energy wants to pull me back to the mood I woke up in. I don't let it, and instead,

I finish editing the rest of my video with the free app I downloaded.

An ad comes up for Canva. Instead of clicking off like I usually do, I go to the site on my computer. "These are bold fingers I have here!" I chuckle at my own joke, sending Chuggers into his happy turns. I smile at him, allowing his innocence to spark my day. Rekindling my fire usually takes a while, but these tasks have lit a fire like no other.

After only thirty minutes, I've used the free Canva version to create a cute introduction to my videos. After a half hour I have something. The animated pug bats a ball of yarn around on the screen as a cheerful song plays in the background.

I next piece together a logo that I've had dancing around in my head. The one on the screen isn't exactly like the picture in my mind, but it's close. "I wonder," I start, but finish the sentence with an email to my friend, Zooey. She's into graphic design and does this exact type of work. I hit send with the message asking if she could create the idea I've described.

"Another video idea!" I grab my notebook and scribble some bulleted ideas about conquering your fears before they fly away. "To demonstrate…" I grab my phone and hold it away from my face, ready to record another short for YouTube.

"We all have them: fears," I say with a curt smile. "When you're unsure how to do something, just go for it. What have you got to lose? The worst thing that can happen is that it doesn't work and you'll be in the same situation you're in now. The point is that you've faced that fear and taken a step toward your dreams."

I hit upload, follow my instincts yet again, and strap my shoes to my feet on our back porch. Chuggers flies from the sliding glass door, charging after the red and brown birds who peck at the feeder.

Six laps around my property equals a mile, and I go for it. I definitely have the time to exercise, which I need to do more for the mental benefit rather than the calorie burn. A sleek physique is important to me, but it's way down on the list. Not all of us need to be super skinny. My grandma fell a couple of times toward the end and was fine.

"This extra cushion around my hips that I've fought my whole life is now saving my bones," she said.

Just in the few days I've been home I've gotten much more movement in with all my cleaning and project work. I don't mind being squishy around the edges, but it's nice to feel a slight looseness around my middle instead of my pants digging into my sides.

My eyes stay on the oversized, blue garage in the backyard as I walk around the path around our yard. My mind brings up images of the mess beyond the closed doors. "Now there's a project to tackle."

The front part of the garage holds Patrick's tools, but I've needed to clean out the quarters that Nana lived in. There's plenty of space for someone else to live there unless it's my mother. "Ha, as if she'd ever stoop to that level!"

What if I spruce that up to be a rental? "Could be possible," I say, answering my thoughts. I let the idea percolate for a bit. This could close some of the gap needed from my missing paycheck. That would reduce the pressure off me to rush and get a job, AKA be more useful in Patrick's opinion. I have a couple months' severance pay. This would extend that even further!

Ignoring what will undoubtedly be Patrick's protests for having a tenant on the property, I use the garage's side door with Chuggers on my heels.

"Step one, assess the damage…" I tell Chuggers, who resembles a sausage, in a dramatic, deep voice. The space isn't as messy as I remember. I have a few bags of forgotten yarn here, but other than that, it just needs a good scrubbing. The bottom floor is one big open room with a kitchen and living room. The layout is spectacular, with a roomy loft upstairs for a bedroom.

Someone might really like this place. "Except for the sea of red and green. Sorry, Nana. I love Christmas, but this décor needs to take a break," I say.

The living area is quite bare, with just an old desk. I parted with Nana's furniture after she passed away, with it getting quite old. "Oh yeah!" I type out a text to my friend, Joanie. At the last PTO meeting, I remember she wanted to sell her furniture, which was too small for her huge house. She moved to Garden Valley about a year ago and I remember her saying they've finally upgraded their furniture.

If the stars align, Joanie's overstuffed white couch will fit perfectly in the living room. It's a small space, but the tall ceiling gives that open feel.

My optimism about renting the place increases every second. One of Patrick's friends, Matt, moved in for a few months last year. We didn't charge him rent, but in exchange, he fixed up the place. Matt upgraded the space with new flooring, installed a dishwasher, and revamped the adjacent bathroom with a modern sink and a brand-new shower. We for sure won in that deal!

I look out over the apartment from the loft. "This place could really shine. All it needs is a little inspiration." I hold my finger in the air and trot down the stairs with Chuggers on my heels.

Just the thought of visiting the fabric store flings my depression over a cliff. My severance pay will be money well spent in the decoration aisles. "Not yarn, Lisa. No yarn this time!" I chide. I have enough skeins that I could make a blanket to cover Garden Valley.

My sour mood fades into the background, replaced by the spark of this new project. This could be the lifeline I've been waiting for, the income that buys me the time to focus on my passions.

***

It's been a month since I've been at Joann's, and not because I've forgotten about my favorite place on earth. I always want to steer my car to the enormous building that offers much more than fabric and yarn. Scrapbooking supplies, small furniture, decorations for the current season, and everything you could want to decorate pulls me in. I'm in *'the'* destination to spruce up the back garage. One thing about Garden Valley: there are enough crafty people in this town to keep this place in business.

I have to stop myself from dashing to the yarn aisles to see what's new, instead heading to the decorating section. Shelves, colorful pictures, and cute pieces of furniture would look fantastic in the back apartment. "This would be great for my yarn!" I say, crouching to inspect the wooden unit thoroughly. The sales price has me sold in a second. This cabinet would be great in the guest room, but the price is so reasonable that I want to buy one for the back garage as well.

I grab a fake topiary, a couple of pictures, and a few pillows with birds and trees on them. There's even an aisle with bedspreads. I pick out one that will be perfect for the loft. There, that should be a good start for the apartment. I want to leave room for whoever moves in to put their own touch on the place, but at the same time, I want to market it as move-in ready in case someone is just starting out.

Once my cart's full, I can finally skip over to the yarn section. This is where the magic happens! My imagination runs wild, and I wish I could slow time down just to dive into every project I dream up. I know I'm not the only one who can crochet, but it's my thing that I know I'm good at.

My phone buzzes with a message from Joanie about her furniture. *You have terrific timing. My puffy couch and loveseat need a good home.*

We type back and forth to secure a drop-off time. Joanie insists on delivering everything free of charge.

My phone also dings with a message from Zooey. *I love your logo ideas! I'll get started right away. I'd love to exchange the designs with one of your crocheted blankets!*

I fill my cart with yarn in colors and textures that match my positive mood. Retail therapy works in my case. I've also replaced a layer of depression with the hopefulness of getting a tenant in the back garage.

I'm nearly done when I pass a young girl checking out the hooks and gadgets. For a moment, I wonder why she's not in school before figuring she's older than she looks. She seems confused as she picks a hook up, looks it over, and puts it back.

"Hey, do you need some help?" I ask with a smile. The girl turns to me and freezes. "Are you okay?" I laugh.

I figure she's about fifteen, given how small she is. Her baggy black attire doesn't automatically match her to a hobby of crocheting. Still, I don't like to judge people by their 'book,' so to speak. I was this way once, swaying to the punk-rock side, mainly to tick my mother off. They called us 'tree frogs' in high school because we hung out to smoke by the big oak tree across the street from the school.

"You're Lisa," she finally says.

I shake my head back in surprise with an extra blink. "Yes, I am. Do we know each other?"

"I've watched your channel." She threads her light brown hair behind her ear and looks down in embarrassment. "I've posted comments on your videos. I'm, um, 'Mermaid On Land.'"

I recognize her name instantly. "I know who you are! It's nice to meet you in person. You're the first fan I've met! Well, aside from my friends and family, who make up ninety percent of my subscribers. I guess I didn't realize that you live in Garden Valley." The girl looks around as if checking to make sure no one overheard my traveling voice.

"I just moved here," she says softly. "I'm staying at the inn down the street." The psychology nut in me kicks into high gear. Coupling her twitchy movements with her outer appearance, I'd say this girl is either lost or a runaway.

An idea pops in my mind like a firework. "Staying at the Inn, huh? Well, I'm going to rent our back garage soon if you don't have a place lined up." Her eyes show interest. I feel slight guilt since I need to charge rent, but this is the way of the world, after all. "Are you a fellow crochet-obsessed person?" I ask, running my hands over the bundles of yarn in my cart.

"Not really. I mean, I'm just getting started. I've followed your tutorial video a dozen times and can't get it to start."

"Well, maybe I can give you a lesson now that you're in town."

"Really?" she asks with wide hazel eyes.

"Sure, just send me a message sometime. It was nice to

meet you, 'Mermaid.' I better get going to pick up my daughter."

"I didn't know you have a daughter," the girl says in surprise, walking next to me as I wheel over to the register.

"Yeah, I don't put her on camera. It's a decision I made when I started the channel."

"That's smart." She keeps her eyes on me as if not wanting to let me go. "You never know what kind of creeps are out there."

She says this in a far-off way like she's thinking through something. "It was nice to meet you. I'm glad you said something. Meeting a fan has given a boost to my day!" I say, unloading my yarn at the register.

"I hope to see you around." It's more of a question than a pleasantry.

"I'm sure we will," I say with a cheery voice to the lovely girl. This is precisely why I don't judge people on their outer appearances.

It's more than flattering that I was recognized by a fan from out of town. This means I'm on the right path! I reached someone young, and she was here to buy a hook! Now that I think of it, I didn't even help her pick one out. I still need her real name in case she's interested in the apartment. Darn, she's walking out the door as I'm about to pay for my purchases.

I let Janet know I want to buy two cabinets for my yarn and walk out with Charlie in tow, pushing my purchases on a cart. Yes, I know everyone by name at this store. Sue me.

I see the mermaid girl looking lost on the sidewalk after we throw everything in the van. She looks one way, takes a few steps, and then turns around and does the same in the opposite direction. I pull up next to her and roll down my window. The clouds above signal that it could rain at any moment. I'm not about to let this girl get lost in town.

"Are ya lost, hon?"

"Yes!" she says with exasperation. Tears form in the corners of her eyes. She's so young and seemingly alone in this town. It makes me think back to when I was on my own for the first time. Nana gave me a room when I got away from my parents, something I returned when she got older and needed a helping hand.

"I could have sworn the inn was that way." She points in the wrong direction.

"Yeah, you're turned around, sweetie." I try to make light of the fact that she's mixed up, even in this small town. Her quiet, timid ways make me wonder if she's ready to be on her own. Large raindrops splatter on the windshield, indicating more to come. "It's a few blocks that way, and it's about to rain. Do you, um, want a ride?"

I don't know what to expect from her. In her eyes, I'm a stranger. She's a stranger to me too! Her eyes light up, showing she'll take me up on my offer. It's not like me to do this. I usually stay laser-focused on my schedule, barely noticing what others around me are doing. But my world has been shaken up, freeing me from the grip of a hectic routine and giving me a clearer view of those around me.

She nods and climbs into the passenger seat. The way her clothes hang on her has me suspicious that there's a skeleton of a body underneath. I briefly think about grabbing her a fast-food meal on our way, but I need to get to the school.

The girl clutches her bag to her stomach as she sits next to me. It's an odd duo here in my mini-van, a woman in her thirties with vibrant colors and the young new girl in town dressed in black.

A dozen questions pop to mind, with me writing in her

chart as if she's a patient. A fear that she'll flee holds me back from prying. It's undeniable, though. There's something about this girl that makes me want to help her.

Chapter 9 Leira

The Secrets We Keep

Why did I tell Lisa my code name on YouTube? What if she tells someone? This could link someone to the name Ariel, which gives clues to where I am!

I throw these worries aside, allowing myself to revel in the fact that I found her! Or, rather, she came up to me in the store. I wanted to meet Lisa but had no idea I'd be so lucky. Here I am in her car on one of my first days. It's odd, but I feel comfortable with her. She and maybe the tall guy at the college are probably the only people I'd like to talk to. Well, I guess there is Bailey at the salon, who was nice. And Amber at the inn seemed trustworthy.

I sit quietly in Lisa's van, a smile warming my insides. I've met people I can trust in this town. Already!

I don't think I was too much of a fan girl when I met Lisa. At least I didn't jump up and down crying like some people do when meeting their idol. I want to play it cool, but not too cool! I want her to know how much she has meant to me. Well, without me telling her that I ran away, that is. Because of her, I've taken hold of my life and am running toward my dreams.

"Thank you for the ride."

"No problem-o. The inn is just a couple of blocks away." A beeping noise interrupts us. "Crappers, I need gas," she sighs. Her posture physically sinks in her seat, like it's one of the worst things that could happen right now. "It's a good thing this is a small town. My husband says I'll be walking one day." She giggles in the same way that shines through in her videos. She's exactly the same with her kinky black hair and dimpled cheeks. For not the first time, I want to get to know her. "I have a few minutes before I get Adrienne," she says as she pulls into the gas station. "If you don't mind?"

I shake my head, glad I'll be able to spend more time with her. "Is she your only child?" I ask, easing my hold on my mini backpack. It's awkward to be in her car. Even if I trust this woman, it's not like we're friends.

"Yup, I only have one little sweetie," she answers, her face visibly brightening. "Do you have any siblings?"

I shake my head. "I always wanted one." But I'm glad I didn't. They would have been caged up like I was, and it would have been impossible for me to leave.

It would have been nice to have someone to be friends with at home though. I wasn't allowed to do anything or go anywhere with anyone. But that's all behind me. I'm ready to move on and give my life a spin. I'm following Lisa's advice about turning trauma into no-drama. She says a person can turn any situation into something positive. The positive was that I wasn't homeless, and the dads gave me money for food.

Besides, don't most teens feel trapped by their parents? Probably. But most teens don't list 'drug dealer' as their parent's occupation.

"What about you?" I ask.

"I have a sister," Lisa says, digging around in her purse for a credit card. "Ten gallons as quickly as you can with regular, please," she says as she hands her card to the man. "They sure are busy here today, huh?"

"Do you ever see her?" I ask with curiosity.

"My sister? Only when my mother makes us get together for a holiday or birthday."

"I always thought it would be fun to have a sister," I say.

"We aren't close, but that's because she's so much like my parents. Oh my gosh, I'm going to be late if these guys don't get it together! It's like they're moving in water or something. School gets out in ten minutes, and that's almost how long it'll take to get there." She looks around the van, seeing that we're blocked in by a car in front and behind us.

"I'm sure I can find the inn from here," I say, unclicking my seat belt and taking my bag.

"No, it's starting to rain, and I said I'd give you a ride, um…" She looks up ahead, back down at the clock, and then over at me. "How would you like to meet Adrienne?"

"Me?" I ask in a high voice. "Sure!" I nod emphatically in agreement.

A few minutes later, Lisa takes her card with her left hand and puts the van in gear with her right. "Off we go!"

She practically peels out of the gas station while talking a text into her phone, telling me beforehand that she'll ask one of her friends to wait with Adrienne until she gets there. Her phone dings a moment later, and Lisa sighs back in her seat. She's so worried about getting to school on time that I can feel her stress.

No one ever worried about me like this, and I mean ever.

"Good ol' Amy. Crisis averted! So, I'm guessing you haven't seen much of the town beyond that block you made to get here?" I nod in agreement. "I think you'll like it. It's a combination of being a small, beautiful town but with plenty to do. There's always some kind of event happening on the weekends. There are city-wide yard sales, movies in the park, 'lake day,' markets every other week during the nice weather, craft fairs… a little something for everyone."

I nod. This is why I came here, to experience the wholesomeness I have only heard about through Lisa's channel and on those far-fetched Hallmark movies. I never thought there was such a thing as warm smiles and helpful people. Yet, here it is in Garden Valley.

"Oh my gosh!" she screams. "I don't even know your name. I can't exactly call you 'Mermaid.'" She laughs, and I nearly join her this time. It's a sound that means she's not uncomfortable with having a stranger look like I do in her car. That is, the way I dress. Bailey's hairstyle has taken me into the 'normal-looking category.'

"It's Leira," I say softly.

"Similar to Lisa… I like it!" she hollers. Little does she know that the reverse is my real name, Ariel. I've been second-guessing my 'reverse name change' that I once thought was clever. What if the dads do the same thing when looking for me?

Lisa continues to talk about the town, cluing me in on the best place for pastries and how many residents there are. She's a sweet sparkle of a person, shining her light to guide the way for others. That's what she's been for me, at least.

For just a moment, I pretend she's my mom. I haven't had my mom around for a while and have forgotten what it's like to have another female around. It's not too far-fetched. Everything from her outfit to the smile on her face screams mom to me. She looks comfortable in a baggy blue shirt and jeans. It's plain, but the light rainbow scarf around her neck makes me want to hug her, and I'm *not a* touchy person.

Over the years, maybe a teacher or two have reached out to me, but I'm the type of girl who always finds a crack to slip through. I'm the type who is easy to forget over a long weekend or holiday break. It's just how I've wanted it, though. Questions come with too much attention. Questions about home life and why I act and smell the way I do.

I realize I've been staring at her and need something to say. "I like your scarf," I say quickly as if the compliment was stuck behind my tongue. "Did you make it?"

"I sure did. I think I'd crochet a house to live in if I could."

"Do you sell the stuff you make?"

"Eh. I've tried at a few events in town, but there's only so many tissue box covers and fuzzy sweaters these people want."

"I mean on Etsy or something."

"It's a bit over my head, but I'm working on it!" she yells excitedly. "I applied for an LLC and everything. I haven't taken the next steps of setting up a bank account under the business name, but that'll be next when I get my papers. I've had time since I've been off work for a few days."

"Oh yeah, I saw the video about your job. I'm sorry."

"Things are supposed to work out for a reason, right? For example, what brings you here to town?"

"College," I say simply. It's plausible but not the whole truth.

I look out the window at one green pasture after another. Tractors plow through fields and horse tails swish. Dots of puffy sheep graze in pastures and people do God knows what in the stables. My thoughts take over, not allowing me to fully appreciate the beauty of the town. I'm glad I finally took the leap to run away, but I wonder if this blissful time is only because I know the dads have no idea I've left yet. They'll soon find out I'm gone. And then I know they'll be looking for me. And… they'll be mad.

"I really like your videos," I say.

"Thanks! I'm getting new subscribers every day. I was thinking of naming them something like the crazy crocheters."

"Good idea," I nod. "Maybe the crochet-iacs, like maniacs who like to crochet."

Lisa laughs. "That's a keeper! Did you get a hook at the store?"

"Not yet. But I saw that they have openings there."

"You're in the market for a job, huh?" Lisa says with a glance. "If you're serious, I can give you a good word."

"You'd do that?"

"Sure! I mean, we just met, but I have a feeling you're a good worker." I shrug, having no idea if I would be or not. "Never had a job before?" I glance out the window again in embarrassment. "That's fine. Hey, where did you say you're from?"

Great question. I hadn't thought this closer proximity in the car thing through. "California," I lie.

"Oh yeah? Whereabouts?"

Lisa doesn't take the hint from my drab tone of voice.

"Just in a town, uh, by the border." There.

Lisa gives me a nervous smile and switches the topic back to the fabric store. "I'd love to work at the fabric store, but I think we'd literally be swimming in yarn at home if I did. Ahh, finally, we're here."

Yes, finally!

She pulls down a street lined with houses and the greenest grassy yards I've ever seen. I remember spray painting our grass at home, um… 'back then.' Even at eight, I knew we lived in a broken house. Ours looked nothing like the ones in the nice parts of town or the ones here. In Garden Valley, it seems nothing has been neglected. It makes me wonder if there is even a bad part of the town or anything resembling my old neighborhood.

"There's Amy with her kids and Adrienne," Lisa points out as she throws her seatbelt off. She pops out of the car immediately after she parks. "You can come too, Leira!" she shouts before trotting to the three kids surrounding a blonde woman.

I slowly follow, feeling like I'll put my dark stamp on these squeaky-clean people in bright oranges and yellows. I don't even own a shirt with yellow *on* it. Lisa's questions weren't too prying, but I have a feeling they are the first of many coming my way. One thing's for sure, I need to get my story straight.

"I'm sorry I'm late!" Lisa shouts. I love how she's out there with her personality, unafraid of who hears her. "I was low on gas, and… oh, let's face it, I was at the fabric store." The other woman with blonde hair laughs as Lisa snuggles with her little girl. I inch up to them, watching Lisa fawn over her daughter, which was never a greeting given to me. "Guys, this is my friend, Leira. She's new in town." Lisa holds her hand out to introduce me.

I freeze. Why the hell didn't I stay in the van? I don't think anyone has ever introduced me like this. All eyes are on me, and even the children's are intimidating. I can feel the judgment coming my way. I glance to the left and see a mom look away. The same happens to the right me. Gosh, they're just dark clothes. Doesn't anyone around here wear black with extra zippers?

"Hi," I say without a smile, tightening my grip on the strap of my backpack. I try to smile, but my lips stay in a tight line that probably does nothing to hide my discomfort.

"I'm Amy," says the woman with a bright smile. "Where are you from?"

And here's the start of the questions. Isn't this the icebreaker of them all? Yet, I still need to think through my answer, which will be the backbone of the lie of a life that I need to fabricate.

"Oh, um, California." This is an acceptable answer, right?

"Oh? My husband and I want to take the kids to Disneyland," Amy says. "Which town are you from?"

I scrunch my lips together. It's not exactly a friendly gesture, which is what I'm going for. I hate to get all 'teenage girl' here, but leave me alone, lady! I look around and shift to my left leg. Of course, I don't want to tell her where I'm from, but I can't come up with one single town name to save my life. Who cares if it's fake? What, does this woman know all of the names of every town in that state?

"By Sacramento," I say when her stare hasn't backed down. I don't care if it's not a friendly one. Being on the spot is not my thing.

Lisa gives me an odd glance and I realize Sacramento isn't anywhere near the border, which is what I told her.

"I have a couple of friends who live there who are teachers. Which school did you go to."

What the heck, lady?

Smiles seem to be constant in this town, something that isn't really my thing.

"Hey, Amy, thanks for staying with Adrienne," Lisa interrupts. I wonder if she knows she's saving me from this inquisition.

The women chat for a few minutes about school and schedules while I stand in awkwardness, wishing for a cigarette.

"Want to see my playground?" It's Lisa's little girl, Adrienne. She stares at me with deep brown eyes full of trust and innocence. Eyes that remind me of what I saw in Jordan's, the tall wonder of a boy at the school.

When my mom left, I was even younger than her. Her outfit, complete with matching heart pants and a T-shirt, screams little girl through and through. A ribbon in her hair has fallen slightly askew from what I can imagine was a day of play and work. I can't possibly say no to such a cute face.

"I guess," I shrug. It's not like I need to be anywhere.

"Mommy, can I show Leira the playground?"

Lisa looks between the two of us before answering. "It looks like the rain is already off to dampen another town. We can for a couple of minutes if Leira has time."

"It's fine," I say dully.

Lisa and Amy say their goodbyes, thank goodness. All I need is to be questioned further by Miss Nosey.

Adrienne walks alongside me. She seems not to notice how she bumps into my side with every other step. She begins chattering about her day, showing no signs of stopping anytime soon. Good, less pressure on me to fill in the silent gaps.

"We have quail eggs in our classroom!" she says with a hop. "They're going to hatch in a couple of days, and then we'll hear their tiny peeps. I like that jungle gym!" She makes peeping noises before sprinting off to the playground up ahead.

Other kids play, scream, and have fun on the swings and play structure. A strange feeling wells up in my chest. It feels like a lifetime since I've been on a playground. The teases from my classmates echo in my ears. I never had the same look as the other kids. Messy hair and ratty clothes made me stand out like a shining beacon of light, and not in a good way.

I kick at a rock in bitterness of the laughter around me. Kids swing and play like nothing is holding them back. I never had this type of childlike innocence. My mom left when I was five, three days before kindergarten started. I showed up on the first day with a dirty dress, messy hair, and no school supplies in sight.

It's a sob story I've held in my heart since, no matter how grown up I act. Moms are supposed to pretty their daughters up, as Lisa obviously does with Adrienne.

The other kids on the playground are well-groomed, with trimmed hair and nice sneakers. I envy them and how their lives are set up for greatness without them knowing it. My plan to run away started formulating not far past their age. Probably none of them will have an escape plan and a secret stash of money as I did.

As it should be.

Apparently, the dads couldn't be bothered to do anything for me. Throughout the years, a mom would take me under her wing and give me some hand-me-downs. Once the school year ended, I was sent home for the summer, forgotten by those moms. Or, they moved from our town, a good choice since it was overgrown with weeds. More accurately, the weed the dads grew and sold. I would start a new year with the charity bag of supplies from the school. I'd bury myself in a book, wishing I could hop into the pages and escape the life I was dealt.

I quickly learned to shower and do my hair after the kids teased me with names such as 'Pigpen' or 'Dirty Pants.' Yeah, that one was mature. But it did the trick, whipping me into shape, introducing me to maturity at a young age. I looked after myself, learning that the only person I could depend on was… me.

Some kids become the class clown in my situation. Some bully or get in trouble all the time. I did the opposite, fixing my nose firmly in books and barely coming up.

When I started school, I didn't even know the letters of my name. Sure, my mom left when I was five, but it's not like she was loving and doting like Lisa or Amy and taught me anything. I lucked out that I was a quick learner. I was fascinated by the alphabet, numbers, reading, and all the school subjects.

I quickly became the best in the class, even though sometimes I would dumb myself down so the teacher wouldn't make such a fuss. I was the girl who read books while walking down the hallways and on the playground. I grew to not care that the other kids teased me; I barely even heard them. What I did hear were the whispers from the characters in my books. I saw them in front of me instead of the words that created their stories. I dove into their worlds, pretending they were my own to escape the crappy hand I was dealt.

A scream of play snaps me back to my place outside the playground. Adrienne waves from atop the play structure. I give her a small smile back. I'm happy that she has a good life and am glad all these kids will have a better upbringing than I did. Well, I'm assuming they will. Their moms staying after school and allowing them to play speaks volumes about the type of people they are.

A kid plays by himself, glaring at the other kids as he walks along the outskirts of the playground. It makes me wonder what his experiences have been and if they've been similar to mine. I wish I could whisper in his ear that it'll all work out, even if I don't know the end of my story yet.

It's enough to spark an idea for my future. My upbringing could connect me with kids who have had it hard like me. I couldn't take them all in and shelter them from the evils of the world. But I could help them by sharing my story of how I grew up and broke free. I'm doing it now, breaking the cycle of destruction. At least, that's what my goal is by being here in Garden Valley.

"Hey, you have your psychology degree, right?" I blurt to Lisa when she comes my way.

"I sure do," Lisa says, smiling at her daughter. It makes me wonder if she's thought of having any more children. I'm terrible at guessing people's ages, but she seems to still be in that range.

"Did you go to the school in town?"

Lisa glances my way. I've known her for less than an hour, yet I can sense her studying me, trying to click the pieces together to see the whole picture. It feels like she already knows more about me than Charlotte does.

Warning bells go off in my head. I like Lisa, but I don't want to share too much with her. I'm sure she can easily connect the dots of my past to create a complete picture.

"I did a mixture of schooling," she says, her hands circling in front of her as if she's stirring soup. "My parents wanted me to attend the university in Eugene, where they live now and where I grew up." Now, it's my turn to analyze the bitterness in her voice. "I started at the big fancy college in Eugene, but then I met Patrick and moved to Garden Valley. I finished at the college in town. It's pretty good." She raises her eyebrows as if in question.

I don't bite.

"I'm sorry about your job." A subject change is needed here to get the spotlight off my life.

"Yeah, that's been tough for me to deal with." This woman is the brightest, bubbliest person I've ever seen. Yet she again shifts into a different frame before my eyes, one I feel bad for bringing up. Her shoulders slouch before perking up when she talks. "I've been making more videos, though, and have scrubbed my house clean." She laughs, rolling her shoulders as she straightens again. "And I'm going to give the back garage a much-needed makeover to rent out. My grandma lived there for a few years before she passed."

"I'm sorry," I say after a few moments of silence.

"Thank you. It's be a good project for me and a good way to compensate for my not working. So, if you know of anyone interested in renting a place."

She gives me a sweet smile, driving the idea to my core. I never thought I'd be here in Garden Valley, let alone standing next to Lisa. And yet, here she is, taking me under her wing, just as those moms did long ago.

Chapter 10 Leira

A Stroke of Fortune

Today I have an interview for a job at the fabric store. I opted for my new green shirt and jeans that actually fit my petite frame. I clip my hair in a barrette, a big change for me. I'm not used to showing my skinny face with the pointy chin and barely there eyebrows. I remember I put my hair back once at school and got teased about how small my face was. Like I could help it.

Now that I'm here in Garden Valley, I hop out of bed every morning with the first chirping of the birds. Even the annoying racket of the woodpecker makes me curl my lips in a good way.

I've wanted to explore the town to drill in some landmarks and bearings, especially since I've already gotten lost. I can't imagine a better place to hide out from the dads. This town has a college, cute mom-and-pop shops, and apartments that aren't very far from the school. I've kept my interest in moving into Lisa's back garage but have yet to tell her.

I pull out my phone, wondering if I should text her. We exchanged numbers the other day upon her insistence. Seriously, how does somebody get to be so nice?

I remember Lisa's expression and how her voice dropped when talking about her family. It made me feel like I'm not the only one with a difficult upbringing. Of course, I'm not! There are services for neglected and abused kids and therapists to help them deal with it for the rest of their lives. That doesn't happen for only a few dozen kids.

It helps to know that I'm not alone, even if I'm not going to actively seek out those who are like me. I won't do this *yet*, at least.

I'm going to enroll in classes for the next semester.

"No, that's lame," I grumble, deleting this text.

I bought myself some clothes.

I delete this. What, do I want a gold star for picking out matching clothes?

I allowed myself to shop at the thrift store down the street, taking a few tips from how the college kids are dressed. It's worlds different for me to want to fit in. During the first few days here, I stood out in my clothes, which brought unwanted attention and glances.

It's funny how a simple wish can turn into a whirlwind of change. Here I am, in this town, after years of tucking money away and planning. I've applied to college, hunted for a job, revamped my look, and refreshed my wardrobe. It's all exciting, but it's a lot more work than just cooking dinner for the dads and hiding away in my room.

My phone lets out a ding with a text from a number I don't recognize. My stomach erupts in nerves as I assume the worst. They've already found me!

Guess what? Your application flew through the system. You're in!

My suspicion of who this is settles my stomach. I know the dads are going to find me eventually. It's like having a bad cell in the body; it's in the background, waiting for the perfect moment to pounce. I know the dads are going to pounce, but there's nothing I can do about it. Now that more people know where I am, I'm much more vulnerable. I have to move on at some point. I'm eighteen, for crying out loud! It's not like I was going to stay home forever. Plus, even if I moved overseas, I'd leave an identity trail.

I can't help the smile and warmth that fills my body upon seeing Jordan's texts. What can I say? The guy practically spewed rays of sunshine from his small-town charm.

I'm assuming this is Jordan? Leira

How did you know? Jordan

The woodpecker told me. Leira

The smile stays on my face as I watch the three dots pop off and on the screen. I can picture him texting me, erasing, pausing to think, and then texting again.

"Yes?" I say, waiting for words to appear.

Let me know if you'd like a tour of the campus. Jordan

"Oh!" I say in surprise.

Okay, thanks. Leira

Does that mean yes? Jordan

Wow, this guy's persistent.

It wouldn't hurt. Leira

How about Sunday at ten? The campus is pretty empty on the weekends. Jordan

I give this some thought. Can I officially add this friendship to my list of new things?

"Yes, yes, I can." I text him back that I'm game. He tells me how to sign up for classes through the school website, but I'll have to return to campus since I don't have a laptop.

I have plenty of money to enroll. It's weird making these decisions about classes and clothes. I've pinned three courses I want to take, not a full load, but it's a good start. At the very least, I'll learn how to cook in the culinary class. I have only a couple more basic English and math classes, so I added just one of those. And then there's the psychology class, which I'm the most excited about. No cape, no mask, but every step I take feels like a leap across skyscrapers.

After the back-and-forth with Jordan, I feel comfortable typing a text to Lisa.

I have a job interview today. I put you down as a reference, so you might get a call. I hope that's okay. Leira

I hit send before I can second-guess myself. My phone dings in the middle of curling my hair. I never knew how much fun it would be getting myself ready.

I'm so excited for you! Adrienne and I are cheering right now. I hope you get it! Lisa

She ends with a heart emoji that holds my eyes for a few seconds. The only other person I have texted ever is Charlotte, and she would answer with as few words as possible.

Thanks. I'm really nervous. Leira

I hesitate before hitting the send button. I usually don't put myself out there like this, freely giving away my emotions. I nearly drop the phone when it rings. My eyes bug out when I see it's a call from Lisa!

"Hello?"

"Leira, I have so many tips for your interview! I hope you don't mind me calling."

"It's fine!"

"Good. What type of outfit are you wearing?"

I look down at the clothes that actually fit around my body. "I have a dark green top with dark jeans."

"Are they super ripped jeans? And I don't mean muscular," she laughs.

"No, they're just regular jeans."

"Sounds perfect. Not dressy, but not ripped jeans either. I'm sure Janet will be interviewing you, and she loves animals. Do you have anything like that you can add?"

I think about the clothes I bought, knowing I don't. "No," I say with a somber voice.

"That's fine, I'm sure you look great."

"Wait! I bought cat earrings." I dig through my suitcase, which looks like it exploded with clothes, and pull out the calico danglers. It's unlike anything I've ever worn. When I bought these, I hoped they would somehow bring me a cat one day.

"Good! When they ask you questions, say something about yourself, but then bring it back to how you will benefit the company. If they ask about your experience…"

"I don't have any experience," I interrupt with a flat tone. Unless you call dropping bundles of weed off experience, I give myself a score of zero here.

"That's okay because you can use this to your advantage. You can say you're fresh clay to mold the way they want. They can teach you how to be a good worker. Something along those lines."

I nod in response, taking it all in.

"So, even if you're unsure how to answer, just say something about the company. You can talk about the departments you like if you have special knowledge about something…"

"I don't have any special knowledge," I say with worry.

"Of course you do! You were just in high school, right? I'm sure you had to organize your homework a certain way, which would be great for the section with stickers and stuff for scrapbooking. I remember reading a ton in school, and they have a section with books."

"I like to read!" I practically shout, finally feeling like I have something to offer.

"There you go! And, you're young, don't have kids, and can be somewhat flexible with your time. As long as that's true."

"It is," I say with another nod. "I can take the late shift."

"That's perfect!"

It's exactly what I need—to have someone in my corner rooting for me. It's not a stadium full of fans, but I don't even want that. I barely know these people, and here they are offering their support.

I finish getting ready. Even if my screams of doubt were winning the battle, Lisa's voice reassured me that I can do this.

***

Lisa's encouragement stays with me right up until I walk through the doors of the fabric store. Somehow, I make it to the breakroom, waiting for my name to be called. I've never been so nervous in my life! I prepped by watching some videos about etiquette, from what to wear, what to say, and how to act. Still, I suspect nothing could prepare me for the in-person grueling session.

"Leira Jones, come on in." I'm far from being used to this name, but it's easy to answer since I'm the only one waiting. I walk past the woman holding the door, but she's so large and looming that my confidence scurries off to hide in a corner somewhere. She wears a long, black skirt and a dark orange shirt, her outfit resembling the season.

"Hi Leira, I'm Janet," the other woman in the room says. She extends a hand out to me across a dark wooden desk. Her shirt with leaves matches the one dangling from her ears. Having not explored this fashion that matches the season, I have to say, I like it.

We enter a decked-out office with cushy, flower-filled chairs and a desk. It looks like most of the items come straight from the store. Everything goes together perfectly, giving off an inviting feel. My main goal is to keep a smile on my face, even if it feels as foreign as getting dressed to match the fall season.

"I'm Eleanor, the hiring manager here at Joann's. I'm not sure if you know anything about the company, but…"

"I studied it," I blurt, interrupting her. "I'm sorry," I say, looking down at the mini backpack I use for a purse.

The women smile in response. "No need to be sorry. This will be a pretty informal interview, Leira." It offers only slight relief. This interview is about me, after all. "We'll be easy on you. We just want to get to know you."

Great.

I wish for something to ease my clenched stomach. I remember the cat earrings. I thread my hair over my ear and shake my head slightly to make them dance.

"Oh, I like those earrings!" Janet says. It worked! The break in the intensity of the interview does wonders to ease my nerves. "Let's see, the first question," Janet says, looking down at her paper. "What can you bring to the Joann Fabrics team?"

I practiced answering questions like these, and the results were a bunch of fake-sounding responses. Nevertheless, I'm on the spot again and must answer. I borrow Lisa's words for my answer.

"I haven't had a job before, but I'd be excited to start here. Everyone so far in town has been nice." It's a good answer, but I've forgotten one thing. "And I can offer that to the customers," I say quickly. "I, uh, checked out your book section too. I read a lot and can help in that area."

"Okay, good," Eleanor says, jotting down a note in her notebook. "Let's say a customer comes in with a complaint, and no matter what you say, you can't make them happy. What would you do?"

"This one's easy." Oops. From the looks on their faces, I shouldn't have said this out loud. "I mean, I've dealt with angry people before." This isn't a lie. The dad's business customers weren't exactly the upmost citizens. "I'd stay calm and come find the manager on that shift." Phew, I didn't blow it any further.

"Good," Janet nods. They ask a couple more questions before getting to my schedule.

"I'm enrolled in college classes, but they aren't every day. I'd be available to work all day Wednesday, some Friday, Saturday, and Sunday. Oh, and nights, too." I hope I don't sound too eager but I want them to know I'm interested.

"You've listed Lisa Carnell as your reference."

"Oh, I just love her," Janet says. "Have you seen her channel about crocheting on YouTube?"

"I haven't!" the woman says, jotting down a note on her page. "I called her just before you arrived, and she said she would stand behind you. You don't have the other two references filled in, but I think Lisa's word is strong enough to make us overlook that. Listen, Leira," she starts. I brace myself for the bad news. Nothing good ever follows these words. "We don't mind allowing people to start their work experience here. We have a few shifts a week that we need help with on the register. We can start you there and then move you around as you get used to everything. How does that sound?"

I stare at the women for a few seconds before responding. "What?" I ask with a flat voice. The women laugh. "I'm sorry. I thought you were going to say you don't have anything."

"We'd love to have you join our team," Eleanor says with a smile.

A lump forms in my throat. I try not to cry but lose the battle. Oh no, are those tears I feel on my cheeks? I swipe at them frantically, knowing they saw. "I'm sorry. It's my first job."

"Welcome to the team, Leira! When can you start?"

It's no long a book I'm diving into to escape my reality. Right now, I'm writing my own story.

Chapter 11 Lisa

Highs and Lows

I haven't convinced Patrick that the back garage will be a success. Regardless, I'm moving forward with my plan. It's not like he's here most of the day, so I'm free to do whatever I want.

"Do you hear that, Mom? I can do what I want!"

I've added a few decorations to the apartment, but it still needs a pop of color here and there. I've cleaned the entire place from top to bottom, put out a glowing ad with pictures, and… nothing. No response at all! Not even one. Maybe Patrick isn't too far off base.

This also describes my job search. I've applied to more than a dozen openings, called them back, and received the same response: we've already hired someone. It makes me wonder if the real reason is that someone has been dragging my name in the mud around town. It wasn't like I was a model employee at the clinic.

My phone jingles Beethoven's Fifth Symphony, the noise I've assigned to my mom's texts. I thought it was funny to assign her to this dramatic noise. To this day, whenever I hear it in a movie or in a cartoon, I get chills.

We're having a party for Aunt Beth, and you need to be there.

You'd think that with my mother's high-class standing, she would have more, well, class. Her message could have been, 'Hey, come join the family,' or, 'It's been a while since we've caught up.' I'm surprised she didn't tell me to make sure I don't embarrass the family. I've always been a master of untangling knots, but I haven't figured out how to break the knuckles my family and I have created.

Wonderful. When is the party? As I tap my phone, I say this out loud with a dreary voice. "Tomorrow, great. Thanks for the warning."

No need to bring a present. We've got it covered.

This is actually a relief. I know it's because my mom is afraid of what type of present I'd give rather than her helping me out. No one in my family appreciates a handmade scarf. They all respond the same, holding them up like a piece of toilet paper smeared with poo.

After lunch, I prop my phone on a book to film my next video of my hands weaving a Halloween-themed blanket. It's exactly what I need to overcome the anxiety from my change in plans for tomorrow.

The picture of the finished blanket is quite beautiful, with purple, black, and orange colors featuring a witch flying on a broomstick. She hangs in the air over a field of pumpkins and a haunted-looking house to her right. A full moon is in the left corner of the blanket. It offers me a challenge, but I know I can do it. I rarely feel this type of confidence, but I'm embracing it right now, using it as another shield against the depression lurking in the corner.

I gather my supplies and Chuggers and sit in my cozy chair to get started. Soft rain falls outside, offering the best background for my hour-long session. Yes, it will be a long video, but people don't have to watch the whole thing if they don't want to. These types of videos are popular in the YouTube world these days.

I position my phone to only show my hands, blanket, and lap in the frame. I open a window to have the sound effects of rain in the background. "No need to worry about copyright infringement when the sound is straight from nature!" I close my eyes and fill my lungs with the damp scent of the outdoors, settle into my cushy chair, and click record.

"Hi there!" I say, bending down so my face is in the camera for the first few seconds. I'm going to continue my work on this blanket. I'm not going to chat much throughout this video. I hope you can sit back, enjoy the sights and sounds, and finish some of your projects with me."

The minutes fly by when I get into the groove. It's been an up-and-down day for me, with the threat of depression waiting for a hole to make its way in. I take a deep breath, knowing that said hole always follows a visit with my family. It's inevitable: I work myself up before the party, rehearsing the perfect lines, wearing clothes that aren't my normal, and trying my best to be the way they want me to be. Then, the crash comes after expending all of my energy.

This blanket project is the perfect way to get through the sting of news that came with my mom's invitation. I already know, from experience, that it's a party I won't be welcome at. We agree on at least one thing: it's hard to fit in when you're being looked down upon by people who think they're better than you. To make it worse, these 'people' are my family. Sometimes, I feel like my challenges are as knotted as Christmas lights.

I make a lot of progress on the blanket, enjoying the feel of the weight resting on my body with every row I complete. "Okay, I think that's it for the day. I hope you used this time, as I did, to soothe some of your anxiety. This is what I got through today," I say, holding up the portion of my blanket I completed. "I'm gathering more subscribers than I have yarn, if you haven't noticed. I was thinking of calling my awesome following the 'Crochet-iacs.' What do you think? Anyways, if you enjoy this video, please give me a thumbs up! If you're interested in having a piece of my work, visit my Etsy store, Coping With Yarn. Bye."

I hit the stop button, sinking into my chair with that 'feeling sorry for myself' attitude. Not even crocheting could weave all my troubles away today.

I watch over a couple of minutes of footage. "What's this 'make your video into a short' button?" I say, figuring I'll give it a try. After a few clicks, I upload the short, which yet again does wonders for boosting my ego.

I watch a few minutes of my long video and deem it good enough to upload after adding my new beginning. It's easier to finish the video description and add my links from the computer, so I move to the kitchen counter where I can stand and work.

My last step is to add my Etsy link. This reminds me to check my store. It was easy to set up after opening a bank account for Coping With Yarn as a business. It felt good to finally cross this item off, which has been on my list for ages. Sadly, my shop hadn't seen any action the last time I checked.

"Ten sales! Holy crappers!" I shout, causing Chuggers to start spinning. "That's how I feel right now!" Not only have I made ten sales, but one was for a hundred dollars for my entire farm. "People are going to want their things!"

I hadn't thought much of how I would ship my stuff out, figuring I wouldn't get any sales in the first place. I gather everything I've sold, sticking notes on the items to remember who bought them. It's baffling that people want the colorful creations I loved making. These people aren't even my friends!

A burning question hits me. I pull up my store and check how many people have visited. "Three-hundred? With a few comments!" I'm in shock while I read one aloud.

I've seen your YouTube channel, too, and it's great! You're the Bob Ross of crocheting. Just don't tell anyone about that tree. We'll keep him a secret.

I throw my head back and howl a laugh that's enough to knock my sour mood into next week. I check the rest of my five messages of people asking if I can make this and that type of blanket or scarf in specific colors. I type out responses, saying I'm thrilled to make their requested items. This gives me the double-whammy of an idea to make YouTube videos while I crochet them.

It takes me an hour to get everything ready to ship out. I spend extra time adding colorful tissue paper and confetti to each order. I print my new logo at the top of a few pages that I use for thank-you notes. I fill my arms and head to the car with a new feeling that I can conquer the world. I added five dollars for shipping to ensure I'd make a profit. I have money in the yarn itself, but I would have spent that anyway. Overall, I made a total of two-hundred and forty dollars. I'm thrilled!

Just before I leave, Joanie pulls up with the furniture for the rental.

"Hey there!" I shout. My wave gives away how elated I am with my sales.

"Hey yourself," Joanie says with a hug. "I have your furniture. I think the two of us can move it."

"I'm on cloud nine, so I'm sure I have strength like Wonder Woman right now."

"That's fun to hear. Did you win the lottery or something?" Joanie asks, pulling her long brown hair in a ponytail. She's a couple of inches taller than me and inches smaller around the middle. I always praise myself when noticing this without and envious word in site. People are who they are regardless of their size, and that includes me.

"I might as well have. I got some sales on my Etsy account and am on my way to mail them. You have good timing because you almost missed me. It's funny; now that I'm not working, I'm busier."

"I felt that way when I first moved here," she says, nodding in understanding. "I had the whole house to renovate, and a list a mile long." We ease the couch out of her trailer and walk it to the back gate.

"How's your furniture-making business? I can tell by how heavy this is that it's one of your creations. Geeze-Louise!"

Joanie laughs. "I did make the frame for this. What can I say? I don't cut corners. And it's going very well. It's exciting when people buy your creations, isn't it?"

"Yeppers!"

We carry in a chair and a loveseat next. It all fits perfectly in the space I hope someone will be interested in one day soon. Joanie and I say our goodbyes, and I head off to the post office. I feel as light as if a fresh breeze has swept through me, carrying away the heavy, dark negativity that wants to settle in. The feeling prompts me to open the windows, inviting the cool breeze to dance through my van.

"Woohoo!" I shout.

It's a release like no other. My mood has been up, down, and all around since I got fired. I've been getting more subscribers, but it hasn't given me this feeling of a win I've desperately needed. For the first time since I started my channel a couple of months ago, I sense that things are working out for me.

I park and carry a box of crocheted goodies in to the post office.

"Hi, Betsy," I say to the woman at the counter. "Can you believe I sold all of these items on Etsy?"

"Yeah, I can believe it. Look how cute this is," Betsy says of my crocheted cat. "I saw your Etsy shop and love your things. I think I'll get a few as Christmas presents."

"Thank you. I'll need to pick up extra packaging. I hadn't thought I'd get any orders, and here they are, rolling in."

"A word of advice?" I nod. I will always take free advice. What I do with it, however, is up to me. "I follow your channel. This is good quality stuff here. I think you should raise your prices."

"Oh, I don't know," I say, looking sheepishly at the counter.

"How much did you charge for this?" She holds up the three pumpkins I remember making next to the fireplace this time last year.

"Five dollars."

"Five dollars? Lisa, this would have sold easily for fifteen, probably twenty at the crafter's market."

"Twenty! I can't charge that."

She shrugs in a way that says she's right. "Your stuff really is that good."

It's a nice change to get this compliment. Lord knows I've never gotten anything like it from my family members, Patrick included. Nana believed in me, but it's been a while since I've heard her voice of encouragement.

Besty's words are of the kind that I've never attached to myself. Now that I've gotten these orders, I wonder if it's in my capacity to believe them.

We get everything squared away with me purchasing a few extra bags and boxes to ship my future sales items.

I spend my extra minutes before I need to pick Adrienne up in the fabric store next door. To my surprise, I see a familiar face. "Leira! It looks like you got the job!" I eye the familiar tan and green vest around her slim shoulders. The poor girl looks like she needs a few home-cooked meals.

"It's been fun!" I've only seen her once, but she looks different. I can see her whole face with her hair pulled up in a ponytail. Her skin is flawless with small features, and I've got to say she's quite striking.

"Hot diggity! It looks like my reference worked. I'm glad."

"That and your advice beforehand. People would pay money for that, you know. Is it time for more yarn?" she asks.

"It sure is! This time, it's to fill out some custom orders. I sold some of my items on Etsy!"

"Cool! I saw that you've doubled your subs." She gives me a sweet smile. She isn't even trying to bite it away with her teeth as she had done the first time I met her.

"I know, it's been making leaps and bounds every day! Last week I crested the two hundred mark, and now I'm almost to four hundred."

The automatic doors open, and in comes a woman using a walker. Her teenage son hunches over as he rests one hand on her back and the other behind her right elbow.

"Beatrice! Today is full of bonuses! I feel like it's been ages since I've seen you." I hug my friend and smile at her son, noticing his eyes are glued to Leira.

"I see you all the time on your channel. I guess it's not a two-way system, is it?" the older woman responds.

"Jordan, how's life treating you?" I ask Beatrice's son.

"I'm good. I start school next week. It's my sophomore year," Jordan answers. He doesn't even try to look away from Leira. How cute. A customer enters the line to check out, and Leira springs into action as I chat with Bea. I know she loves her craftwork, and I'm glad she hasn't slowed down despite her arthritis and handicaps. When Leira's done, she turns my way.

"Hey, can I ask you something?" she asks when Beatrice and Jordan filter into the store.

"Sure."

She hesitates and looks down before continuing. "Do you, um, still have your back garage up for rent?"

Except for that nasty party I have tomorrow night, I couldn't have asked for a better day. "It's as free as the wind dancing through open fields! I'd love for you to check it out. I have a dumb party tomorrow, but you can come on Sunday." Leira laughs, a true sign that she has settled into the Garden Valley atmosphere.

"That's fine."

"How about ten?"

"I, um, have a tour of the college in the morning," she says, her eyes flicking to where Jordan and his mom are, "but I can come afterward!"

"I'm home all day. See you then!"

***

I do my best to dress up for my parents' events, but mixing up my four fancy outfits is a struggle. This skirt with that top gets rotated with a different top and set of shoes. At the clinic, I wore scrubs, and when I go around town, I wear jeans. It's easy. But easy doesn't mix well with my mother's elite

119

requirements.

My mom cares about one thing: lipstick. I could wear a potato sack but have my lips decked out in cherry red, and she would somewhat approve of me. As such, I keep a special drawer of every color from my makeup artist friend, Monica.

As I get ready, my phone repeatedly dings with that special jingle from YouTube. "Okay, I'll look at you in a minute," I say, smiling.

"Lisa, honey, we're going to be late," Patrick hollers from the foyer. I'm always the last one to be ready, trying to will the mirror to turn me into something I'm not.

I grab my phone and the Coach purse my mom got me last Christmas. This luxury item would be fun to show off, except for how it was given. I distinctly remember my mom's words when she gave it to me: 'At least you don't have to tote around that dingy yarn bag you use as a purse.'

I disapprove of my dark blue outfit, but it's as good as I get. I fasten in for the forty-five-minute drive to Eugene with a sigh. "Goodbye, house," I say with sorrow.

Patrick laughs. He somehow finds my misery with my parents amusing. He doesn't understand how deeply these interactions affect me. These parties make me feel like I'm on one of those reality shows. I'm the poor girl who stands before the judges, awaiting their critical opinions, which my mother and sister are full of.

"It's not like we won't be back."

It's true, but I always lose a piece of myself after meeting with my family. And I'm not looking forward to the inevitable crash afterward.

My phone dings again, reminding me of the message I missed. "Holy schnockies! I have twenty-five new subscribers since this morning!"

"Wow, that's cool," Patrick says.

"You're popular," Adrienne says in her sweet voice.

"Wait a minute… I have thirty-eight. The twenty-five that it kept notifying me about was because those people already have channels. Oh my gosh! They like my content!"

"Good job, hon. That's a fun hobby."

"Well, it'll make me money once I get to one thousand subscribers and four thousand hours watched."

"That might take forever and a day." Patrick, always the encouraging husband. He's always been like this, convinced his dumb comments are comedy gold. The jokes lost their charm ages ago, leaving just the sting behind. Still, he's a galaxy away from how my parents treat me.

"I don't know," I say with a hopeful tone. "Some people out there take just a couple of days or weeks to get to that point. The pay is based on how many people watch and how long they watch. But I think I can get more views with my 'thirty-one days of Halloween' series, which I'm going to post every single day next month." I scroll through my videos before clicking on the analytics button. "Whoa, that ASMR crocheting video I just put out already has a thousand views! That's semi-viral for me."

"What does that stand for?"

"Oh, it's that new craze stands for autonomous sensory meridian response. It's when people listen to certain sounds, and it relaxes them. It's actually not all that new, but it is for the social media crowd. I remember learning about it when I was in school."

"I'm glad all that schooling paid off so you can make crocheting videos for people to *listen* to." Patrick laughs. I know he's been stressed about me not bringing an income in, but he doesn't have to be a jerk about it. He gets a bit cranky this time of year when the cold weather settles into his achy joints. He mainly works outside, and he *hates* to be cold. Still, he doesn't need to take it out on me; I didn't choose his profession.

"You know, that's not very nice, Pat." I turn in my seat to face him after glancing to ensure Adrienne is engrossed in playing a memory game on her device. We've had many fights in our relationship. I've tried the yelling. I've attempted to guilt him into doing things. Simply calling him out with a calm tone works best to get my point across.

He glances my way and sighs. "I'm sorry, I was just trying to be funny."

"I know you're still sore about me not working, but I'm trying other ways to make money. And I've been working hard on the house, and you haven't even said anything about it."

He nods and reaches over to give my hand a squeeze. "I've noticed. The house looks good! The fresh paint has made a big difference, and you fixed the screen door!" he chuckles.

I let this sink in for a bit. It takes a lot to get under my skin and affect my feelings, but they heal quickly. "I have a friend interested in renting the back garage, and..."

"Wait, what? You never told me that." It's not an accusation as much as surprise in his voice. This flips the conversation from a blame game to something way more chill. I've learned over the years that Patrick mirrors my approach. When I bring good vibes, he shows them back. It's way easier to talk when we're both riding the positivity wave. Who says you can't apply a psychology degree to a relationship?

I nod with enthusiasm. "Yup, I spent a ton of time back there this week sprucing it up. Joanie brought some of her furniture in, and it looks great. You should take a peek. The girl who is interested can add a few touches of her own to make it look nice. She has a job and everything. I'm going to charge a few hundred a month."

"Well, that's something!"

"Oh, and my Etsy shop sold another hundred and forty dollars yesterday! You came home after I was already in bed and I didn't get a chance to tell you." As much as I've been dreading this long drive to my parent's house, this car time gives us a much-needed heart-to-heart.

"Wow, really?" he asks in shock, rolling his right shoulder to work a kink out.

"In fact," I say, reaching into the back seat to grab my blue yarn bag, "I need to work on my next project while we drive. I have orders! No need to just sit here when I could be making money." I give Adrienne's knee a tickle, coupled with a smile. She smiles back beyond her video game, which is keeping her attention.

"That's actually pretty neat," he says with a nod. There, something nice!

"It is! I'm no longer making my critters for the boxes in the spare room closet." He chuckles and looks at me with a smile that crinkles the corners of his eyes.

Combining this conversation with all my good news improves my mood. It's probably not enough to completely shield me from the negativity I'm about to endure, but I'll take every pocket of good news I can get. Sometimes, I wish I could crochet something around myself to shield me from my mother's criticisms.

***

My parent's mansion is flawless, right down to every flower

petal, like someone hand-picked them with a ruler. Waiters in suits float around with trays of appetizers and champagne while perfectly polished guests exchange pearly white smiles and small talk. The place is massive—vaulted ceilings, grand rooms for schmoozing, and a white-and-beige color scheme so pristine it's almost scary. The towering columns and fancy archways still make me feel like a kid who doesn't belong. I feel even less at home now than when I was living under my mom's designer-driven dictatorship. I've got to give her credit, though—her constant redecorating has made the house impeccable, even if it's not my vibe. And here I am, standing in the corner with my frumpy blue outfit, trying not to be noticed.

"Lisa, what's wrong?" It's my mom, and she's come to throw whatever the night's theme of criticism is at me. I'm convinced she has a grab bag labeled 'things to nag Lisa about.'

"Nothing is wrong, Mother," I answer with attitude.

"Patrick and Adrienne are having a good time. I don't know why you can't." It's not like she's being mean. Her tone remains pleasant yet in command. It's her words themselves that are rude as hell.

"I'm having an okay time."

"Oh, you are not. You aren't talking to anyone. Here you are in the corner sulking."

"Mother, just because I don't have a mile-wide smile and I'm not faking a happy conversation with someone doesn't mean I'm not happy."

"Come on, Lisa, mingle a little," my sister, Diane, says with a glass of wine perched in her hand. My Mom manages the team of surgeons my Dad and Diane have working for them. It's like a secret club, and I'm not invited.

Diane is everything they've always wanted, pretty and skinny with my mom's inherited fairer skin and light hair. I swear I inherited all of the Indian blood from my dad's side of the family. I'm not complaining since I love my black hair and natural tan. But why do they keep pestering me to be just like her? I fit in less with them than I do a size six.

The two resemble money with their perfectly tailored dresses, manicured nails, and dangly earrings that probably cost more than several months of my mortgage. It's the life they envisioned for me, but it was never the right fit for my journey. I'm starting to appreciate the hard U-turn I took from losing my job. I'm having a blast skipping down my path that's filled with wild flowers and unexpected twists, embracing the adventure around every bend.

"I was just telling Lisa to let her guard down and have some fun," my mom says with a touch of irritation. Her hand full of diamond rings pats perfectly groomed hair. She portraits the surgeon's wife to the 'T,' with long, slender arms and the most proper etiquette. I know she hires her own personal makeup artist for these events.

My mom flits away to greet guests with her light pink fitted dress and tulle shawl drifting behind her. I'm left with Diane, who has a more petite body than Mom. She has less effect than my mom but is still just as much of a nag.

She leans forward to whisper in my ear for effect. She's always done this when she has something juicy to tell me. "Tired, huh? From all your *work?*" I stare in shock, hoping she doesn't know the secret I desperately didn't want them to discover. "Oh yes, I found your *little* YouTube channel and stumbled upon your blubbering 'I got fired' video," she says in a high voice as if mimicking me.

"You're not going to tell them, are you?" I look at her with pleading eyes, hating that I'm a grown woman who still uses such desperation. It throws me back to our childhood when Diane was obviously the favorite. There she was with her perfect hair and proper manners, skipping grades and being granted to medical school at an early age. I was off crocheting and playing outside, baking with Nana.

"Your secret is safe with me." She pats my shoulder as if it's a comfort. "But seriously, give me a call if you need a job. Our receptionist was promoted and we haven't filled her position yet."

"I have a psychology degree, Diane," I say with a scoff.

"That could come in handy. Our patients need guidance to handle the emotional impact of their surgery news."

I roll my eyes and attempt to turn away. My sister and I have never gotten along. Growing up, she was straight A's and captain of every academic club out there when I wanted to do my crafts and take art classes. I followed my parent's rules since I was required to get a college degree, even though they were vehemently against it being in psychology.

"Are you having a good time?" Diane's husband, Gordon, joins us and threads his arm around my sister's tiny waist. I never understood how she and mom have a fast metabolism while mine is more like Chuggers'. Or is it more that they have the willpower not to eat and I allow myself to enjoy these indulgences of life?

"Yes, dear. Isn't that what I'm supposed to say?" He looks my way and laughs, not seeing me, as always. He's a top-notch lawyer in town and looks every inch of it with his tan suit and perfectly manicured look. They are a stunning couple who match each other with their firm bodies.

Diane nuzzles into her husband's neck, a sentiment I rarely see. She whispers something in his ear and they share and intimate chuckle. One glance at my mother shows her glowing smile as she talks with one of her guests. A woman comes to her side and she embraces her with a hug.

My dad joins us and gives me a hug. "Hey, pops," I say, giving him a real smile. He's never been as critical as my mother, accepting me for who I've become.

"There's my crafty girl." He lifts my hand and inspects my fingers. "Still the straightest crew I've ever seen. I don't know how you can do all that crocheting and not have knots in your fingers that match your blankets."

"It's because they get a lot of exercise," I say, dancing my fingers in the air. He chuckles, and as always, I love the distinguished lines on his face. His flat nose and dark features mirror my own. We're not deeply connected to our Indian heritage, but I've always admired how my dad has carried it with quiet pride, a part of him that's woven into who he is without needing to be spoken aloud.

My ultra-cynical side has given me reason not to reconcile with them over the years. In actuality, I'd love for us to be on the same side, to mingle as effortlessly as these guests do.

My dad sees someone he knows, gives me a squeeze, and leaves.

"Seriously, sis, give me a call sometime," Diane urges.

"Maybe if I get tired of my hobbies. As for now, I'm enjoying my time without a job." Diane's eyes grow big as she looks over my shoulder.

I glance back, hoping to see Patrick coming to my rescue. But it's not my husband, it's my mother. She stares back with huge brown eyes before glancing around her, no doubt worrying her guests have overheard her unemployed, frumpy daughter. It seems I don't have to worry about her telling my parents about me getting fired since I just did.

Chapter 12 Leira

Winds of Change

I am more nervous about touring the school with Jordan than I was about my interview. A glance outside shows a break in the rain, which was going to be my excuse to cancel. I chose a new fuzzy violet sweater to go with jeans, hoping this will be warm enough for my fat-free frame. It's simple but cute, and this color is one I've never worn before.

I've gotten used to walking around town. One evening, I strolled with a map on my phone, learning street names and landmarks. It's a small place with streets named after trees and fruits, so it's easy to navigate. The school is less than a ten-minute walk, and the fabric store is just a few blocks away. While I'd love to stay this close to everything, living at the inn isn't practical, and I'm excited to check out Lisa's apartment.

Somehow, my legs work through a bundle of nerves to get me to school. I feel dorky with a new backpack hugging my back, but it's my safety net.

Jordan was right; this place is empty. It's not a large campus, so I can't imagine it taking too long for him to point the buildings out to me. I'm ignoring that I'm more excited to spend time with Jordan than I am to see the college.

"There you are." I spin and am greeted by his broad

smile. He's dressed in jeans and a button-up blue and white striped shirt.

"Morning," I say simply, trying to funnel my excitement upon seeing him into the clutch my hands have on my backpack.

His eyes flicker down my body and back up to my face, his ever-present smile acting as the key to my soul. He could ask for the combination to my very being, and I'd give it to him if one existed. It's a strange feeling to have someone genuinely happy to see me. No one's ever been in that position unless you count the dads when I showed up with beer, but that's a different story.

"Ready to take the tour?"

"Yup."

"I see you've signed up for math, a culinary class, and psychology. Those are all in different buildings, but it's not a big campus. Everything is easy to find." He starts walking backward, facing me as he talks. Naturally, I follow, hardly able to take my eyes off him.

"I might get a kink in my neck from staring up at you all day." It's the longest sentence I've said to him. And flirtiest! Thank goodness he laughs in response.

"I'm only six-two."

"To a girl who's barely five-three, you're a giant."

"I've been called that before," he says, pointing a finger at me. I wonder if people try to be charming or if it's just their natural way. For Jordan, it seems like it comes easy. "Let's get started, shall we?" He holds his left arm out to display a building while guiding me gently with his right hand on my upper back. Whoa!

"To the right, we have the Stevens building. This is where you'll find all the art classes: theatre, music, and the creation of wonderful food. Your culinary class will be here. You'll find that everything is state-of-the-art with updated technology. The school itself isn't ancient, having been founded in 1950. It was more of a group effort by the city council instead of one person saying, 'Hey, we need a school.' We're a small town, but people around here and proud of this school. Others like to donate and have deep pockets, let me tell you." He thrusts his hands in his pants, forcing a frown and pulling out the empty pocket as if to say he's poor.

My teeth can no longer bite my smile away. He seems so effortlessly happy that I wonder if he's ever gone through anything complicated in his life.

"Up that hill is the science building. It's named Science, so let's not get confused here." I bite my lip in an attempt to keep my laugh in. He looks down at me with an amused grin. I'm trying not to get my hopes up, but it appears that he's enjoying this time as much as I am.

The campus is larger than it looks at first glance. There are ten two-story brick buildings scattered across acres of green grass. Tall trees with sway gently overhead, dropping orange and yellow leaves on the smaller shrubs lining the paved walkways. The huge library is something I can't wait to check out. I can see myself checking out a book and ducking away on one of the cozy-looking couches. An amphitheater outside rounds out the college experience, adding to the praise I've given myself for choosing this town. Stepping onto campus feels like a treat, wrapping me in a sense of excitement and belonging. It's like I'm exactly where I'm meant to be.

"Why can't you be open?" I say quietly as I peek in the library windows.

"You're a reader, huh?" He elbows my shoulder gently with the comment. It's a simple gesture that propels us to the next level. At least it does in my book that hasn't even had the first page read, so to speak.

I nod in response, not wanting to delve into anything related to myself. I mean, I know this tour is for me, but since Jordan is driving and rattling off a well-known script, it allows me to follow quietly.

"And here's Psychology. You'll know what classes are here because it's labeled 'Psychology.'" He says, making a rainbow across the sky with his hand. "Here, you'll study every nut job and learn about all the ways parents screw up their kids."

Now this, I do not find funny. I know what people say about mental diseases and psychologists. I also know from experience how much they're needed.

I glance in the window to hide my pursed lips. I take a deep breath, knowing Jordan didn't mean any harm with his comment. People like him haven't been dealt the harsh realities of others. I have a feeling his Saturday mornings are filled with fluffy homemade pancakes instead of delivering bags of weed.

I turn away from the building and start toward the opposite direction. A glance at my phone shows that it's about time I get to Lisa's house.

"I better be going," I say, my arms swinging to the vigorous pump of my legs.

"Really? Do you want to grab a bite to eat first?"

"Nope." Uh oh, it's my snotty voice. One glance at Jordan reveals that he's picked up on my mood swing that has come at us like a giant wave rushing to the shore.

"Uh oh, what'd I say? I have the tendency to strike a chord at these tours. Was it my 'nut job' comment?"

"It's fine. I just have to be somewhere, is all."

"No, I need to know so I don't repeat it. Come on, I can take it." He widens his stance and crosses his arms like it's some sort of game.

I guess if he wants to know… "Not everyone has had a privileged five-star Garden Valley upbringing. Psychologists are here for a reason. Kids even need them for Christ's sake."

Some people say they can take criticism, but the shock on his face shows otherwise. Or, maybe it's the topic at hand.

"Hey, I'm sorry. I meant it as a joke," Jordan says quickly, looking me up and down with a serious expression.

"I don't exactly think that child abuse is funny," I blurt it out and immediately regret it. My voice cracks—fantastic. Now my childhood memories are leaking everywhere like a busted piñata.

He stops less than a foot from me, craning his head down with a softened expression. Just having him near me is a comfort I've never experienced before. It's like he's my guardian angel, coming to protect me.

"I'm sorry." It's only two words, but it isn't what wins me over; it's the genuine voice he uses to say them. His finger catches the splash of my tear. I nod and look down before our eyes connect us to the moment.

Gosh, it's not like Jordan meant to personally attack me. If I take this psychology route, I'll need to be more immune to these types of comments.

"Anyway, it's fine. I really do need to be somewhere." I start off toward the entrance of the school, realizing I have no idea how I will get to Lisa's. Jordan follows but stays silent. Why wouldn't he? I basically just told him that I was abused as a child. Of course, Mr. Small Town has no idea what it's like having your birthday forgotten or crafting an escape plan at the age of ten.

"Do you need a ride?" he asks in a small voice. I hate how I've brought him down from his natural high. I make a mental note to not be that girl who flies off the handle simply by words being spoken.

I slow and look left and right over the open town, seemingly showing my dilemma. You can see just about the whole town from where the school is on this hill. Wide open fields and pastures surround me. Narrow streets veer off into dirt roads that are people's driveways. It mimics the country towns I've conjured in my mind, and I love it. Lisa gave me her address, but I have yet to venture into her neighborhood that I'll somehow get to. I can't imagine there would be a cab service running on Sunday in Garden Valley.

"Um."

"It's the least I can do."

"You've already wasted weekend morning giving me a campus tour." I offer a slight smile that I hope he takes as a peace offering. It's not Jordan's fault that the dads are douchebags. He gets down on one knee and holds his hands up as if praying. "What are you doing?" I ask with worry, looking around to see if anyone is watching.

"It would be my honor to drive you wherever you need to be right now, Leira Jones."

I clutch my backpack strap with my right hand to prevent a smile from taking over. I nod, feeling uneasy about this decision, and it's not because I don't trust him. It was awkward enough being in the car next to Lisa. I can't imagine what it'll be like to be within inches of Jordan.

***

I don't have to imagine for too long since I'm strapped in next to Mr. Tall and Leggy three minutes later. "How do you even fit in here?"

The small Toyota speaks volumes. It's nothing of a privileged kid's car. Even a car is a privilege, but it's not like it's a Lexus. It's clean inside and out and doesn't have a scratch on the pastel color.

"Light blue, huh?" I tease.

"It was my moms," he says with a smile. It's not one of shame, either. Points for that. "So, where are we going?"

"I'm not sure. Lisa gave me her address, but…"

"Oh, Lisa Carnell? I know where she lives."

"You're kidding?"

"I've lived here my whole life. In a small town like this, you pretty much know everyone."

"It's why I'm here," I say quietly, wishing I hadn't.

"Oh? I thought you came for the top-notch college," he says with a wide smile.

"That too," I smile back, this time thankful for his joke.

Jordan mostly fills in the silence with stories about the neighborhoods we pass and points out the vicinity of his house. He talks about working at the college, shows me his high school when we pass by, and seems to know every historical story surrounding the town.

My phone dings with a text message. I figure it's Lisa asking when I'll be at her house. Nope, it's from Charlotte!

How's it going? Charlotte

Jordan looks between my phone and watching where he's going. He doesn't say anything, but I can sense his curiosity.

"It's just my friend, Charlotte."

Fine. Leira

I haven't wanted to check in with her, aiming to cut ties with my life of 'back then.'

"Is that code for Charlie?" I look over at him quickly, and he lets out a laugh. "Just kidding. I live on the other side of town," he continues. He laughs, but I don't get the joke yet. "Not that there's a 'that side of town' here."

"What do you mean?"

"I mean, there really isn't a bad neighborhood."

"How lucky for you." I mentally kick myself for being irritated by his comment. Once again, it's not like this is in Jordan's control. Still, the way he's said it comes off like he's bragging.

He glances at me several times, probably to gauge my feelings. I show I'm okay with a forced smile that I hope looks genuine. This is fast, and I'm not talking about his driving.

"Definitely not the driving," I say out loud. "You drive like a grandma."

"I'll take that as a compliment. My grandma didn't know a speed less than fifty." He revs the engine a few times, pulling a giggle from me. "Lisa is just up here on the left. Soon, you'll be rid of my dumb jokes." I spy a bit of a falter in his smile this time. Disappointment, perhaps?

"They aren't dumb," I smile. "They're, you know, kind of cute."

"She thinks I'm cute!" he says, rolling his window down and fanning himself with the added breeze. "It's okay if you're not as talkative as me. I know I'm high maintenance."

I look out my window to hide my smile but turn back to explain a moment later. "I'm sorry. It's a lot of change right now."

"I get that, I get that," he says with a nod.

No, you don't! You have no frickin' idea what I've had to go through to get here! I push this aside, trying to end whatever today has been with him on a good note.

Jordan turns left into a long gravel driveway with a cute blue and white house at the end. I do my best to play it cool and keep my gawking to a minimum. Lisa's house and lot are much nicer than I'm used to, and the kid in me wants to scope it out.

The outside is clean and spacious. Green grass, bushes, and wispy flowers add a homey feel—the opposite of what I grew up with. A white fence runs the length of her property, going beyond my vision to the left, where a back garage sits. I assume this is the space she has for rent.

"Thanks for the ride," I say, grabbing my bag. "And for the tour." I aim to scramble out of his truck as quickly as possible. Jordan rests his hand on my upper left arm, stopping me immediately. This isn't anything like Amber's touch from the Inn. This, dare I say, is welcome.

"Leira, I'm sorry if I said something wrong today. If I said a couple of things wrong."

Oh no, I'm *that* girl. The one who gets all upset by everything everyone does or says around her. Nope! I will not be her!

I soften my posture into the passenger seat. "It's totally fine. There really isn't anything to be sorry about. It's not like you know my past. I had fun. Thanks for the tour." It's a simplistic take on the day, but it ends our morning the way it should.

Jordan gives one last wave as I stand in the oversized gravel driveway. Watching him drive away is awkward, but I need to settle my racing thoughts before stepping into yet another doorway of change. I knew everything would be different here, but slowing things down would be nice.

I ring the doorbell, igniting a flurry of barks beyond the door. I step back, having never had a good encounter with a dog. At least, they've never liked the site of my dingy car rolling down their driveway to deliver illegal packages.

"Hang on, boy," Lisa says from inside. She opens the door a moment later, holding her very round and happy-looking pug. "Leira, hello." She sticks her head outside with a worried expression. "Oh my gosh, I didn't even think about how you'd get here!"

"It's fine. A friend dropped me off," I say, hoping she won't pry into this statement.

"Come on in. I'll get you some water."

I step into her foyer, pausing at the bright white and blue living room. It's cozy with wooden side tables, large windows with not a drape in site, and a TV. The windows are in two sections and extend from the floor to ceiling, allowing natural light in. It's what a house should be.

This room leads to a dining area or a hallway to the left and the right, where I assume the bedrooms are. The central part of the house is pretty much one large, interconnecting room. My home 'back then' was choppy, with walls separating everything. I like this open look much better.

Lisa chatters about this room and that, all with me feeling awkwardly out of place. It's all in my head, and I know it.

"This is Chuggers. He's more fat than brain, which makes him the sweetest guy ever." She uses that dog voice that people who adore their dogs have. The pug wiggles in her arms, panting with his tongue out. I'm not much of a dog person, but the excitement this 'stranger dog' has for me is flattering. I hesitate before bending to pet the chunky pug.

"Stay still. I want to pet you," I giggle. He's dancing around me so much I can barely touch him. I stand and look around. "It's clean."

"It's a first! I've had a lot of time on my hands."

"Leira!" Adrienne comes running from the hallway and plows into me for a full-on hug.

"Hi, Adrienne." I can't help but give the girl a genuine hug in return. She's as sweet as they come. I haven't been around kids much. One can hardly ignore when a kid looks at you with as much adoration as she's showing right now. "Want to see my room? Come on!" Adrienne pulls me away from the rest of the house and into a sea of pink and white.

The white canopy bed with stuffed animals brings out the little girl side that I thought I left behind years ago. Shelves lined with trinkets, a rainbow beanbag, and an area made just for llamas draw me in.

"You like llamas, huh?" My voice is dull compared to the fairyland I'm in. I hope it will come with time, that spark in my voice that matches the natives in Garden Valley. My imagination runs free of its own accord. I suddenly have the urge to grab a stuffed animal and make it float in the air.

"I *love* llamas!" Adrienne says with excitement. "We went to a farm that had them a couple of hours ago. Hours?" she giggles, covering her face with her hand. "I mean, a couple of weeks ago. One spit at my dad, but they liked me. They were so fluffy! Look, I just learned this twirl," she says with a spin that makes me smile. "Are you going to live here?"

"I don't know. I'll have to check it out."

"I'll come with you!" She takes my hand and leads me back to the kitchen. "Mommy, can we see Nana's garage?"

Lisa's smile falters, revealing the sadness of this statement. "Sure, honey. My grandma lived back there. Don't worry; it has none of that ointment smell. She had it decked out in Christmas colors and lights year-round, but I've cleaned it up." Despite the sad topic, she and Adrienne share a smile. "Let's go see! I hope you like what I've done with it," Lisa says with a skip. "Patrick's shop is opposite the garage, with the living area in the back."

We follow a stone path in the grass to the two-story garage amidst the trees. A light breeze sways the tall evergreens with a whooshing noise I swear I'll never grow tired of. There are a few neighboring houses, but they're so far away that I couldn't throw a rock at them if I tried.

If I take this place, it'll be just me back here. Lisa's house is only a few paces away, but only experience will determine if I'll like the privacy or be terrified to be alone.

The blue building with white trim matches the house. I instantly love it before seeing what is beyond the side door. I follow Lisa in with Adrienne by my side. I feel a great deal of comfort with her holding my hand. It's like her super power is to comfort me, helping me make this transition, showing me it's okay.

I'm sold the moment I see the place. What it lacks in space, it makes up with in charm. Besides, it's loads bigger and better than my dingy room from 'back then.' This will be my own tiny home. I've felt envy when watching videos of people showing off their tiny homes. It's their own sanctuary, with every nook and cranny decorated.

"I just painted the walls this beige, but you can feel free to add an accent color if you'd like." I shrug, having no idea which color I would choose. "I can help if you want. The bedroom is upstairs." My eyes drift up the narrow wooden staircase on the far wall. That will be my bedroom! "My friend, Joanie, dropped these couches off the other day."

The main floor is basically a kitchen, bathroom, and living area. Vaulted ceilings and windows open the whole area up. A spattering of rain starts tinkling against the windows, inviting me into the cozy atmosphere in a way I couldn't have predicted. I don't say a word as I walk around to assess the place.

I like it, I like it, I like it!

It's me in every way. It's plain and simple yet warm and comfortable. Nothing is too fancy, but it's clean. It's small, but it will soon be mine!

"The kitchen is small, but everything is new and works great. Right here is the bathroom. I know it's right next to the kitchen, but that's how these things go with plumbing. Want to see upstairs?"

"That's my favorite!" Adrienne says, pulling me to the staircase.

"No jumping around up there, missy," Lisa warns. "There's the balcony, as you can see, so it has that open feel. It's not an actual room because there's no door, but at least there's some separation since it's upstairs."

We climb the staircase, which gives me a better view of the downstairs. The white furniture and hardwood floors offer a clean and tidy look that is a stark contrast to the brown-stained carpet and dusty couches I'm used to.

I had figured there wouldn't be any room to stand upstairs with a low ceiling, but this is bigger than my old bedroom. A down comforter with swirls of purple calls my name. I can see myself snuggling in here with a book, listening to the rain tapping against the skylight above. The dresser will fit my new wardrobe. I'm set!

Lisa and Adrienne watch me with hopeful expressions, waiting for the answer to the obvious yet unspoken question. This will be my own oasis, my own place in the world. That alone means more to me than all the super powers combined.

"I like it," I say with a nod once we get back downstairs. I'm thrilled inside, hit with the energy to run back to my room at the inn and bring all my things over. That thought poses quite a problem: how will I get my stuff here?

"Yay!" Adrienne shouts with a tug on my hand. I bite my lip as the smile pushes through my guard.

"That's great! You can move in anytime. I'll help you. We can load up my van and…" Lisa's phone dings a dreary song, causing her smile to vanish. "Oh, you've *got* to be kidding me," she says with a tightness of her posture.

"What?" I ask in surprise.

"My mom's here." Dread fills her eyes first before she forces a smile. "Grandma's here," she says to Adrienne in a forced upbeat tone.

"Yay! I wonder what she has for me," the little girl says, rushing outside.

"Probably something I couldn't provide," Lisa mutters. "It's fine if you stay out here to look around. If you come out, be on guard." Her eyes give an additional warning. They hold nothing of the warmness she usually has. I definitely can't miss this!

The second we get outside, I hear a woman hollering at the house. "Hello? Is anyone home? I know you're home, Lisa; your car is out here."

Lisa walks with steps of urgency to the side gate. "Mom, I'm out here."

"What took you so long?" the woman asks. Adrienne opens the gate and gives her grandma a hug. The woman is dressed in the nicest black and white checkered suit I've ever seen. Her soft brown hair is perfectly curled at her shoulders, and her makeup is as perfect as Monica's was at the salon. In the driveway, I spy a Cadillac. I've only seen the rich people who work with the dads drive these cars.

"I wasn't hiding from you. We were in the back garage."

"You still have that old thing? I don't know what your grandma liked about it so much or why she preferred to live out there instead of with us."

"Yeah, it's a real mystery," Lisa mutters over her shoulder. I tuck my lips in to keep from smiling, loving the family dynamic before me. Don't get me wrong, I feel bad for Lisa. It's evident this is a strained relationship, as she's alluded to. I guess it proves that no family is perfect.

A movement to my left catches my eye. A grey cat runs across Lisa's driveway, ducks under the wooden picket fence, and dashes into the bushes by the garage. From what I could see, it looked more like a kitten. I start toward it, but Lisa's mom goes in for another round.

"I came to see what this ordeal is with you losing your job. You avoided me for the rest of the party last night. Do you want me to call the clinic and see what happened? I hope you weren't wearing your hair like that when you went to work. And where is your lipstick?"

It's a strange mix of her mom offering help while splashing in rude comments. Lisa's hands are clenched at her side, giving away her feelings.

"I did my hair for work," Lisa says, bundling her thick black hair at the neck as she heads for her house. "They wanted someone full-time." Her voice mimics mine with a lack of enthusiasm. It looks like we can't have giggles all the time.

"I thought you liked that job." Finally, a sympathetic voice. "What will people think if they find out you got fired?" And there it is, the reason for her 'concern.'

"I did like the job. It just didn't work out." Lisa shrugs. If I hadn't watched her confession video filled with tears, this wouldn't know of her disappointment from being let go.

"Well, you know you're always welcome at our practice." Her mom shows her first smile since being here and even offers Lisa a pat on her shoulder. Her eyes drift to me. Their coldness freezes me to my spot, making me regret following Lisa out here. I'm no match for this woman. "Who's this?"

"Mom, this is Leira. Leira, this is my mother, Nancy."

"Nice to meet you. Aren't you going to take your shoes off at the door?" Nancy asks after Lisa walks inside.

"I'm not dirty, mom." Lisa promptly picks Chuggers up and takes him to what I assume is her bedroom.

"Well, your house does look clean today," the woman says, stepping into the house with caution as if something is going to fall on her.

"Grandma, do you have anything for me?" Adrienne asks with hopeful eyes.

"You know I do," she says with a hug. While the woman doesn't fit in with the pleasantness of this town, she's at least grandmotherly to the little girl. She pulls a beautifully wrapped pink and purple gift from her purse. Adrienne tears into the gift to reveal a pair of earrings.

"These are pretty, grandma."

"I thought you'd like those. It's your birthstone, after all."

I peek into the box that holds a pair of dangly blue topaz jewelry. It's the same as my birthstone, yet I do what I've done best and keep my mouth shut. I definitely don't want this woman's claws sinking into me. Lisa comes out from putting her dog away, only to roll her eyes at the wrapping paper on the ground. I suspect her reaction has nothing to do with the mess.

"Mother, you don't have to give her a present every time you see her."

"Of course I do. She is my only grandchild, after all."

Nancy says this with obvious disapproval.

"Diane's older than me, and she doesn't have any children. Why don't you harp on her for once?"

"I do. Nothing I say makes any difference to either of you." Her lips form a thin line as she looks over the kitchen, dining room, and living room. Geez, what's with this lady? "Anyway, I was in town to go through your fabric store. It's the only place that has decent silk flowers."

"I agree. Leira just got a job there."

Oh no, don't bring me into this!

"Oh?" It's not a question from Nancy as much as a condescending tone. "That must be nice." She keeps her eyes on me as if expecting an answer.

I quickly switch to my stoic nature, which doesn't offer a hint of a smile. This is one of those times I wish I could hide in my black clothes and bushy hair.

"I'm sure it'll help with the college bills," Lisa offers, stacking a few papers on the kitchen counter.

"Well, good for you, dear. I'm sure the community college here will do you well. Anyway…"

"It's a state college," I correct with a boldness that comes out of nowhere.

"Oh?" Nancy's face has fallen as she looks from me to Lisa. "I always thought it was a two-year community college."

"I've told you it's a four-year college, mom. How else do you think I got my psychology degree?"

An odd silence follows, with the mother and daughter staring each other down. It's not a stand-off. It's more like they are trying to understand each other with their eyes. Nancy looks down first, and I swear I spy regret in her expression. Maybe the psychology degree isn't wrong for me. I've been able to read these two as plainly as if they were written in a textbook.

"I have tea with the ladies at the club soon, so I better get going. Adrienne, you stay as sweet as can be, okay?"

"Bye, Grandma. I'll walk out with you."

The little girl leads the woman out the front door, chattering about school and leaving Lisa and me behind. Lisa collapses on the couch with an exasperated sigh. "Ugh, it's so painful to be around my mother."

"Yeah. What a bitch," I say coldly.

Lisa breaks into a belly laugh. It's not one of her cute giggles; it's a full-on laugh. "Halleluiah, someone agrees with me!" She slouches forward and clutches her stomach before standing and shaking her head with a smile.

"Welcome to my mother. You sure are perceptive for a girl who doesn't say much." She continues for a few more seconds to let all her laughter out. "Oh, I really needed that." She pats me on the shoulder before going to collect her daughter. "I can tell that I'm going to love having you here. I hope your childhood was happier than mine."

I'm not about to start a debate, but I highly doubt it.

Chapter 13 Lisa

Weaving Through the Changes

It was unexpected to have my mom barge over. Leira acted as a buffer to the usual letdown when she leaves. Adrienne usually saves me from my mom completely chomping down on me. There was something different about our visit. I swear I suspected a bit of softness in her tone, not once but twice.

My mother usually chews me up one end and down the other, leaving me raw. It takes days for me to recover, but not this time. I also didn't have the expected letdown after last night's party. The combination of my YouTube and Etsy successes and Leira renting out the back apartment has held my depression at bay. Imagine that, distraction has worked yet again.

"So, what's your final consensus of the apartment?" I ask Leira once I gather Adrienne back inside. "I think we should call it something other than 'the garage' if you decide to move in, don't you? I love it when I go to the lake, and all the cabins have different names, such as 'Serenity' or 'Escape.' Maybe we can do something like that."

Leira stays quiet. I don't mean to bombard her, but I'm excited that she's here. It's not because of the money either.

Well, that's not the only reason. The rent will help us immensely. It's nice to change things up, and I'm not going to turn down the extra body now that I'm home so much. Adrienne seems to like her, too.

"How much are you charging?" she asks flatly. She's so young to be jaded with this type of voice, but I know nothing of her story and upbringing.

"Yikes! I'm sorry I didn't mention that. I keep thinking you saw the ad." I reach out to touch her forearm to show my apology. I've done this for most of my life, adding a connection with someone through this touching gesture. Leira flinches, looks away and tucks her hair behind her ear. "It's three hundred a month. I hope that's not too much."

"That's fine!" she answers with excitement. She's so young that I feel bad not reducing the amount for her, but at the same time, we need something steady if I'm not going to work, and this is less than the going rate in town.

Is that what's going on here? Am I not going to work anymore? The thought jump-starts my passion even more for my videos and sales. The idea of being my own boss is enticing and not for the first time.

"Is Leira going to live here?" Adrienne asks with a hop. I nod in confirmation, and my little girl lets out a hoot. "Yay! I can't wait to play with you! I just started a new game that has Care Bears and dinosaurs."

"How's that for a combination?" I mutter to Leira. She smiles briefly but remains quiet. She digs into her side bag and pulls out a wad of cash almost too big for her hand. "Whoa, that's quite a load. Where did you… I mean," I stop, feeling that her private ways won't like this question. "You should get a bank account, girl. Even in Garden Valley, where our crime rate is in the single digits, you don't want to carry that kind of cash."

"I've never had a bank account," she responds with big, panicked eyes. She looks from Adrienne to me and backs up a step.

"It's a cinch. I can help you if you want. You should have an account since you have a job. It's easy. I was afraid to open one for my Coping With Yarn business, but it only took a few minutes. When would you like to move in? We're free today if you are."

"I actually have to work in a couple of hours. But I can tomorrow."

"It's settled then! I don't know about you two, but I'm hungry. What do you girls say to some grilled cheese sandwiches and chicken tortilla soup?" I scurry to the kitchen and pull out the ingredients. A glance at Leira shows she's rooted to her position in the living room, her fingers clutching her bag.

"You can sit next to me, Leira," Adrienne says sweetly as she pulls a chair out at the table.

"Um, okay." She keeps her eyes focused on something out back but takes a seat. "Lisa did you make these?" she asks, holding up a candycorn critter in one hand and purple bat in another.

"I sure did! And I've been trying these cute little bookmarks. What do you think?" I ask, holding up the crocheted cat with the long tail that allows the reader to thread between the pages.

"I think I want one of those for each of my textbooks!" Leira says genuinely.

One thing is for sure: Adrienne and I will help Leira come out of her shell. I know nothing about this girl, but I do know that I need to help her.

***

Since Leira had to work Sunday afternoon, I convinced her to let me help her move after I dropped Adrienne off at school Monday morning. I also convinced her to take a quick trip to the bank.

Leira had three large stacks of cash that she pulled out of her bag. The account manager and I exchanged glances full of questions. It's not her place to ask the source; I suppose it's not mine either. Leira said something about having a job where she's from. Still, something was off with this.

All in all, she ended up depositing almost five thousand dollars. And good for her! Here she is, going to school and working. No matter what her past, and I sense that she has quite a history, her actions have shown that she's making her way to a brighter future.

We stuff all of Leira's things at the inn in the back of my van. She doesn't have more than a couple of suitcases and bags. She checked out of the hotel with the girl, Amber, who looked about her age. They exchange a few words about seeing each other in a class they have together. It warms my heart that she has a friend.

I have a million questions, with my psychology brain kicking into gear. I don't want to scare her off, but something about Leira makes me feel like she needs the interaction. I know everyone isn't a talker like me, but we all need someone to be there for us.

"That should do it," I say, bringing the final load into the back garage. "Maybe this place can be called 'Oasis,'" I offer, wiping my hands on my jeans. She's been quiet most of the morning. I back out of the apartment, figuring Leira could use some time to settle in. "If you want to come over, just knock on the back door. We usually eat around six, and you're more than welcome to join us."

"You're leaving?" Leira glances at the apartment space before looking at me with frightened eyes.

"I don't have to," I say quickly. "I don't have plans today and can help you unpack if you'd like."

"I pretty much just have clothes," she says quietly, her shoulders sinking. We stand in awkward silence for a few seconds, looking around for another task for me to help with.

"I know!" I hop to the kitchen, pull out a drawer, and grab a swatch book I stashed in there the other day. "Colors! I kept this book for whoever was going to live here. Maybe you can pick something you'd like to see day in and day out."

Leira joins me at the small counter island in the kitchen. I'm glad I convinced Patrick to use a creamy quartz for the countertops. There's not much counter space, but what is here is classy. "I've never painted before," she says with worry.

"There's nothing to it! We have all the supplies you need, so we just need to buy the paint." I flip through the book, glancing at Leira every few pages to see if I can detect a spark in her eyes.

"I like that yellow," she says softly, tapping one of the colors.

"Ooh, I like that too." I flip the swatch over to read the name. "This is one of my favorite parts, to see what the colors are named. This one is 'Buttermilk.' That sounds right since it's such a soft yellow. Can you believe it's someone's job to develop these? How fun would that be?"

I mark the page with a sticky note and continue to go through the book. She points to a color in the purple section.

"Let's see. This one is 'Field of Lavender.' I don't know if lavender tastes good with buttermilk, but we'll find out." Leira bites her lip with a smile. "These are quite cheerful. I like it!" She smiles proudly back at me.

It's the second time I've seen brightness on her face. I'm glad to be a part of this transition for her. I suspect there's a story behind her quiet voice and one that I'll weave my way into. It's not for curiosity. I feel like I can help her through what life has given her.

"What do you say? Want to make a trip to the home store and get these colors whipped up?"

"I'm working tonight."

"It's only ten o'clock. What time do you have to work?"

"Six."

"Plenty of time! I'm pretty caught up with my stuff, and I'm one of those weirdos who like to paint. What do you say?" I don't want to be a total spaz, but I'm failing at trying not to be overly excited here.

"Okay," she says with a shrug. So far, she's been pretty flat, but I've seen glimpses of the true Leira. It makes me wonder what her favorite things are in this world. Does she have hobbies or interests? Does she have a favorite food or drink? What else is there in this world that she loves?

We load into my van and head to town. "So, um, how are you going to get to work tonight?" Her silence tells me that she hasn't thought this far ahead. "I don't mind being your shuttle."

"No, it's fine. I don't want to be a burden."

"Are you kidding me? I'd have an excuse to go to the fabric store! What time does your shift end?"

"Ten-thirty, it's too late for you to pick me up. I can just take the bus."

I bark a laugh, not at her but at the sign of how small our town is. "We don't have bus service here, sweetie. I don't mind picking you up. It's not like I have to work tomorrow," I laugh. I honestly don't mind being her shuttle for now. "We have a beater pickup that you could borrow, but I'll have to ask Patrick if he's okay with that."

"I don't want to put you out. I'll pay you."

"No way, silly, I won't take your money." It feels strange to be taking money from a teenager for her rent, but being responsible for bills is a progression of life.

I'm the one in charge of things at the paint store. I give Leira a couple of chances to order the paint, but she practically shuffles to the corner. I give her leeway, assuming she's never been in charge of something like this.

In no time, we return home with our two gallons of paint and new brushes.

"See? Easy. We have four hours until I need to pick Adrienne up. That's plenty of time to get the first coat of color on." Leira stares out the window, not sharing any of my enthusiasm for our upcoming task. "You okay?"

She snaps her head back to me with a self-conscious expression. "I'm fine. Why?"

"You're a bit quieter than Adrienne. It takes some getting used to. I'm not saying that's bad. Most people are quiet compared to me. I think I could talk and drink water at the same time if I tried," I laugh.

"Maybe we can call the back garage 'The Hideout' or something," she shrugs.

"I like that. So, uh, is this your first time being out on your own?" I ask with a sideways glance. Leira answers with a nod, which seems like her preferred method of communication. "I remember moving out of my parent's house. They weren't happy at all that I came here. It's too bad they couldn't see that this was my best decision."

"Did they eventually come around?"

"Eh, sort of. Their opinion really bothered me at first. Consumed me is probably a better way to describe it. Nana was always on my side, though. She was my grandma. She pushed me through and assured me it was okay to do my own thing. I had just turned twenty. It's young, but you don't realize it at the time. All you can think about is branching out and making your own decisions."

She nods, but this time, I can see more of a connection to what I'm saying behind her eyes.

"Sometimes all you need is that one person to cheer you on. And, sometimes, it's good that the person isn't someone your own age." I give her a smile, hoping she understands my whole meaning.

We spread drop cloths and get started. I show Leira how to use the roller and put myself on trim duty. "I pride myself for not using tape. I have steady hands, and it beats spending a ton of time taping everything. Okay, this is the fun part…" I open the can of yellow paint, oohing when I see the color. "Beautiful! Shall we look at the next one?" Leira nods with a smile this time. It's not difficult to read her expressions, like deciphering all the meanings of 'I am Groot.'

It's not a combination I would have immediately chosen, but the purple and yellow look nice together. "I'm going to let you do the honors of making the first swipe."

Leira glances around the place with worry on her face. I remain quiet, allowing her to be in her thoughts. "I think that wall should be the violet color," she says, pointing to a wall in the living room. I'm glad it's the smallest one in the room, so we won't have to be on a tall ladder. "Then maybe the yellow one can go on that wall by the kitchen. And then…"

She takes a couple of quick steps to the bathroom. I allow myself to smile as I follow the girl who is probably making her first-ever decorating decision. She looks around the small room, which is complete with a shower and tub.

"I think it would look good to have that wall yellow and that one violet in here."

"I like that idea. It brings it all together to have both colors in here. You can paint the bedroom area too if you want." Leira's eyes light up. She blows by me and runs up the stairs. "What are you thinkin'?" I ask when I join her. I have my own opinion, but I want her to develop hers.

"Violet would add a nice touch-up here," she says with a confirmational nod.

"It's better than white, for sure."

"And black." Her eyes gloss over, not seeing our surroundings. I study her, wondering what's going on behind her mind with this comment. It's a topic I want to explore, one that's probably necessary for her to work through.

"Let's get started!" Before I get there, Leira rushes downstairs and holds a paintbrush above the yellow can. Her face has a big, goofy smile as if stretching out the anticipation. I laugh in happiness at how she's finally joined the party.

"Which wall shall we do first?"

Leira sidesteps to a wall in the living room comically. I laugh again, loving the bond I'm making with her. It's almost like I can see the aura around us, interlacing and connecting us. Hers is shy, as you'd expect a beautiful violet to be. Mine is yellow, vibrant, and outgoing as ever.

"Lavender goes well with yellow. Don't you think?" she asks, looking between her color and mine.

"It sure does."

Chapter 14 Lisa

Life's Twists and Turns

I leave 'The Hideout' to get Adrienne with Leira finishing the first coat in the bathroom. I've propped the windows and front door open to allow the fumes to escape. We've been blessed with a warm fall breeze to help blow out the fumes. We got the type of paint that is less stinky, but still, I don't want Leira's first night to be a fumy apartment.

Leira's place.

The thought stops me briefly on the stone path from 'The Hideout' to my back porch. It's no longer 'Nana's place,' as we called it before. Really, we should have named it 'Christmas Central.' I can almost see the red and green flashing lights with the memory. I let it be a happy thought instead of the sadness that wants to take over. I don't want this to happen today, not when my day with Leira has been fun.

Leira opened up, even if it was just one petal of a bloom. She seemed to like hanging out with me. And then I falter again, believing my next thought as the truth.

This teenage girl, who is just starting out, isn't going to want to hang out with an old mom. The 'Negative Nelly' inside pontificates her feelings and brings me down a few notches. More like it brings a mirror in front of my face to see what's going on.

Am I really this desperate for friendship?

Instead of taking it as the truth, I fight back.

Why can't she be a friend? "Why does it matter her age?" I snarl.

It's not like I need someone to be over thirty to be friends with them. I'm sure the lack of regular interaction I got from work is something I'm missing. I'm not complaining. I've found joy in my videos, crocheting, and now my Etsy shop. It's not only about the potential to make money. I'm doing what I'm passionate about and am building a community, one subscriber and order at a time. More importantly, I'm having fun!

I grab my phone to check my numbers to confirm that this is working, a visual representation that I'm on the right path. I struggle to keep myself from obsessively checking how many subscribers I have and sales on Etsy. Still, I allow curiosity to win a couple of times a day.

"I have twenty more subscribers! Almost to five hundred." I know this isn't much to brag about, but hey, you've got to start somewhere. I check my Etsy account next and see I have four more sales!

I scroll through my comments with my ego-boosting with every one of them. "Darn it," I sigh, stopping on my only one-star review. My heart sinks as I read how one of my pillows unraveled.

My son pulled on the string, and the whole thing came undone.

"Well, yeah. You can't go yanking on the strings of almost anything," I say in irritation. It's logical reasoning for the customer to give me a low rating, but it still dampens my spirits. Maybe I should stay away from the reviews. Of course,

I'll get a bad review or comment occasionally. "Get thicker skin, Lisa!" I should have thicker skin, having dealt with my mom and sister my whole life. They've knocked me down plenty, but this soul only got weaker, not tougher.

My phone buzzes with the reminder to pick Adrienne up, thank goodness. I had to put this alarm on my phone for fear of getting too deep into a project and losing track of time. It's completely different punching my own clock as opposed to being on someone else's schedule like I was at the clinic.

I rush to the school, looking forward to seeing my daughter. Adrienne comes out with a bright smile. It's always this way for her, something I take credit for since this is the side of me she sees ninety-nine percent of the time.

It makes me wonder what has happened in Leira's life to not put one on her face. Did she have a mom who picked her up? Did she have anyone in her life who made her happy?

When we get home, I take Adrienne and Chuggers out back to check on Leira. Pop music blares from her phone, giving off a teenage vibe. I'm not sure how Adrienne will react to seeing the changes we've made. She spent a lot of time out here with Nana.

"Leira, I love these colors!" she says, running to hug the girl. Leira grins in return. It's a simple gesture that isn't fake. Their instant friendship makes me wonder if Adrienne has made her feel like a little girl for the first time.

"Well, hot diggity, it looks great in here!" I exclaim.

"I just got done with the second coat and am going to start on the bathroom." It's Leira's first day here, and we're almost done with the painting! She flits around in an energy high, moving to the music as she swipes the new color on the wall.

"Your school starts on Monday, right?"

"Yup. I'm glad I'm getting this done now." Leira's eyes switch to fear, and she looks at the ground with worry.

"Don't worry. The first day is the hardest. After that, it gets easier." It's Adrienne taking the words from my mouth. I've said this to her every first school day in the last couple of years. It feels good hearing her repeat my words of wisdom.

Leira and I lock eyes for a moment before laughing lightly. "That's good to know, thanks," Leira responds. There's a difference in her voice when she speaks to Adrienne. It takes on a light, friendly tone instead of the lower tones she hides behind. "I like this painting process, so if you have other things to do…"

It's her way of dismissing us. "I need to get dinner started. You're more than welcome to join us. And then," I say, looking her in the eye again, "I'll take you to work." Leira nods with a slight smile of surrender in return.

I turn to leave, pausing to take in the bright colors. We've turned 'The Hideout' into a cheery place in just a few hours. I can only hope that it offers Leira as much joy.

"It looks really nice in here." Her face lights up and I give her a nod before leaving. It's good for her to do this independently and prove to herself that she can do it. That goes for school, too. I hope she doesn't push it too hard, trying to balance school with her first job and being on her own.

It's an easy dinner I have planned for tonight. I pride myself on having a freezer full of homemade casseroles that I can pull out on days like this. My cheesy lasagna will hopefully win Leira over if she joins us.

A noise in the guest room brings me in to check it out. "What are you doing in here, missy?" I ask Adrienne in the spare room with a hand on my hip.

"Halloween!" she replies, holding up two witches I've crocheted. I laugh in response and help her bring down my bins of decorations from the closet.

"I seriously need to get rid of some of this stuff. We don't have enough room to display it all." I absolutely love Halloween and have crocheted every type of ghost and candy corn out there! I love all the holidays as they give me inspiration for crochet projects.

"You should sell these decorations on your Etsy shop," Adrienne suggests. It's funny to be getting business advice from her sweet voice.

"Good idea! Better yet, I should make a video that they are on my Etsy shop!"

We sort through all the bats, witches, spiders, and ghosts, putting aside our favorites. I grab my phone, hit record, and spring into action. "Hello fellow Crochet-iacs! I have all these little guys for sale on my Etsy shop if you're interested. Starting October first I'll be doing a 'thirty-one days of Halloween.' I'll take you along as I make a project a day. I'm taking requests!" I move the camera from one item to the other. I only have about a minute for this short, so I plug my shop's name, hit the stop button, and upload. "It's worth a try!"

I take pictures of the items for my Etsy account, considering what Betsy said about hiking up the price. I pick up a bat to inspect it, ensuring everything is tight and cinched up as it should be. "This is good craftsmanship here," I say out loud. "And I'm worth it," I say the words, solidifying their meaning as I allow myself the compliment.

"It would be fun to make a video of us decorating," Adrienne suggests.

"I'm going to hire you as my idea girl." She smiles at the

compliment. I make a note to throw compliments Leira's way for her during her time with us, which I hope will be a while.

"Can I record you?" Adrienne asks with a smile.

"Hmm," I say with a tilt of my head.

"I'll keep the camera straight," she adds.

"I learned this new trick for taking the jiggle out. I'll get my tripod!" I rush to the living room where I last had my things and hook the phone up to the tripod. I push a button to help with this, give Adrienne a couple of instructions, and get started.

"Ready?" she asks.

"Ready." Adrienne points to me after hitting record. "Hi, I'm Lisa with Coping With Yarn, and I thought it would be flice…" I start laughing, which makes Adrienne start up herself. "I was going to say fun but then changed it to nice in my head, so flice. How does that sound, young camera person?"

"It makes sense to me."

"I have my daughter on the camera to help me out today. Anyway, I thought it would be *fun* to show you how we decorate our house for Halloween." Never mind what my mom thinks about our tiny house. Never mind that there's clutter on the kitchen counter that seems to breed overnight. "I usually hang these bats from the ceiling. I have spiders and pumpkins and… bonus! Here's the witch I couldn't find last year!"

We spring into action, getting the place set up in no time. "'Tis one advantage of having a small house; you can transform it quickly." I take the camera from Adrienne when she gets antsy and wants to decorate. "This spooky house is my favorite. As you can see, you can even use yarn for this sort of thing. I've crocheted a lot of these items around cardboard to keep them sturdy. I'll show you how in my next video. I've put a couple of LED lights in the house, and they blink. And I made that spooky tree and pumpkin patch that goes in back of the house."

I move the camera around, showing the bats and spiders hanging from the ceiling. "It's not as complete as usual, so I'll show you the house when we're done. In October, I plan to put out a video a day of me making everything you see here one at a time." I look over all my creations that I made with love and passion. This hobby is turning into a business I'm ultra proud of. I never knew over the years that I've been weaving my reality, one knot at a time.

I put the camera down so I can use both hands. We hang purple lights around the house, lighting up the table behind the couch where we strung spider webs from our quaint foyer. After only an hour, our living area resembles the kid version of a haunted house.

I take a video of our newly decorated house, wishing I knew how to overlay spooky music in the background. This time, I keep an open mind. I've recently learned that if I want to do it, it can happen. It's a new thought process I've proven to myself over the last few weeks. Every goal I meet is a step closer to my belief that I can achieve these dreams.

"That was fun! Want to help me edit?" Adrienne and I have a blast watching the video back and figuring out how to add spooky sounds and effects. I hit upload and finish dinner with my daughter next to me on her stool the entire time. I'm lucky to not only be Adrienne's mom but also to have her as a friend.

I haven't let Patrick know that we decorated. I also like to 'warn' him about this so he's prepared for the different-looking house when he comes in the door. I decide not to send him a text. It's an experiment of mine to gauge what his reaction is.

"Daddy's home!" Adrienne yells, propping herself on the couch by the windows that view our gravel driveway.

Here goes.

Patrick comes in the front door and jolts to a stop when he's nearly engulfed by the fake spider webs.

"Whoa, someone's been having fun!" It's a statement that could go one of two ways. He could simply acknowledge that we've decorated. Or, he could be upset about the change.

"Mommy posted a video of us decorating on YouTube, and she's going to sell her extra bats and ghosts on Etsy," Adrienne blurts in a rush.

"That's a good way to get rid of your overflow," Patrick nods. He really does seem in favor of this, boosting my ego considerably. This is a big win in my book.

We sit down to eat twenty minutes later in our Halloween-themed dining area. I glance at the back garage every minute, hoping Leira will join us. So far, no such luck. I didn't have the refrigerator in her place stocked with anything, so the poor girl will go to work hungry, and she doesn't look like she should miss any meals.

My phone dings throughout dinner, indicating I have new subscribers! I've kept it across the room to keep from sticking my nose in it the whole time. So far, I've kept the evenings free for my family, but tonight, I sense I'll be checking my numbers and packaging the items I've sold with Adrienne.

"Seems like a busy day for you," Patrick says in response to my phone dinging.

"It's been a good day! Leira moved in, and she seems happy about the place." Happy is a bit of a stretch for her. Is

Leira going to be happy here? It's not like she will live here forever, but I hope she will join our family fun time from time to time.

"It's cool you got it rented," Patrick says before shoveling a bite in.

"See? I told ya it could happen. I'll take Leira to work soon. I hope that's okay. She doesn't have a car and I was wondering if she could borrow the pickup to go to and from work."

He thinks about this for a second. I know I didn't send him a text first, but this is how life is. I shouldn't have to warn him about every topic I want to discuss. "It needs a little work, but I don't see why not. It's just sitting there, and it'll do it some good to be driven. I can take a look at it after dinner."

"Thanks. That's nice of you to do for someone you haven't met." I reach to my right and give his forearm a squeeze. It's something I've always liked about my husband, his generosity to others. Sometimes, my mind stays on the negative side of Patrick. It's like the needle gets stuck in the groove of a record, unable to jump to the next track.

"I think that's her right there." Patrick points to Leira. She's dressed in jeans and a simple sweater with her black backpack slung around her shoulder, as usual. She shuts the back garage door behind her, locking it and giving it a tug.

"She looks young," Patrick observes. "How much did you say you're charging for rent?"

"Three hundred a month," I say, jumping up, having just finished my dinner.

"Sweet! How's that for a bonus?" Patrick says, rubbing his sore shoulder. I make a mental note to give him a massage later.

I open the sliding glass door and wave my hand. "Leira,

come on in. This is my husband, Patrick. Patrick, this is our new tenant, Leira. She just enrolled in school and will be starting on Monday."

"It's a good school. We're happy to have you here," Patrick says formally.

"Nice decorations," Leira says, eyeing our living room.

"It's a bit early if you ask me," Patrick says, "but I stay out of it."

"Good move," I say with a smile and nudge to his shoulder.

"It's the smart one," he responds.

"We're going to head out. Honey, want to come?" I ask Adrienne.

"No, I want to keep playing my game," she answers.

"And have ice cream with me," Patrick whispers across the table.

I grab a bag of snacks and a sandwich I threw together right before dinner and hand it to Leira. "I hope it's okay that I made a 'to-go' dinner for you."

"This is for me?" she asks in surprise. She looks at the bag as if it's a foreign item. "Thanks. Hey, I saw a grey cat in the backyard. Is she yours?"

"No, I think she belongs to someone around here. I've been seeing her around here too but haven't been able to catch her."

"She's pretty skinny," we say together. Our eyes lock, and we both offer a warm but sad smile. I wonder if she's linking herself to the scrawny stray cat as I am.

"Bye, Leria!" Adrienne says, with a hug to her new friend.

"Bye, Munchkin," Leira says down to her. It's easy to see that the two of them have bonded. I've always thought it sweet for a teenager to befriend a little girl, but Leira strikes me as someone who isn't quite ready to grow up yet. I envision them spending more time together. Perhaps I have a built-in babysitter!

Leira looks around the driveway, searching for something on our way to my van. "Are you looking for the cat?" She nods in return but doesn't look at me.

"I might get some cat food," she says. "I don't want her to run away." The phrase sparks a flurry of butterflies in my stomach, connecting the cat to Leira. I don't like the idea of Leira straying or fleeing our town. My mama bear instincts have kicked in, and I want to throw a cloak of protection around her.

"Sounds like a good idea." Leira and I get in the van and start up the sloped driveway. "Hey, Patrick said he'll tinker the pickup back to life. If you're interested. I don't want to force you into anything."

"He would do that for me?" It's more of a statement to herself than a comment to me.

"He's good like that. He perked up when he had a reason to finally work on that old thing."

"I, um, saw your short about your Etsy shop. And then your video about Halloween."

"Already, huh? Thank you."

"Did you really make all that Halloween stuff?"

"I did," I say with pride. "I can teach you if you want."

"Really?"

"Sure! It'll be easy now that you're staying with us."

"I wonder where I'll get all my supplies." She puts her finger to her chin before letting out a scrunched-up laugh. I join her with relief that she's already coming out of her shell. She stays quiet for a minute before speaking again. "Your videos have really helped me, Lisa. It's one reason why I got the courage to come here." She clears her throat and looks out the window before turning back to me. "You should be a life coach or something."

It's the second time someone's mentioned this life coach thing, and honestly, it's flattering as hell. 'Wow, thanks,' I say, though the term's always been a bit fuzzy. What exactly does a life coach even do? Once the wheel of curiosity starts spinning, it's hard to stop—and now, it's turning full force, wondering if this is something I should look into.

Chapter 15 Leira

Another Step Forward

My nerves are on fire on my first day of school. I've had many firsts lately and am nowhere near used to them.

On my first day in this town, I was scared shitless. But it was like seeing color for the first time. It was like that scene in The Wizard of Oz when Dorothy goes through the traumatic storm, only to shift from black and white to vibrant greens and golds.

My first day at a real job was scary for a couple of hours, but everyone was friendly enough to hold my hand, and now it's an easy job. Figurative hand-holding, of course, because otherwise, I would have run out of the store with the heebie-jeebies. Physical contact is not in my language.

My first date, or whatever that tour day with Jordan was, made me wonder if I actually am likable. This thought is about the size of a grain of sand, but it sits where there was nothing before.

All these 'firsts' have solidified my opinion of this town being a slice of heaven right here in Oregon. It's my first day of official college, and I'm wearing my first blue shirt. I got up early today to primp myself. I feel like a fourth grader with my new outfit and bag. I even did my hair in a barrette this morning. It's been fun messing with new hairstyles instead of allowing my bushy hair to lay on my shoulders and in my face.

A quick glance in the mirror reveals a new look that I'm thrilled with. If the dads came searching, they'd have a hard time recognizing me. I'm dressed in clothes that actually fit my slim figure. My honey-brown hair is swept away from my face and goes well with my chosen periwinkle sweater. In less than an hour, I'll be blending in with college kids. Or so I hope.

I've been in Garden Valley for over a week and love it. The dads will be back to their shitty house in two days. I'll keep the festering at bay until then.

I wasn't sure if I could sleep alone in the small apartment. Knowing that Lisa and her family are just steps away, I've been okay with it, especially loving falling asleep to the sound of rain on the skylight above my bed. And I have my trusty wooden wedge to shove under the door.

So far, I've been keeping to myself, reading the assigned texts to get a head start. I bought my college books five days ago and haven't put them down since.

Patrick had their loaner pickup up and running within a few hours. When they called it a beater, they were right. It's white with pinstripes down the side. At first, I thought it was the ugliest thing I'd ever seen, but appreciation set in after it got me to and from work. I know it's not mine, but I gave Lisa a couple hundred dollars for it.

Movement in the living room window has me startled to a gasp. Everything brings me back to the dads. I wonder if their sixth sense has kicked in, and they're lurking around, waiting to pounce.

Instead of the dad's being outside, it's a cat balancing

along the windowsill outside! I throw the wooden wedge out underneath the door and desperately rush out. The action of opening the door startles it away.

"Wait, don't leave!" The cat flees across the green lawn and is under the fence in no time. I look down at the can of food I set on my porch last night. It's halfway gone! It feels good to know that the cat's tummy is full. Animals will always be back if they know where to get their food. I chuckle at this correlation to the dads. Those are two animals who will surely want their cook back.

I step inside with a shiver as I thread my arms in my new beige jacket. I'm not used to the chilly mornings. Dark clouds above indicate more rain for the day. For me, it adds to the coziness of the town, and I feel snuggled in my sweater and jacket. I've enjoyed the tinkling raindrops on the roof as I read under a blanket on my cushy couches.

First day. Are you ready? Jordan

It's one of the several texts I've gotten from him since the campus tour. He's asked about my schedule, work, and even how I will get to school. He's chatted about his mom and a friend here and there. He hasn't mentioned one word about either of the times we butted heads the other day. And why should he? It's not like we were screaming at each other or even all that upset.

As ready as I'll ever be. Leira

You'll be fine. All you do is find a seat and listen to inflated egos for a couple of hours. Jordan

I can only hope it will be that easy. Memories of those dreaded back-to-school 'What did you do over the summer' speeches still linger. After a few years, I perfected my go-to story about how I spent my time off: 'I read books and hung out by the pool,' was what I said. The reading part was mostly true, but the crystal blue waters were really bags of pot filling my bike basket before I had a backseat to stash them in.

Jordan sends a smiling emoji before a *'See you soon.'* I've never been one to swoon over a guy, but here I am, staring at the violet wall with a head tilt as I fantasize about seeing him today.

I tuck my pack of cigarettes in my bag just in case today tickles my nerves too much. It's a nasty habit and something that draws a straight line from me to the dads. I've cut back to only six smokes a day. I've heard this leads to a higher success rate of quitting than going cold turkey.

"Small steps," I say to myself, straightening my collar. I laugh as this phrase doesn't describe my last weeks. More like Jordan-sized leaps.

As I reach the pint-sized pickup, my careless footsteps disturb the perfectly formed morning dew. Sweet songs from birds that frequent the backyard feeders land on deaf ears. I have only one focus now, and it's not nature.

Lisa's voice carries to me from the driveway to my right. She's talking to Adrienne in a fun, peppy voice that I've grown used to. I can see that the two of them have a good relationship. She's such a great mom. I'm not going to lie; being around her doting, motherly ways has been a challenge. It reminds me of missing memories I don't hold from my own mom. It's probably the main reason I want Lisa's approval this morning.

"Um, hello," I greet. I've created a routine of sneaking through the side gate when it's time for work. The path is out of site from the back door, and that leads straight to the truck I've named 'Grit.' It's not like I don't want to see them. I've just wanted a few days to settle into my own.

"Leira!" Adrienne runs to me and squeezes my middle. I

would never allow anyone else to do this, but Adrienne is the little friend I never had. I really hope she can't smell that I'm a smoker. It's yet another reason to quit!

"Hey, Munchkin," I say, returning her hug.

"You look really nice," Lisa says with a gentle nod.

"Thanks. My first class starts at eight, so…" I've said these words, but here I am, staying in the driveway as if my feet are stuck.

"You'll be fine," Lisa encourages. She begins to reach her hand out but lets it fall, much to my liking. "The first day is always the hardest. You can feel free to come by for dinner tonight, too, okay?" Lisa asks with a hopeful expression. There's a touch of sadness there as well. She and I had a good time painting together last week, but we've barely spent time together beyond that. Maybe she's as open to my friendship as much as I am to hers!

A glance at my phone shows it's already 7:40, and I want to give myself enough time to find my first class. "Okay, I guess I'll see you later."

"Do you work today?" Lisa asks.

"Yeah, from two to five." I've lightened my schedule to three-hour shifts during the week and six to eight hours on Saturday or Sunday. Twenty hours a week is perfect to go along with twelve credits at school.

"Have a great day!" Lisa chirps. "Ahh, the college experience. I can't wait to hear all about it. We might see you tonight then," Lisa says hopefully, opening the car door for Adrienne. I give her a small smile, not wanting to commit myself to anything.

Her words are as sweet as honey, and enough to give me enough courage to get in the car. I don't need superpowers; the strength to face my fears is the only power I need. I know that once I pull out, there's no going back. Every mile I drive heightens my nerves. The song 'A Little Bit of Sunshine' plays on the radio, introducing my first spark of energy for the day.

Unfortunately, it only lasts the duration of the song.

I find a place to park. Too quick for my taste. let out the breath I probably held during the drive, willing myself to go in.

I allowed myself a cigarette on the drive, keeping my window open to filter the smoke. But now, in the quiet of the truck, I'm all nerves, wanting another one. This is ridiculous. I should drive straight back to Nevada and forget this ever happened.

But… I want this. I don't know what my purpose is yet in life. I'm only eighteen! I have three classes to get a taste of this and try and figure it out. Probably literally a taste since one of the classes is an introduction to culinary arts.

I step out, facing the vastness of the campus ahead. The towering buildings seem to loom over me, aiming to intimidate. I shrug on my backpack, gripping the straps tightly, refusing to let my jitters get to me.

I force myself to look past all this and find something more positive. The rain from last night has left behind a smell of freshness. I welcome it as I, too, embark on this fresh start. The buildings look like they've been built around the trees. Grass surrounds a maze of paths. I take my first steps, taking one of those paths to the science building where my first psychology class is.

I pass several other students on the way. Most of them reflect a look of terror that I'm feeling. It's good that I'm not the only one with excited dread for today. I'm glad Jordan showed me around. At least I don't worry about showing up in the wrong class.

The hallway is filled with murmurs from the other students who seem to know each other. I quicken my steps and enter the room, aiming for a seat in the back that screams my name. I unpack a notebook and pen and tuck my phone in the front pocket of my backpack. It's not like I need to worry about being interrupted by any friends.

"You made it, huh?" I look up to see Jordan walking my way!

"What are you doing here?" My voice is high, coupled with a genuine smile.

"Surprise!" His smile reveals straight white teeth in a wide, adorable mouth that could make a cupcake bite-sized. It's not a flaw. He's attractive with his wavy blonde hair and small, stylish glasses. Well, they look small on him, but he's a big guy.

"I'm technically a sophomore, but this class was full all last year. I got some others out of the way in its place." It's a relief that he has so many words inside. Lisa is the same way, allowing me to my quiet ways. And… it gives me a reason to stare at him as he talks. It's hard not to feel an inner warmth in his presence. A lime-green shirt with tiny palm trees and light brown slacks gives him a look of going to a tropical island instead of it being the first rainy day of school.

"I hear Mr. Strickland is nice enough but assigns a ton of reading. You said you like to read." He awaits my response, but I'm too nervous to give much of an answer.

"Yup."

The teacher saunters in, appearing to not have a heightened nerve in his body. It saves me from thinking of more words to say to Jordan, even though the signal of the class starting sends a rush through my body.

"Hello, class. This is Beginning Psychology, so if that

doesn't sound familiar… you're late for your actual class."

Some of the students chuckle at this icebreaker. Humor is a good way to ease people into the first day of class. Even though I didn't laugh, it works for me.

"I'm going to pass out your syllabus. You'll see that there's a lot of reading in here. That book you bought isn't just for looks. You'll be getting through every page. Well, those of you who want A's will."

I glance at Jordan, who raises his broad shoulders as if to say, 'I told you so.'

Mr. Strickland walks along the rows of desks, handing out the papers. Everything about him seems ordinary but friendly at the same time. He's middle-aged, medium height, and has brown hair. See, nothing scary here.

"I'm going to give you five minutes to pair up with someone." And there he goes, ruining my good first impression of him! A glance at Jordan shows that's he's pointing at me. "Studies show that having a study buddy keeps you on track, helps you learn more, and prevents drop-outs. So, I'm all for it. Go ahead, start getting to know each other."

I don't want a study buddy!

"So, uh, what do you say?" Jordan says, scraping his desk across the floor towards me, not giving me a chance to answer.

"Hey, Jordan, want to be study buddies." I look beyond him to the next aisle and see a girl leaning across her desk towards him. Great, one of *these* girls.

A few things happen in this position for her: her curly brown hair fans over her shoulders, her boobs spill out of her barely-there top, and her hip pops out behind her. She's coming on strong, and honestly, if I was a teenage boy, I'd probably be all over her easy advances.

"I think I'm going to pair up with Leira. But thanks, Mia." Jordan looks back at me with large eyes and a slight shake of his head. I don't know him well enough, but it seems like I helped him dodge a bullet. "She always wants to be study buddies with me. Nooooo!" he whispers.

I laugh slightly in response, my hand covering my mouth. He turns his head to the side as if studying me. I look down at my desk with embarrassment flushing my cheeks. Wipe the smile from your face, Arie… Leira!

"So, study buddies?" he asks with a hopeful raise of his eyebrows.

This is a fear wrapped in a rainbow. The teacher comes around, and all I can do is nod in agreement. Something is satisfying about the way Jordan exhales.

He's just chosen me over the hot girl.

***

It's my first lecture, and it's a good one. We were assigned two chapters of reading even before the first day. I got through eight. I couldn't help it. I first studied the table of contents before diving into the text itself. One thing was for sure, my childhood is all over that book.

"So, algebra is next, huh?" It's Jordan, following after me when class is over.

"Do you memorize everyone's schedule?" I ask, turning away so he can't see my grin.

Jordan laughs and reaches to put his hand on my shoulder. It's new to have the people of this town adding a touch of kindness. At least, I think that's what he's doing. I pretend to drop my bag to shrug from his reach.

"This thing weighs a ton," I say as a coverup.

I allow myself to look over him again as he chatters about his work at the registrar's office. It's normal to look at the person who's talking, right? He's more than half a foot taller than me. He's both tall and broad without an ounce of fat. Kind of like me except for the advanced height. I'm guessing he's one of those guys who shot up as a freshman in high school and will take the next ten years to fill out.

His nerdy, friendly look *should* make him easy to talk to, except my awkwardness throws a wall between us. Thick, wild hair adds to his height and approachable nature.

"What's up, Bodie!" he chants, giving a fist bump to a guy in a sports jacket. I look at Jordan with large eyes. Oh no. Please tell me this guy isn't a jock! "Anyway, study buddy, want to meet to discuss the chapters assigned this week?"

He looks me in the face before his eyes flicker down my body once and then twice.

"I, um, already read the first few chapters."

"Oh, smart girl," he says teasingly. "We have a half hour before our next class. Want to grab a cup of coffee or a donut or something?"

I can't help but grin at his efforts to be my friend. He's not making a move, and he's not giving me a bunch of cheesy lines. He wants to study with me. Simple.

"Okay, I guess."

"Have you checked out the cafeteria yet? It was closed during our tour."

"Nope." But I have a feeling that's where we'll be *talking*.

"There are booths where we can sit. Well, of course, there are. It's not like they're going to expect us to stand and eat."

It's my turn to laugh this time, doing my best to stop myself by biting my lip. His dorkiness adds to his trueness.

The girls who check him out confirm that I'm not the only one who thinks he's cute. He doesn't notice them. He does, however, keep his eyes on me. He's coming on strong to be my friend, but it could be worse.

A few minutes later, we're sitting in a booth at the cafeteria, the aroma of food wafting through the air.

"So, did you leave your laptop at home today or something?" I stare at him blankly, not sure how to answer. "You do have a laptop, don't you? You won't want to spend all your free time in the computer lab."

"Of course, I have one. They didn't let us bring them to high school." I tuck my hair behind my ear, hating myself for bringing up where I'm from. I mean, I didn't really say anything specific, but I sure opened the gate.

"Oh? Where was that?"

See!

"Oh, you know…" No, he doesn't, and I'd like to keep it that way. I fiddle with the keys in my pocket. The jingle is a dead giveaway of my nerves. In all my fidgeting, I fumble my pack of cigarettes out.

"Oops, you dropped something." Jordan drops down to pick them up and hands them to me. I study his face for a judgmental expression but don't find one.

"Uh, thanks. It's a bad habit," I croak. I flinch back, my voice sounding like there was a piece of gravel stuck in my throat. Oh no! I will not sound like the dads with their rough voices. I've gotta kick this habit, and fast.

"Yeah." That's it? Just one syllable? Not even a scrunched-up face?

"I want to stop. I'm cutting down," I continue to explain.

"That's good." He keeps a smile pointed at me. It's irritating. Here I am, confessing to this nasty habit, and he doesn't even care. "What?" he barks. I shake my head and dart my eyes away, not knowing exactly what he means. "You seem to be bothered by something."

"It's nothing." Yes, it is! "It's just you didn't seem surprised by the cigarettes."

"Oh, that? I could smell smoke on you the other day, so I figured you either smoked or lived with someone who did."

"Oh." It's a disappointing discovery. This means that everyone can smell me! This might be the clencher I need to quit.

"Why so glum?" He asks, bending his face towards the table so he is in my view. "It's not like I won't like you because you do this." He brings his long fingers to his lips and puffs an imaginary cigarette. My face erupts in a smile before I can squish my lips together. "I'm glad I know. Maybe I can help."

And then, something happens: he reaches across the table and covers my hand with his monstrous one. I don't pull away. I don't even flinch. It's not an unpleasant touch.

"I don't have a printer." What? This is where my mind has gone?

Jordan laughs before scrunching his face as if this is horrible news. "You might want to get on that. Jeffrey's Electronics is pretty much the only place in town to go for printers… and laptops," he says, eyeing me suspiciously.

He seems genuine enough, but still, he's a teenage boy. Everyone knows they are after one thing. Right?

At the moment, it doesn't matter. Right now, Jordan's warm hand is covering mine. He's among the nicest people I've met besides Lisa's family, maybe minus her mom.

Jordan knows that I have the flaw and weakness of smoking… and he likes me anyway.

Chapter 16 Leira

Adulting, For Real

I can't believe it's one o'clock and my school day is already over. I only have classes on Mondays and Wednesdays, with labs on alternating Fridayss. The rest of my life will be rounded out by work and gobs of homework that has already been assigned. My algebra class was as expected, with a combination of numbers and letters that some poor soul spent his life coming up with. It's just as confusing now as it was in high school.

I have an hour until my shift starts, so I drive to the electronics store that Jordan suggested. He said it's the only one in town, so it's not like I couldn't have figured this out on my own.

I pull into a parking spot and send the shopping carts in front of me flying. Oops. I inspect the damage. With all the other bumps, scrapes, and dents on the pickup I named 'Grit,' it looks like this is the car for me.

I have no idea what I'm looking for regarding printers. That's what these nerds are here to do, though, help me figure it out. And I say 'nerd' in the nicest way. There are all kinds of groups out there; we all fit into at least one stereotypical category.

I tap the keys of various laptops, and sure enough, the little guy comes scurrying over to help.

"Hey, are you looking for a laptop?"

I nod with my reply. "I need one for school. And a printer."

"So, you probably need one for writing papers and printing research." Of course, he has it pegged. He's on the sale with what seems like a gallon of coffee in his system.

"Sounds about right."

He shows me a couple of options, and I land on one that does the basics. It's a pretty straightforward process that adds another point to my list of accomplishments.

I lug the boxes to the pickup, realizing they will sit in the parking lot while I'm working. I might as well put a sign on the pickup that says 'expensive electronics inside.' This would be a problem in the town I used to live in, but I doubt it will be here.

My shift is slow, which allows me to put my earbuds in. It's Lisa's day to upload her Mental Health Monday video, so I listen as I organize merchandise next to the register. Lisa always offers me a bit to think about. It's like she has a window into my past, giving me customized advice on how to deal with what I've been through. This time is no exception.

The video centers on a theme that followed me around today. Lisa says we all go through trauma in life, whether it be something big, such as abuse, or something smaller, such as being lied to. It stirs unwanted emotions from my past that was only a couple of weeks ago.

"Turn the trauma into no-drama," she says. "Only you can break the cycle."

Some might consider this an oversimplification of what they've been through, but I get it. Yes, I've had to deal with crappy stuff, but it's not like the dads beat me or screamed at me. Neglect is real, but I'm not the type of person who needs a ton of attention anyway. It's a much-needed spin to get my situation twirling. I've gone through the disappointment of my parents not being there for me. But I did grow up, and now I'm making my own choices instead of wallowing in my past.

I finish my shift and excitedly steer the truck toward where I now call home. Eagerness courses through me. I'm looking forward to the adult projects of setting up my laptop and printer and diving into homework on the cozy couch. I took computer classes in high school and feel good about my abilities. Plus, I have that 'nothing will stop me now feeling.' I'm starting to feel like nothing will. Instead of floating through life like a puff of smoke, I'm living it.

The song 'Fighter' comes on by Christina Aguilera. I turn the knob, sending a warbled version through the old speakers in the pickup. I sing along without holding back, visualizing myself stepping into my own. These songs have good timing today.

My phone beeps with a sound I still need to get used to. It's a text message from Jordan! I practically swerve off the road to read it. I put the phone down and wait until I get into the driveway. I snuff out my last allotted cigarette of the day and read my text.

How's it going? Were you able to find a printer? Jordan

I smile as I type a text in return once I turn the pickup off. *I'm going to set it up right now.*

Great! Let me know if you have any questions. Jordan

I've never been around somebody my age with as much energy as he has. It's not fake, either. Of course, he hasn't had my type of upbringing. All this talk about mental health is getting me to address my own so I can move on in life. I'm not surprised, nor am I afraid. I flash on a sentence in my psychology book and how it said it all starts with how we are treated as children. "Duh. How else is life supposed to start?"

"What's that?" It's Lisa's voice, but it comes out of the darkness and startles me. "I'm sorry, Leira. I turned the light on out here and was dragging my feet, trying to get you to hear me. Chuggers wanted to come say hello."

I'm not a dog person, but seeing the wiggly dog with a sock in his mouth wins me over. "It's okay." It's nice to be welcomed home.

"What have you got there?"

"I bought a laptop and printer!"

"Nice! Do you want help setting it up?" she asks, full of hope. My instinct is to turn her down, but I remember how excited she was to paint with me and introduce me to her husband. I think Lisa wants a friend as badly as I do.

I nod in agreement. "Sure." I swing my bag onto my shoulder and walk to the backyard with her. "I've never set up a laptop before."

"I'm no techie, but I'm sure the two of us can figure it out. How was your first day of school?"

"Pretty good. I already have a ton of homework."

"Ah yes, the promise from every teacher to make you grind away for two hours at home for every hour in class." I stop and stare at her as she literally repeated what I heard three times today. Lisa laughs in response. "Looks like they haven't changed, huh?"

The can of cat food I left out is completely gone. But, sadly, "No cat in sight," I say quietly.

"I've pet her a few times and set food out every now and then. They always seem to come back to their source of food."

"I hope so." I want to eat my words with this answer, thinking back to the dads. Just like in all the mystery books I've read, I know the bad guys always find the one who has run away.

A car I don't recognize pulls into Lisa's driveway. Headlights shine over her property and my door, causing shadows to dance around us. I fumble with my keys, wanting to get inside before being seen. I'm convinced this is them, that all this goodness I've created will be snatched away. They've found me and will pose a threat to anyone who stands in their way. Which, right now, is Lisa! I finally unlock the door and push my way inside.

"What's wrong, Leira?" Lisa asks, following me inside with a worried expression.

I rush to the window to pull the blinds, seeing that the car is simply turning around. I breathe a sigh of relief, except now I need to feed a lie to Lisa.

I turn to her quiet stare, wondering if she's figured me out yet. I stay mute, unable to form anything logical. She opens her mouth but doesn't say anything. Then, she does something unexpected: she takes the boxes from me as if nothing happened.

"Is the couch okay?" she asks, heading that way.

"Uh, sure," I answer in surprise.

She sets the box on the coffee table, and I join her. Together, we pull my new items free from the packaging.

"This is the best part: pulling all these little stickies off the screens. Go ahead, this one's for you."

I reach over and pull the screen protector off the face of the printer. "Ooh, that is kind of fun." Lisa laughs. I'm glad she's here. Her demeanor and cheerfulness lighten my previous scare.

"I've thought about asking Patrick for a new laptop, but I'll struggle through using my dinosaur until it dies. Maybe I'll start making tons of money and will be able to buy my own," she says sarcastically.

"You never know," I say with a shrug. "You said you've been getting a lot of sales and subs."

"The numbers are going up every day," she says, switching to a confident tone. "Hey, let me know if you need extra pots or anything for your kitchen."

"I'm not much of a cook, but I noticed this place is pretty stocked," I say casually.

"Yeah, Nana only bought top-quality kitchenware. She claimed it enhanced the quality of the meal," she says with a shrug.

"Anything will help me. I almost have no clue what I'm doing in the kitchen beyond one or two meals."

"Oh? I'd be happy to help sometime."

"Thanks, Lisa," I say earnestly.

"So, my birthday is coming up. I'm throwing myself a party this weekend. I'd love it if you could come." Lisa looks at me with those hopeful eyes once again.

I've had a lot of social interactions lately, but what the hell? It's only Monday. I'm sure my social battery will be recharged by then. "Only if there's a white cake," I joke.

"It's the only kind in my book. None of that fake-tasting chocolate," Lisa responds without skipping a beat. We laugh together, thoroughly easing the car in the driveway debacle that scared me. Lisa has proven that she's one hundred percent on my side.

Chapter 17 Lisa

Guided by Youth

"This stupid thing!" I complain, tossing my phone on the bed. Here Leira is, going to school, getting a job, finding her purpose, and I'm futzing around with this stupid old phone. But that's not what is really wrong. I'm almost thirty-five; you'd think I wouldn't feel this lost in life.

I lay in bed after picking Adrienne up from school, cursing my phone and its small storage space. My phone is full, the edited video won't upload, and I completely messed up on my Halloween project and need to rip part of it out.

These are surface problems, like little gnats that get stuck in wet nail polish. They are insignificant to the bigger picture and shouldn't take my energy. "Time to practice what I preach," I say between gritted teeth. I begrudgingly take deep breaths to switch my mindset. I know every experience is here for a reason. It's the tough times that motivate us to push further. Deep down I know nothing is really wrong, but darn it, sometimes I just want to be mad!

The breathing exercise takes a few minutes, but it works to calm down. I change my focus to my party. I'm excited, but it's a bit of a letdown to be throwing a party for myself. Patrick is clueless in this area. Still, I can't wait to spend time with my friends on my birthday. I need more social interaction now that I'm not working. What better than a party to fill this hole? As I stated in my email invite, I'm not expecting presents. I just want a casual dinner of my favorite appetizers and a big ass white cake that I can eat as much as I want.

I put my sneakers on and get Chuggers for a few laps around the backyard to stomp away my cranky mood. I don't want to be negative. It's time to change this around and breathe my gratefulness into existence.

"Adrienne, honey, do you want to walk with me?"

"Yeah, I'll come out in a minute," she answers.

Walking has been my go-to lately for snapping me out of funky times. After my second lap, I feel better. Adrienne's playful screams ring out as she plays tag with Leira. We make eye contact, and she trots over to me.

"Hello," she says in a breathy greeting. I can't pretend I'm happy that Adrienne is looking up to Leira with an aroma of smoke around her. I hate to judge these things, but she has so much potential, and I hope she won't go down the drug path.

"You two look like you're having fun."

"I haven't played much of these games. It's so fun!" Leira says between breaths. It's an odd statement. Don't most kids, well, play with other kids growing up?

"Hey, you still need to join us for dinner. It kind of feels funny not to have a 'welcome to our back garage meal.'" Her smile stays instead of wavering into uncertainty as it usually does.

"I'm free tonight," she says in her shy voice.

"Great! It's casserole night if that sounds good. Most nights are casserole nights if I'm honest." I get a shrug in return. It's been these hot and cold moments with her, but I feel like she's coming around. For all I know, she hasn't had many adult encounters. "Dinner will be ready in about an hour, so see you soon!" I go in through the sliding door and am overly excited to have a guest. Slowly but surely, Leira is warming up to us.

With renewed pep, I throw the casserole in the oven, whip up four salads, and make parmesan bread. I set the table for four, using our fun place settings with scenes of Italy on them. It's a massive shift from a few moments ago when the threat of depression was knocking at my door.

"Hey, babe," Patrick says, popping through the front door.

"Look who just shows up for dinner!" I tease.

"Wow, you're using the fancy stuff tonight," he says, pulling me in for a side hug.

"I figured, why not? Leira is joining us tonight. I hope that's okay."

"Of course. I get the feeling she needs a second family. You know?" Patrick intuitively states.

"I've thought the same thing. You go get in the shower. I'll finish up here," I say, smacking him on the bottom with a napkin.

"Care to join me?" he says, nuzzling my neck.

"Raincheck," I say, smacking his bottom as he trots away.

I feel as light as air as I get dinner ready. It seems silly, but I visualize a past ream while preparing this meal. I've always wanted a family of four. The way my female parts are, I was lucky to have Adrienne. Boy, was Patrick proud of himself when I got pregnant with her. I smile, remembering all the funny sperm jokes he made during that time.

Time flies with me putting the final touches on our dinner when I hear a soft knock on the back door. I wave

Leira in so she can get used to coming in as she pleases. I smell a hint of smoke again mixed with a coconut scent. This is her decision, but I hope she'll consider quitting once things settle down for her.

"I hope you've come with an appetite!" I welcome.

"Hi, Leira!" Adrienne says, sliding her foot along the floor. "I can tendu now."

"Nice. A fancy Munchkin," Leira compliments. Her face becomes fearful as she looks over the table, which is nicely set with multiple forks and glass goblets.

"I had time to add a few touches, but it's just an easy family dinner. Patrick is taking a shower but he'll be out soon. Go ahead and take a seat." I take drink orders, and Adrienne helps me by filling our water glasses. I'm buzzing with excitement but trying to play it cool. I sneak a glance at Leira, watching her reaction as my dinner makes its grand entrance. "It's zucchini and meat casserole. The secret ingredient is cheese."

"Amen to that," Patrick says, joining us with slicked back hair, the fresh smell of soap floating around him. He plops in his seat and starts the meal by dishing himself a large heaping of food.

"Would you like me to get you some?" I ask Leira. Her eyes shift from the casserole to the bread to the salad as if she's in a foreign country.

She nods and holds her plate up. I add a piece of bread and let her know she can choose from the three salad dressings on the table. She leans towards me and whispers a request. "Um, do you have ketchup?" Patrick and Adrienne look at me with shock.

"On casserole?" Adrienne asks with a giggle.

"Hey, you like what you like, Leira," Patrick says,

popping up to get the bottle. "Growing up, I loved dipping my sandwiches in ketchup. Everyone made fun of me so I'd get a big blog on there and take a huge bite right in front of them."

"Even for peanut butter and jelly?" Adrienne challenges.

"Sometimes," Patrick teases.

With the surrounding laughter, Leira seems more settled. After five minutes, I noticeably see her shoulders lower as we dig in and share stories about our day.

"This is really good," she says, looking down at the food as if it were the best dish she's ever eaten. It's a simple recipe I make a couple of times a month.

"Thanks!" I beam.

"So, Leira, how's the truck treating you?" Patrick asks.

"It drives," she nods. The rest of us laugh lightly in response. She looks between us and smiles in surprise.

"I guess that's what's important," Patrick answers. "Lisa says you're taking classes at the college. What are you taking?"

She looks between us before answering, "Algebra, psychology, and a culinary class. It looks like Lisa can help me with that one." We all get quite the kick out of this comment, as I've said dozens of times over the years I never consider myself a good cook.

Patrick laughs with exaggeration. "Lisa, teaching you how to cook? Now that's funny."

"Hey," I say, tossing my napkin at him. "You're eating hot food that you didn't have to make, aren't you?" I blow this comment off. I'm used to Patrick thinking he's funny when he really isn't.

"We should have a cooking day!" Adrienne exclaims.

"That would be fun. Maybe you can help me get ready for my party, Leira," I offer as an idea.

"When is that again?" Patrick asks.

"Saturday," I reply flatly. He gives me a wink. "I need another napkin!" Adrienne hands me hers, and I again throw it in Patrick's direction. "I hope you can still make it," I say to Leira. "No pressure, though!"

"I'm looking forward to it," Leira answers quickly with a nod.

"It might get rowdy," I forewarn.

"As long as you stay away from the fire, we'll be okay," Patrick says teasingly, poking me in the side.

"I told you that we're not to bring that up!" I exclaim.

It sounds odd, but I'm excited that Leira will be joining my party. Some fun might just be what she needs.

Chapter 18 Leira

Moments That Matter

The days have been adding more darkness than light. The result is me double and triple-checking my locks. My wooden wedge shoved under the door makes me feel better about being here alone. It'd be nice to have a fish, frog, or something else living with me, to keep me company. After all, I've been spending a lot of time in 'The Hideout' studying and trying out recipes.

I'm down to four cigarettes a day. It's a habit I want to kick, but one that's getting harder. I always smoke outside, which lends to the possibility of getting caught. Continuing this nasty habit has been a commitment in the cold weather system we're under.

I have the afternoon free from work and classes, the perfect time to get caught up on homework. I spent an hour cooking my lunch and reading and re-reading a simple chicken breast recipe. My culinary assignment is far from scratching a box of Hamburger Helper open and stirring the ingredients together. I'm to document my cooking experience, how it tasted, and whether adding ingredients helps or tastes awful.

"Not too awful," I say, an inch away from plugging my nose to get my chicken down.

It was easy to defrost and put the chicken in a pan with salt and pepper. The recommended five minutes a side seemed too short, but my twenty minutes of cooking led to a dry piece of meat. Still, it was good in a wrap with tomatoes, cheese, and ketchup. I smile when I think about the other night when Lisa's family poked fun at my ketchup usage. This habit is one that I won't let anyone make me feel ashamed of.

I crouch down to squash my cigarette butt in the dirt, keeping hold of the "evidence" for proper disposal. Just as I straighten up, a giant raindrop smacks me in the face—no polite warning sprinkles, just a sky full of water dumping without notice. What's peaceful from the comfort of indoors feels far less romantic when stuck in it. I make a break for the door, but my ears catch a soft sound. A meow? Probably just my wishful thinking… until I hear it again, closer this time: a tiny, unmistakable meow.

I'm in excited shock to see the grey and black striped kitty prancing over to me from across the lawn. "There you are," I say quietly, bending down to welcome the cat into my awaiting hands. She doesn't hesitate to find shelter under my body from the rain. She closes her eyes as I run my hands through her matted, wet hair. "Are you a stray, sweetie?"

"Meow."

"Aww, that's cute. Want to come inside with me to get out of this rain?" My voice has raised from its normal low tones to one that sounds like Lisa's around Chuggers.

I scoop the cat up, pulling her close without a second thought. Her tiny bones press against my hands, a clear sign she needs me. I don't need a superpower when this basic human need to take care of something else kicks in. Oh, how I could've used someone to take me in like this. On second thought, Lisa has done that. The thought doesn't just make me smile—it gives me a spark of something warmer, almost like love.

Once inside, we go straight to the bathroom to dab her wet fur. "It's okay; I don't mind cleaning you. Poor thing." I keep the faucet dripping for my damp rag. She wiggles out of my hold to walk onto the counter and bends into the sink to get a drink.

I laugh in response. "Thirsty, huh?" I pull the stopper and allow her to drink as much water as she needs as I continue to dab at her fur. "You'll be okay. I'm sure Lisa will let me keep you." The cat doesn't mind me cleaning her. She gets wet while playing in the sink, but at least now she's mostly dirt-free.

"Playful little thing. Let's dry you off," I say, wrapping her in a towel and taking her to the kitchen. After a quick dry and me cranking up the heater to ensure she's warm, I set out wet and dry food. I bought plenty, hoping for this very outcome. I'm overcome with satisfaction watching the cat eat. I've always wanted a pet but didn't want to keep it trapped in my room 'back then.'

My phone dings with a text from Lisa. *I have a job interview at four today! The problem is, I need a babysitter for Adrienne. Are you free to watch her for an hour or two?*

Adrienne might want to spend time getting to know the cat with me!

Sure, I reply. Lisa asked that I be there in twenty minutes, so I sit on the couch and read a chapter in my psychology book. The cat walks to me with near-silent footsteps, flinching with every movement I make.

She reminds me of myself when I first fled, unsure of everything and how I'd fit into my new life. "It's okay, I'll take care of you." She lowers her warm body to lie next to me, settling in like we've been friends forever. Her purr vibrates the side of my leg, offering a serene, relaxing combination. Add the rain tapping on the roof and windows, and I'm at peace for the first time in, well, ever.

The cat lets me pet her now slightly damp fur as she closes her eyes in post-meal bliss. "I have to go get Adrienne, but I'll be back soon. Okay?"

She stays on the couch as I leave, already comfortable in my place. I lock the door before darting across the yard in the rain to Lisa's house. An uneasiness swarms through my stomach. I've never been entrusted with someone's child before. It's another first that propels me into adulthood.

Lisa waves me in again once I get to the back door. It's odd to walk into their house, but here I go. Lisa talks so fast she would give an auctioneer a run for his money.

"Leira, hi! Thank you for watching Adrienne. I'll only be gone an hour or two. I have an interview at the college for a counselor position. I'm not completely interested since it's full-time and year-round, but it's worth a shot. You guys can stay inside and play or go back to your place." She throws a beige jacket on, threads an orange and brown scarf around her neck, and shoves her feet into shoes.

"Sounds good," I say simply. I plan to take Adrienne to see my new cat but don't tell Lisa. She gives Adrienne a hug and leaves in a rush.

"Want to play in my room?" Adrienne asks. She hasn't let go of my hand since I came in. She's been an incredible comfort in my new world.

"We could do that, or I could show you something in 'The Hideout.' Can you keep a secret?" Adrienne's eyes light up as she nods.

"I'm going to bring Velvet!" she yells, running to her

room to grab her llama.

We dash across the yard through the rain, arms flung wide, feeling as free as only little girls can. I open the door slowly and point to the kitty lying on the couch. It makes me happy that she's in the same spot. "There she is."

Adrienne gasps and slowly goes to the cat. "It's Violet. How did you catch her?"

"Violet? Do you know her?" I ask with a sinking feeling. If she has a name, she has an owner.

"No, that's just what I've been calling her. She's been around the yard. Mommy hasn't been able to catch her."

The cat jumps off the couch to greet us, rubbing her face on our legs. "I love it when they do that." The cat has adopted me quickly enough, and I am already feeling a connection with her. "Do you think your mom will let me keep her?"

"Sure. Mommy loves animals. You rescued her from the rain," Adrienne says, petting the cat who is comfortable on the couch. "Look, she's making bread." I giggle with Adrienne as we watch Violet kneading a couch pillow. "Wanna watch me twirl, Violet?"

Adrienne shows us her new ballet moves as the rain pounds on the roof. A flash of lightning stains our eyes as if it's in the room with us. I scoop the cat up and hold Adrienne to my stomach, anticipating the thunder that will surely follow. Ten seconds later, a clap rumbles overhead. Violet's claws sink into my shoulder, but Adrienne is hardly phased.

"It's just thunder," Adrienne says easily, breaking free and playing with her llama around the place. Despite her easygoing nature, I throw my wedge under the door.

"I don't like thunderstorms." I never have. We'd get violent storms 'back then.' I'm sure they weren't sudden, but I wasn't privy to weather warnings when I was a kid. The dads never offered anything of comfort, leaving me shivering from fright in my dark room. The storms were so close that we'd almost always lose power.

Violet and Adrienne snuggle with me on the couch when there's another lightning strike. Now, only six seconds are between it and the thunder. Great, it's getting closer. "Do you think she knows when her birthday is?"

I laugh in response to the adorable thought process. It makes me feel good that Adrienne is allowed to embody her innocence. "I don't think they know that sort of thing."

"Are those your smoke sticks on the counter?" Adrienne asks. Darn it, I meant to put those away. I hate the idea of adding this lie to the small pile I'm creating.

"Yeah, it's a shitty, uh," I say quickly as her eyes grow large. "Sorry," I say, looking down in shame. If this little girl wants to look up to me, the least I can do is not stoop to the dad's level. "It's a bad habit. *Never* start. I've almost quit." There, my secret is out. Adrienne shrugs and says, 'Okay,' and that's it. It might be weird to some that an eighteen-year-old is genuinely friends with a girl ten years younger. She's easy to talk to, and she doesn't judge me.

The next round of thunder shakes the building and brings a more brutal rain pounding. The lights flicker a few times before going off for good. "At least she's inside now," Adrienne says of Violet.

"Yup," I quickly answer. "Hey, what are you going to be for Halloween?" I ask as a distraction. I'm supposed to be in charge here, and I'm scared out of my mind with this storm. And now the lights are out. Just like they were 'back then.'

"A princess. I want a big, poofy dress. Mommy and I are going to make one."

"Aww, that's sweet." Her wholesomeness reminds me of

Jordan. Being around her genuine nature seems to fill in the gaps of the unhappiness I felt at her age. It's like she smooths out those rough edges that were formed by my neglect.

"The rain is slowing down," she says with a pat on my hand. She must sense how much I hate the storm.

"Good," I say with a deep breath. Thunder rumbles in the distance now. "Maybe we'll get our power back soon."

"Mommy calls them flash-storms," she says, getting off the couch and playing with Violet. "Hey, who's that outside?"

My stomach gives its own flash of electricity. I jump off the couch, expecting to see the dads in the driveway where Adrienne is looking. I move her gently aside, ready to protect her if need be. A woman is out there, looking around Lisa's yard. I have an idea why she's here and want to stop her snooping before she's entirely in the yard.

"Stay here," I instruct, opening the door and stepping out on the porch. Raindrops drip from the overhang, but I don't care if I get wet for this task. "Can I help you?" I've switched to a higher voice, offering friendliness to the stranger, hoping it will help to make her go away.

"I'm looking for my cat." She has a strained voice that matches her brown, dingy clothes. She's been in the rain, but it doesn't look like she started off in a much better position.

"I haven't seen it," I reply as bluntly as her remark.

"You don't even know what it looks like."

"I haven't seen any cats." I hope that Violet won't choose to do some windowsill watching now. I turn to go inside, and the woman yells out again.

"You better not have my cat!"

I shut her out with the door and fully lock us in. That didn't go well.

"Is Violet her cat?" Adrienne asks.

"Maybe," I answer as I pull the drapes. I peer outside and hope the woman doesn't see me shut us further inside. "If it is, she hasn't been taking care of her. I mean, look how skinny she is. I cleaned her up. She looked horrible."

I'm disappointed in how I've handled things with Adrienne today—I wasn't the role model she deserves. It's just one more thing I'll keep working on because this little girl, *and* my new life, are worth it.

Chapter 19 Lisa

Girls' Night In

I only focus on the sound of my shoes crunching on the rocks beneath them. Echoes of criticism have plagued me all morning, and I'm tired of it. It's my birthday, for crying out loud! Why is my negativity choosing today of all days to pelt me?

'Why would anyone want to come to my party?' 'My house isn't good enough to throw a party in.' 'What will I do with my *two guests*, play a stupid game?'

"Maybe I will play a game!" I scold back to the words that always have my mother's voice.

"What?"

I turn and find Leira behind me. Her shoes crunched, too, but I was too engrossed with my lies to hear my surroundings.

"Leira, sorry, hon. I must look like a crazy person."

"You seemed upset. I thought, well, maybe you'd like to have company or something." She shifts her weight and bites her lip.

"I'd love to have company!"

We walk side by side in silence, unsure of the first subject to pursue.

"Happy birthday!" she smiles.

"Thank ya!"

"What were you talking about with a game?" Leira eyes me from the side with curiosity.

"Oh," I say, throwing my hand out to dismiss my stupid comment. "I might play some games for my party, but I haven't figured that out yet."

"Games sound good," she says blandly. This is her way of speaking, with a clipped, monotone voice. She could be excited about something beyond belief and still flatly say: 'Yay.' "I haven't been to many parties."

"You might be the only one there." I give the ground a kick of anger.

"So?" she says with that shrug of hers. "Patrick and Adrienne will be there too, right?"

It's a new perspective and one I'm in favor of. "Yes, and that would be fun. Just the four of us," I say brightly.

She glances at me a couple of times before taking a deep breath. "How did your interview go? Sorry, I didn't ask. I had to go to work when you got home."

It's not the question I expected, but I go with it anyway. "Eh, not great. They won't budge on the full-time status, and I don't want to work that much. Working even part-time will be difficult now that I've gotten in the routine of being home." Of course, Patrick would flip out if I admitted this to him.

"That's too bad," Leira says quietly.

"Not really," I whisper behind my hand. "I'm actually bringing in some money with my Etsy sales. I have such a backlist of crocheted items that it's not like I have to spend all my time fulfilling orders. If it keeps with this upward trend, I might be able to stay home for good!"

"That's nice." Her voice returns to a low tone, and I know why.

"Was there something else you wanted to talk about?"

She looks at me with surprise. I return a sweet smile, hopefully conveying that it's safe for her to open up to me. "It's just that I asked Adrienne to keep something from you."

"The cat?" I respond. Leira's shocked expression makes me laugh. "Yes, she told me about all of that. I'm not going to pretend I'm in favor of lying… or smoking." I raise my eyebrows like a mom who isn't pleased by something a child has done.

"I'm sorry." She lowers her head in disappointment.

"No need to be sorry! We all have our faults. I was beating myself up on this walk before you joined me." I share this with her, hoping she doesn't have her own self-deprecating negative self-talk. "I try not to allow that chatty devil to take over."

"You?" she asks in surprise. "You always seem so happy."

I nod and hang my head. "I'm ashamed of how mean I can be to myself sometimes. Do you get like that?"

"Not really."

"That's good!"

She looks in the distance as if in thought. "I'm too focused on my own thing, I guess."

"That's okay too."

"It's a safety mechanism." I allow her the time, wanting to hear her follow-up. "People won't be able to track me if I keep to myself." Her eyes grow big, and she rushes her following sentence out. "I mean, there's less explaining to do about what I've been up to."

"Ah," I say with a slow, speculative nod. "I hope you

know that you can count on me. Trust is a strong word; I understand it correlates with the time spent with someone. But you can trust me, Leira."

We share a smile and walk a few paces before I speak again. If we're going to trust each other, there's no better way than to open up about some of my burdens.

"It's hard to not think negatively when my family sends me texts about what I should be doing with my life. I'm thirty-five today! They make me feel like I can't do anything on my own." I hate how whiny I sound, but this is how I am with this subject.

"I guess you need to do what I do and focus on your life. It's not like they follow you all day, right? How do they really know what you're doing?"

I raise my eyebrows, wanting to change my rotten inner voice to the irritated teenage tone she uses. "I've never thought of it that way. That's good... really good! That psychology class sure is sinking in."

"It all started from a certain YouTube channel," she grins.

I puff out a laugh. "It's easier to admit this to you than to my camera."

"People who aren't watching are missing out. It helped me."

It's a sentiment that means more than dozens of comments on my videos. *This* is why I produce and upload content, to actually help people. "Thank you, Leira. That means a lot to me and is exactly why I pour my heart into my videos."

"That's why I mentioned the life coach thing."

"I spent a minute searching for one in our area and came up with one guy who does it. It seemed like a dead end if you ask me."

"From what I've seen on all those YouTube ads," she says, rolling her eyes, "is that it's all done on video chats, so it doesn't matter where the person is," she says, matter-of-factly. "I remember hearing someone in the office at school talking about it once. Maybe the guy in town has some tips."

"I didn't realize that. I should have you around more often to knock some sense into me." I knock on my head with my knuckle, and she covers her mouth with a grin. We round the final stretch of the circle, which heads back to the house. "Well, I'm on my way in to go through my menu for the party," I say as we approach the house.

"I'm all done with my homework," she says expectantly. She wants to spend time with me!

"Come on in!" I say, holding the sliding glass door open. "I don't mind if you keep the cat, by the way," I say as she passes me.

Her face lights up like Adrienne's when I've surprised her with something. "Really?"

"Sure, we love animals. And Chuggers is scared of cats, so don't worry about him hurting her."

"Thank you! I didn't grow up with anything," she says quietly. "I mean, any pets," she says quickly. I catch her second not-so-subtle hint, hoping it's the gateway to a deeper conversation. But for now, she leaves me hanging.

"I'm sorry about that, Leira." I can't do much to help her past, but I want to help her walk along this newly paved path. I reach my arms up and take a step toward her. To my surprise, she doesn't back away. She takes two steps toward me and forces me backward with her hug. "You're here now, and you're doing great," I say as I pat her back.

She pulls away a moment later with tears under her eyes.

"Thanks," she says, swiping them away.

"My Nana used to say that we shouldn't just eat our troubles away; we should bake them into our recipes and then throw them in the oven to burn away. I have the perfect recipe for this that we can serve tonight!" Leira smiles and nods in agreement.

This is a big step for us, and I allow it to sink in for a minute.

"It's going to be a snacky meal tonight. I thought that would allow my *dozens* of guests to mingle and eat the night away." Leira smiles at my sarcasm. "I have different types of cheeses, crackers, meats, and fruit. I have a huge white cake, but I thought I could make my famous fudgy oatmeal bars for the chocoholics. That's where we can burn our worries," I whisper.

"I don't know much of anything past Hamburger Helper."

"I used to eat that in college. My mother would have been so ashamed." I say with my head down and a shake.

"Why's that?" Leira asks.

I hesitate, as I always do regarding my family's wealth. "My family had a huge list of snooty expectations. Spoiler alert, I didn't meet any of them." Leira laughs lightly. "Is that how it was for you?"

She flinches and pauses before answering. "Yeah, I had rules for sure. Mainly that I had to be home after school. I couldn't go anywhere after that. It's why I had zero job experience."

I stay quiet, remembering that she said a job was where all her cash came from. "Yikes. That can kind of become stifling after a certain age, huh?"

"You could say that."

I flip on the oven, give Leira the recipe, and gather the ingredients. "The trick to this recipe is to undercook the crap out of it! I don't know about you, but everyone I've talked to loves gooey cookies!" I look at her for a response, but she shrugs.

Her story is filling in slowly. My intuition tells me a lot is hiding behind her hard exterior. I have a thousand-piece puzzle with her and can only click a few pieces together each day.

I flip on music for us to jive to. "Is this your taste?"

"Sure. I'm not picky." After a few lyrics, Leira does something unexpected: she starts humming!

Adrienne dances in from her room, makes a few turns, and returns to her room. Her comedy act hits the mark, and we laugh in response.

"She's pretty good at that ballet stuff," Leira compliments.

"She's picking up on it better than I did as a kid. My mom sat at all my lessons, grimacing like this." I bring my hand up to my forehead, halfway covering my eyes. "There's always a holiday ballet recital if you want to join us this year."

"Sure," she says simply with a nod.

My phone jingles with a text that I take the time to check. "Hey, my friend Elena can make it tonight! Wait a minute," I scroll around and sigh dramatically while letting my arms drop, "a couple of other friends RSVP'd also. This stupid phone doesn't always alert me with messages."

"See?" Leira says snidely.

I always get sucked into my phone once I have it in my hand. "Oh my gosh, Leira! I'm up to five hundred and thirty-five subscribers!! How in the world… it's my Halloween video!"

"It's had quite a few views," she comments.

"And my Etsy shop has a few more sales! Oh…" I hold my phone next to my chest and look up with gratitude. Leira smiles again and looks at the recipe.

"Nana's fudgy oatmeal bars."

"Yeah, my Nana loved those bars. I don't need the recipe anymore; I know it by heart. This party won't be the same without her." I try not to sink to the ground when talking about Nana. It's not my intent to bring others down, but the grief is still raw. "The holidays aren't the same either. I pretty much canceled Christmas that first year she was gone. Talk about a bad mom."

Leira lets out a barking laugh. "Yeah, right, like you could even try and be a bad mom." Yikes. I flinch back from the sadness of this sore spot I hit with her. "Mine left when I was five."

I do my best to not respond in shock. "Oh, Leira, I'm sorry. That must have been so hard."

"It was. But… I'm an adult now." She doesn't mock me with my own words. Instead, she stands taller and says this with confidence.

"And one who is killing it!" We mess around in the kitchen for a minute before I speak again. "I was quite a downer that first year after Nana passed. Last year was better, but it's just not the same. Without her, I don't know how to have a normal holiday season."

We crack the eggs in silence. "Isn't that how things get passed on to younger generations?"

"What do you mean? Nana was the queen of Christmas."

"Exactly. Once the queen passes, sorry, her successors are supposed to take over, right? You spend time passing it on to Adrienne before you die, and so on. It sounds a bit dark, but…"

"No." I shake my head. Leira looks at me with worry as if she's misspoken. "You're right. That's not dark… it's life. Wise beyond her years." I shake my head, giving her a look of admiration. Leira copies me with her face beaming from the compliment. "The queen passes it down. Brilliant!"

"I think I've read every book about princesses and queens. And it's what you say to turn trauma into no-drama, right?"

I answer with a slow nod, mulling my own words over and applying them to this situation. "It's true, thank you," I say after a moment. "Okay, these delicious bars aren't going to make themselves!"

"Fudgy oatmeal bars!" Adrienne screams in her room before twirling out to join us.

It turns out that Leira barely knows a thing about cooking. She soaks up everything I teach her. I tell her about spraying the pan so the bars won't stick. I show her how to warm the butter and take it out of the microwave just before it starts melting. She didn't even know that you start mixing the wet ingredients before adding the dry ones. It's all new and fun for her, and she smiles more than I've seen.

Adrienne stands on her stool, smelling the sugared butter. She holds her hand out as I open the silverware drawer for a spoon. I give myself praise for having this connection with her. It appears that my throne will be passed on perfectly.

I get a call right after I take the gooey, fudgy oatmeal bars out of the oven. "Hey, Bailey."

"Lisa, I'm sorry for the late notice, but I can't come to your party tonight. Monica and I have a wedding this weekend, and we need to work late into the night at my house with all the decorations."

"Oh, it's fine. I'm glad you called. I am in desperate need of a haircut. Can I schedule something now?"

I finish the call and pretend to shoo Leira and Adrienne away from the finished bars. "You two get away from there… on second thought, it is my birthday." I grab three big spoons and hand them over to my buddies. "Cheers!"

"Happy birthday!" Leira's face brightens. This is a present in itself. I feel privileged to be a part of her life, helping her come out of her shell and find her own in this world.

"Happy birthday, mommy!" The three of us clink spoons and indulge ourselves in the chocolaty goodness.

"Was that Bailey from Clippers Salon on the phone?"

"You know Bailey?" I ask.

Leira nods as she takes a bite. "She cut my hair the first day I was here. It used to be as long as yours, but I couldn't take it anymore."

"She's amazing. She has to be to tame this mop of hair." I pick up my hair and allow it to fall over my shoulders.

"I kept wondering how such a young person got to be so successful."

Leira smacks her food as she talks. Adrienne and I glance at each other, and I know she's keeping the same giggle as I am.

"Hey, Leira, want some ketchup for that?" Adrienne teases.

Leira's face changes to one of humored shock. "Little stinker," she says, tickling Adrienne on her neck.

"Bailey actually stayed here when she went to cosmetology school."

"Really?" Leira asks with surprise.

"Yup. She's Patrick's sister." Leira lets her arms fall as

she looks at me in surprise. Adrienne and I laugh in response.

I go through my party list of things to do with a twinge of dread. Why do I always set myself up with stresses like these? "I still have so much to do. I don't even know what I'm wearing or how I'm doing my hair yet."

"Do you ever straighten it?" Leira asks through the dessert in her mouth.

"Not really. It takes forever to get through these thick curls."

"What if you had two people working on it?" Leira gives Adrienne a sneaky glance, igniting my little girl's enthusiasm.

"Let's give Mommy a birthday makeover!"

The two of them being excited about pampering me does my soul good. Adrienne and Leira brush my hair and work the straightener, and they get through my hair in an hour. It's the best present ever to have this time together.

***

Wouldn't you know that eight of my closest friends *and* their families show up at my party? More than twenty people have come, and the party is just starting.

I wasn't sure about decorating outside, but I'm glad Adrienne convinced me to string lights up. It's a bit chilly, but the fire pit and alcohol warm us right up. It's nothing fancy, with music in the background and serving with plastic cups and paper plates. No one cares! With twenty of us sitting and standing around, there's quite a bit of laughter and chatter.

Leira shrugs against the house, mainly talking to and playing with Adrienne. I'm glad she's here, but I'm worried her shyness won't allow her to have a good time. She noticeably perks up when my friend Beatrice shows up with her son, Jordan. Soon, the two of them hang out, laughing as Adrienne dances to the songs in her goofy way.

I've never seen Leira as smiley as she is with Jordan. It punches at a nerve to talk to her about the facts of life and boys in general. She's eighteen, so I know she knows this, but she doesn't know how I made a big mistake at this young age. It sounds like she's doing her own thing for the first time, and sometimes, new love will get in the way.

It's a regular party with food and booze. After one drink, I allow myself another and then another. A glance at Adrienne shows she's playing tag with Joanie's boys, Leira and Jordan. I'm always cautious not to drink too much in front of her. I'm in the clear now since she's into her own fun. Leira runs around with them, being a big kid herself.

"I see you hit five hundred and fifty subscribers today," Joanie praises with a touch to my arm.

"Five-fifty? The last time I looked, it was only five thirty-five!" I yell.

"I don't know how you get all those crocheting projects done," she says with envy. "I wish I could fly through my woodworking projects the same way."

"These fingers are busy!" I say, dancing them in the air. Patrick comes up behind me, mixing his smell of booze with mine. His embrace feels good as he sways back and forth to the music, turning my hair behind me.

"I'd like to help keep your fingers busy," he whispers. He twirls me before pulling me into his body. My long, straight hair flows behind me, adding a light, free feeling. It's funny how a simple change can bring about confidence.

As the song enters its last notes, I allow my loosened-up self to plant a kiss on my husband. The crowd erupts with 'oohs' and a couple of whistles.

"Everyone, I have an announcement," I yell, rising into this high time.

"You're one year older!" a friend shouts.

"Yeah, but that's old news… pun intended." I wait for the laughter to die down before proceeding. I'm happy the kids are still playing in the yard so Adrienne and Leira don't see my foolish speech. "I don't know if you all know this, but I love to crochet." Answers such as 'you don't say' are called out. "I just hit my five hundred and fiftieth subscriber mark this afternoon! Apparently, someone with a bigger channel than mine mentioned my videos, and it's taking off!" My friends cheer, sending my mood souring into the night. A look at Patrick shows his surprise. We connect eyes, and he smiles while raising his glass. "Thank you for being here!"

The night rolls on with more laughter and fun. I'm on center stage with everyone I talk with. The more booze I add, the sillier and louder I get. "Wait, wait, I've got one coming…"

"Lisa, don't you dare," Patrick warns. His huge smile shows the opposite of his words. He even supplies the lighter. I bend over and let a fart rip, sending a flame out behind me. My friends laugh before one of the husbands copies the action himself.

"What on earth is going on here?" It's a voice I'll know until the day I die. Everyone quiets down, leaving only the sound of the music. Standing at the edge of my yard is no other than my mother wearing the most shocked expression I've ever seen.

"Mother, what are you doing here?" I ask in disbelief with the slightest of slurs.

"Nancy, I said tomorrow would be a better time for you to stop by," Patrick says quietly. I look at him in admired shock. Has my husband been running defense for me against my mom?

"What do you mean? I texted you saying I would stop by with your birthday present." Damn that phone. "Little did I know that you were partying it up like you're in a fraternity house. You're behaving like this in front of Adrienne?"

"You're behaving like this in front of my friends." I retort. It's unusual for me to be speaking to her like this. Score another for the alcohol loosening what's been wound tightly inside for decades. "Adrienne is off having her own fun."

"Where is she? She isn't drinking, too, is she?" My mother makes a fool of herself, bending over to look under the table and into the yard. A couple of my friends hold their hands over their mouths to try and keep themselves from laughing. "Oh, you think that's funny, do you?"

"Nancy, maybe it would be best to come back tomorrow." Patrick attempts to take her elbow, but my mother will never allow someone else to decide for her.

"Of course, she isn't drinking, mother!" I give a dramatic sigh and roll my eyes. The crowd laughs, and I feel like I'm on center stage again. This isn't a scene I needed to rehearse—it's been stuck on repeat in my head like a broken record my whole life. "Let's see it," I say with a snotty voice, holding my hand out.

"See what?" my mom asks.

"Let me have the 'gift' you brought. What is it this year, a gym membership? Or how about a trip to your financial advisor? Or, how about when you gave me a handful of self-help books? As if I need those, mother, I have a psychology degree!"

"This is rude of you, Lisa. I'm not going to stand here and be ridiculed." She turns to leave, but I lift the gift from her hand. "Lisa!"

I unwrap it, keeping eye contact with my fuming mother. It's a payback that I've wanted to burst open for years. And, unfortunately, one that will leave me in a world of regret the next time I see her.

"Yup, this is just as helpful." I hold the gift up in my right hand. "It's a book on how to get a job."

"I can see I'm not wanted here." My mother attempts to take the book from me, but I hold it tightly to my body.

"Hey, I might need this since I'm nothing without my career." Those words make me think of Patrick and how he sees me, too. I catch a glimpse of his head dropping slightly in the corner of my eye, but I let the alcohol wash that thought away. It's my birthday, and I'm not letting this moment spoil the night.

My mom turns on her heel and stomps out of the yard toward the driveway. Tension lies in the wake of our argument, tension that I intend to stamp away as quickly as it came.

I hold the book in the air. "Anyone want to light this baby up?" Cheers erupt around me. Do I know how to party or what?

Chapter 20 Leira

A Heart Stopping Moment

I don't know anyone here except Lisa's family, but I'm still having an okay time watching everyone chat and party into the night. The energy surrounding me is unlike anything I've ever experienced. There are at least twenty people here to celebrate Lisa's birthday, and more keep coming. The best part is that no one is high and out of control. Sure, there's alcohol, but it's a tame party so far.

Adrienne has been friendly enough to check on me from time to time. She comes to me now with a small plate of food. "Hungry?"

"Eh, not really." My stomach rumbles, exposing my lie.

Adrienne looks at my stomach and back up to my face. "There's a thunderstorm in your tummy," she says, handing her plate of food to me.

I poke around her plate and end up with crackers and cheese. I take a small bite, dropping crumbs on my shirt, when I hear a familiar voice from inside. Lisa left the sliding door open so people can come and go as they please.

"Jordan, I'm so glad you could bring your mom." It's Lisa's booming voice, announcing that my 'study buddy' is here.

I shove the rest of my cracker and cheese in my mouth. I chew as fast as I can, shifting my weight back and forth, attempting to cool my nerves.

"What's wrong, Leira?" Adrienne asks. She follows my line of sight inside, where it's locked onto the tall wonder of a boy. He glances around a few times as if looking for something while simultaneously trying to stay invested in the conversation.

Was he this good-looking in class? The whole 'nerdy guy with glasses' thing is working for me. That leather jacket shows off some seriously broad shoulders, and those tight pants… well, let's just say they're doing the lower half of his body good. My imagination has been underselling both his looks and my growing attraction.

"Do you like Jordan?" Adrienne asks with that teasing type of voice.

"Shh, Adrienne, he'll hear you."

"Jordan's mom and my mom are friends. He likes to play tag with me."

I stay on the sidelines at first, listening to Adrienne talk until she ditches me for some friends. "Wait, Adrienne!" I scold before she runs off. Great, now I'm by myself without a cigarette in sight. Okay, here goes. I stroll to where Jordan stands with his mom, fixing my eyes on his back. He glances over his shoulder at me before fully turning my way.

"Leira, there you are!" I smile, full of uncertainty. I hope he can't see. "Mom, this is Leira," Jordan introduces. "This is my mom, Beatrice."

I nod at first but realize this isn't enough. "Nice to meet you."

"Nice to meet you too, sweetie. Jordan has been talking a lot about you. You go on and chat, Jordan. I'm glad he has someone to talk to." Beatrice gives me a smile that says, 'Look how cute it is that my son has a little girlfriend.'

I watch as she scoots along with her walker. Jordan follows, ready to catch her if she falls. She makes it to a table outside and sits comfortably before shooing him away. "She got in an accident when I was seven," Jordan informs when he gets back to me. "My dad couldn't handle it, so I've been helping mom ever since."

I'm caught off guard by how much his story mirrors mine—both of us abandoned by a parent. Fantastic, now I like him even more. Falling for someone definitely wasn't on my escape-to-Garden-Valley checklist.

"It's nice that you help her." My main purpose for being here was to be free and start my own life. Making friends barely made the list. I've been independent my whole life. I haven't wanted to be connected with anyone. Yet, whether I like it or not, I'm being lured in by promises of friendship and the possibility of love.

"It's nice to be nice to the nice," Jordan teases. I giggle into this, loving his clever lines. I'm caught between wishing I was invisible and wanting to make a connection with him. Right now, I wish he would look at something else! The plus side is that I'm no longer chilled from the cool night air.

"Want to play tag?" Adrienne bounces to us, followed by three boys.

Jordan looks away as if this sounds boring to him. "Eh, I don't know… roar!" he lunges for them with a scream that scares me. The kids emit a high pitch that I shield my ears from. Jordan takes a few steps toward them before turning and giving me a strange look. "Don't think *you're* off the hook."

My eyebrows shoot up in surprise as Jordan lunges at me.

Thanks to my lightning-fast reflexes, I dodge out of the way before he can snag my jacket. I let out a scream I didn't even know I had in me! I've never played this hard before—here I am, tearing around the yard with kids like it's my own playground.

I played this game a couple of times on the playground when I was little before books took over as my go-to escape. It was easier that way; I didn't have to worry about making friends and hiding the mess of secrets in my life.

But now? I squeal like one of the kids as Jordan chases after me, quickly closing the gap. I dart behind the garage, ducking behind a bush, barely registering the spider webs brushing my face. I glance left, checking for him, my breath sending fog clouds into the chilly air. I hold my breath, staying perfectly still until a rustle to my right makes me jump.

"Gotcha!" Jordan grins, reaching for me.

I bolt from the bush, sprinting for the front of 'The Hideout,' hoping I really did have the power to run like the wind. No such luck; Jordan is right on my heels. He grabs my wrists with his giant hands, lifting me off the ground like I weigh nothing. I feel as light as one of Adrienne's stuffed llamas.

"That's not fair," I laugh, "your legs are twice as long as mine."

Adrienne and the boys come up behind us and kick Jordan in the calves to defend me. "Hey, that's cheating. Ouch!" Jordan says with a hop.

"Adrienne, that's not nice," I reprimand.

Jordan leans down and whispers in my ear. "It doesn't really hurt." His warm breath lingers against my skin. The warmth travels first over my neck before radiating over my whole body. He still has me wrapped in his arms, and I hope to God steam isn't rising from my shoulders.

He walks forward, losing his balance, when he steps into a hole with his left foot. We topple to the ground. I'm lucky he lands on his side with me landing on him to shield the blow. He rolls me onto my back and places his hands on either side of my head. It all happens so fast that I can barely register what has happened.

"Got ya!" he yells before jumping up to chase after the other kids.

I lay there momentarily, listening to my heavy breathing, allowing the earth to cool me down. I've never felt the way that he's making me feel. It's exhilarating and scary at the same time.

But I'm not here to have a boyfriend! I want to get my degree and become a wholesome person like Lisa. I don't want to be a big thorn in the side of society like the dads. A boyfriend will muddy up my clear plan. Still, I can't ignore wanting to be around him.

Our game morphs into hide-and-seek, with Jordan making the rules. "Everyone must stay outside and in the yard. You may not go anywhere beyond the fence. *No* exceptions! Got it?" He's quite intimidating as he towers over the kids. He gets another point from me since he cares so much about their safety. The kids nod with dedicated expressions. "I'm 'it.' One, two, three..."

"Crap!" I say, running off to find a hiding spot. I crouch by the bushes behind 'The Hideout' again. I could pick a better hiding spot since this is where he found me a few minutes ago, but I couldn't think of another place in my haste.

"Pst, Leira. Over here." It's Adrienne, about ten feet from me. I scoot over to her quietly and stay low.

"Are you sure we should be together? He'd get both of

us at the same time."

"We'll just listen and run for base if he gets too close."

"Are you warm enough?" I ask, inspecting the thick jacket over her dress. She's wearing stretch pants, but still, they're thin.

"It's not cold," she states, her breath coming out of her mouth in a cloud of steam.

"This is fun," I beam. Adrienne nods, flashing dimples that match Lisa's. Music is playing in the distance, with the murmur of the party still in full force. I hear Lisa's booming laugh ring out over the other noises.

"Your mom's laugh is so funny." I glance over at Adrienne, who nods, her back to the road on our right. It's not a busy street, but every now and then, a car passes, sweeping headlights across the property. Suddenly, a silhouetted figure appears, illuminated by one of the headlight beams, walking toward us. At first, I think it might be the lady coming back for her cat, but this figure is much larger. My breath catches in the cool air, and my body tenses. Is it Phil? Or worse, Gary?

They've found me! And I'm with Adrienne!

"Adrienne, we've got to get to the house!"

"Shh, Leira! He's going to find us."

"I know! That's why we've got to go!" I scoop her up from her crouching position, plant her feet on the ground, grab her hand, and run for the house.

Jordan is off to the right by the trees that line the fence. He starts running for us the instant we reveal ourselves. As he gets closer, I can see the victory on his face, as if he's going to score by tagging us both at once.

He slows with a worried expression upon seeing me. "Leira, what's wrong?"

"There's a man over there, and…" I turn to look for the black outline I saw seconds before, only to find mere darkness. "He was walking, and…" I can't finish my sentences. What do I say that the dads might be after me? That they will undoubtedly throw me in their crappy car and ensure that I never return to this town? That there's a good possibility of them scooping Adrienne up as well if she's with me?

"Oh, that was probably Mr. Mathis. He walks at night," Adrienne says casually.

"We should probably stay close to the house anyway. Guys, come on in." Jordan raises his arm and waves his hand to bring the other boys out from their hiding places. "I'm sure there will be cake soon," he says to entice them. He keeps his gaze on me, searching my face as if the answer to my riddle is written in plain sight. Adrienne leads the way into the house, saying the boys can be the dinosaurs and she can be the Care Bears.

"Interesting combination, huh?" I say in a shaky voice as a repeat of Lisa's words a couple of weeks ago. It's been a couple of weeks since I've been here. The dads are surely on the lookout for me.

"Are you okay?" Jordan asks, holding my elbow gently. I welcome his light touch. I slowly glance over my shoulder, the fear of being grabbed from behind feeling all too real.

"Yeah, I'm fine. Oh my gosh! What the heck is Lisa doing?" I grab Jordan's forearm as he looks in time to see a spray of fire coming from Lisa's butt. Her guests roar in laughter, Jordan and I included. It's the perfect way to knock my jitters loose in an instant.

The woman beside me laughs so hard that she grabs my forearm for support. "I'm sorry," she snorts, still giggling.

"Oh, no worries."

"I'm Zooey. How do you know Lisa?" Panic sets in for the second time tonight. How do I answer?

"She lives in the garage out back," Jordan chimes. I have a mental head slap. More and more people are learning I'm here and where I live. Coming to this party was a *terrible* idea, Ariel! Wait—where did that slip come from? I've thrown that mermaid back to the sea. I'm Leira now!

"That's awesome. I've known Lisa forever," Zooey chatters on, completely unaware of my internal meltdown. "She's a blast. Her parties get a bit rowdy after the drinks have settled in." Suddenly, one of the other guests lights his fart on fire, sending the group into another fit of laughter.

"Uh oh," I mutter, spotting Lisa's mom storming outside. Things are about to get messy.

***

It took serious guts for Lisa to stand up to her mom in front of all her guests. Admitting she's still living under her parents' thumb, even as an adult, wasn't easy. But it's one of the reasons I've felt so connected to her since I got here. Yep, there I go again—making yet another connection.

It will be hard for my new friends when I am taken away.

The unwanted thought has been repeated a few times this week. It's not just the phrase but dreams of the dads coming to town that haunt me. As much as I've thought that changing my name and look would sever ties with them, I know if they have the will to find me, they will definitely find a way.

The party winds down just after midnight. I still can't believe I'm at a party after dark! I've been chatting with Jordan, but even this has slowed as my body grows tired.

Jordan does his best to gather his mom, but she refuses.

"She doesn't get out much," he says, coming back by my side. "When she gets to a gathering like this, she lets all those pent-up words out to whoever will listen."

I'm a teenager, but I'm not immune to tiredness, especially when my usual bedtime is ten-thirty. I inadvertently wrap my arms around myself and shiver. The cool, fresh air has worn out its welcome in my book.

The song 'Save Your Tears' from The Weeknd plays. Jordan gives me a sideways glance that sends my stomach aflutter, not for the first time tonight. I've seen this look before in movies, but it was never directed toward me. I've never thought that someone would look at me like this. As I've said, it wasn't on my list of expectations.

He better not ask me to dance! All I need is for my first date to have an audience.

"Ae you cold? Do you want to go inside?" Jordan asks, motioning to Lisa's house. My eyes flicker to 'The Hideout,' my body craving being snuggled under my down comforter with Violet playing with my feet under the covers.

"Um," I say, eyeing the back garage again.

Jordan stands to his tallest, following my gaze. Oh gosh, please don't think I'm suggesting we go back there together! It's not like that at all. I'm tired and craving my bed.

"Want to show me your place?"

"Oh, um, well," I scratch my head, shift to my left foot, and don't dare look at his face.

Jordan chuckles. "That sounds like a 'yes' to me." He takes monster-sized steps toward the garage, leaving me slouched in disapproval behind him.

I have no other choice but to follow. A few people are still outside chatting into the night. A glance back reveals that

Lisa's eyes are firmly on me. I quickly look away. It's embarrassing to be returning to my place with a boy. I'd love to text her to tell her that it's not what she thinks, but before I know it, I'm at my door with Jordan waiting for me.

He follows me inside and shuts the door. "Hey, you have a cat," he says, bending down to pet Violet. I keep several feet between us as he walks around. I can't get over how tall he is. Seriously, I think his stomach is at my boob level! Not that I'm thinking of my boobs right now or of Jordan touching them.

Oh my gosh, Leira, get a grip!

"It's nice and clean. I like the layout. I can't believe you live on your own!"

I snap out of my thoughts to answer. "Yup. My bed's upstairs. I mean… we don't have to go up there. Um, I was just letting you know since obviously it isn't here, and it would be weird not to have a bed."

That was smooth.

"I haven't ventured from my mom yet. I can't even think about how that day will go. There will be many tears. I'm such a softie." He eyes me comically, but I barely return a smile. I haven't moved from my position by the front door. It's awkward to have a boy in my space.

"It's nice to be able to cook what I want," I say in return, hoping I can break my awkward streak.

"Yeah, that'll keep me at my mom's for good," he laughs. I can feel my worry grow at the thought of cooking and cleaning for him. Just as I did for the dads. "I'm teasing, Leira. I do most of the cooking for mom and me. It's hard for her to get around the kitchen. I make one or two big meals on Sunday, and we eat them throughout the week."

I've somewhat connected his childhood to mine, with his

dad leaving, but I didn't have anyone there for me. Not for the first time I wonder what Jordan would think about me if he knew my upbringing.

The red and white carton of cigarettes on the counter may as well have a spotlight on them. I dart over, snatch the carton, and shove it in my pocket. I turn my head to the side and shift my weight without looking at him. "I haven't quit yet." Here I was worried about how a boyfriend would derail my focus, and I'm the bad influence.

"Hey, Leira, if you ever need help…"

"I'm pretty tired, Jordan," I sigh, hoping he'll leave as quickly as he invited himself. My eyes catch on the door wedge. I'm embarrassed by what this suddenly symbolizes in my small world. It makes me wonder if there will ever be a time when I don't need this thing I've used as a safety net.

"Well, I better gather my mom. Hopefully, she won't be feeling this tomorrow. It was, uh, nice to spend some time with you. Maybe we can get together next week and talk over psychology."

"As long as it's not about me," I breathe with a sigh of relief that he wants to meet again.

Jordan turns serious with the words I should have kept in. He nods while once again making eye contact. It's not a stare or judgment but one of assurance. He walks past me, touching my forearm while grabbing my eyes with his own. "I like your place. See you soon."

The touch on my arm isn't repulsive as it is with others. It was warm and inviting and confirms one thing: as far as my love life goes, I'm in trouble.

Chapter 21 Lisa

Mixed News

Hangovers are the worst! And I'm not just talking about my body processing the excess alcohol. Dealing with the aftermath of telling my mother off in front of an audience will surely come back to bite me.

I know myself well enough to brace for the post-party crash in energy. It always happens after I've been riding an energy wave like I was last night. After seeing many patients with the same problem, I realized I'm not alone. It's like I have a limited supply of happiness, and once I use it all up, I'm left drained and bed-bound the next day.

I tiptoe out of bed, craving a piece of toast to soothe my queasy stomach and pounding headache. Why does alcohol seem to flow like water after that first drink?

The kitchen is peaceful; the early birds are out hunting worms. I stand by the toaster, ready to catch the toast before it springs up when my phone rings. I grab it quickly, not wanting to wake Patrick or Adrienne. In my rush, I accidentally answer it just as I see my mother's name flash on the screen. Sinking down, I give myself a moment before putting the phone to my ear. Even before I lift it, I can already hear the nagging.

"Lisa? Are you there? I know you're there. You answered the phone. Hello?"

"Yes, mother, I'm here. Good morning!" I say with a chipper voice. It's more for my benefit than hers, to brace myself for what's to come.

"Good morning? You should be hanging your head and attending church for how you behaved last night. Seriously, what was with the fire and flatulence thing? I always thought that was a myth."

I laugh inwardly, knowing my mom won't think lighting farts on fire is funny. "Oh no, it's real. I was just having fun with my friends. Aren't I allowed to do that?"

"If those are your friends, I'm even more embarrassed for you. Seriously, you were behaving…"

"I was behaving like I wanted to behave, mother, I'm…"

"I can't believe you were like that in front of Adrienne," she interrupts.

Darn it! I'm an adult. I was at *my* house. It was my birthday, and I wanted to celebrate. I sulk around the kitchen, getting my toast doctored up and making my triple C combo. Lucky for me, Adrienne is a heavy sleeper. I've shielded her from my feelings for my mom. I want their relationship to develop on its own without my input.

"I don't know how you celebrate when you don't have a job. And even when you had a job, you didn't really see patients. I don't know why…"

"What, mother?" I say in her silence. "Just say it. I know you want to."

"There you go again, painting me as the bad guy when you're the one who, oh, never mind."

"I'm the one you wasted your money on to put me through college. Isn't that what's really wrong here, that I'm not using the degree you paid for? Geeze, Mother, that was fifteen years ago! And that's what parents are supposed to do if they have the means, which you and dad definitely do."

It's not much of a wonder where my negative voice comes from. My mother has fed it my whole life. I've never stood up to her until now. I'm not trying to change her. We are both adults and I'd love for her to see me as an equal.

"It's just, we thought you'd go into the family business, Lisa."

And this is her sob story: I'm not a doting sheep like Diane. "I'm not interested in what you guys do. No offense or anything."

"No offense? How can that not be offensive, Lisa?"

A heavy silence stretches between us as if we're both turning over the same thoughts. I wonder if my mom is trying to piece things together just like I am.

My mother continues to nag, but I'm not listening this time. I roll my eyes and pull the phone from my ear to check my numbers. I need some joy right now.

I tap until I get to my YouTube account. Five hundred and ninety-five subscribers! At this rate, I'll be up to one thousand in just a few more weeks. I also need four-thousand hours watched before I get my first check from YouTube. But upon looking, it seems like my longer ASMR videos of me simply crocheting by the fireplace are quite popular. Maybe it won't take as long as I thought.

My mind is rolling with the next video topic. People are eating up the daily Halloween videos. And my orders of crocheted goblins and ghosts have been through the roof.

"Lisa, are you listening to me?" Oops, I've 'accidentally forgotten' I was on the phone with my mom. I allow myself to think about this as a way to solve this problem with her.

Maybe I just need to play a game. Adrienne handles the same sort of thing by ignoring anyone who bothers her at school, refusing to let their words or actions rattle her.

"Anyway, I set you up with an appointment with my therapist, and I expect you to be there. I know it's a Sunday, but he said he would see you immediately. After what I saw last night, we need to jump on this immediately."

"Wait, what? Mother, you can't make me go to your therapist."

"Of course I can. Hal said he'd be happy to see you."

"I'm not going to see someone today. I have plans."

"While I'm sure you would love to eat crackers and sip mimosas to get over what I'm sure is a hangover, you'll drive to Eugene to see my guy. Lisa? Are you ignoring me again?"

I sure am.

***

I could have pushed back with my mom, but I didn't have the energy. Plus, if I don't go to the appointment today, she'll just keep making them. I don't mind the reason for getting out of the house. Aside from my short trips to the post office or to pick Adrienne up, I haven't been leaving much. I'm not complaining, I've been turning into a home-body and I love it. Besides, talking with someone about my goals, wishes, and desires actually sounds like a good idea.

The appointment isn't until this afternoon, allowing me plenty of time to enjoy a chunk of the day. Leira comes over to play with Adrienne while Patrick works in the yard. She really does enjoy playing with my daughter. Something stirs from her past. I only have inklings of what it could be, but thinking of anything bad happening to her brings out my protective side.

"Hey, do you want to go for a walk?" I still have two hours before I need to leave for my appointment. I'm looking forward to calling my mom out on everything she's done and said to me over the years. I don't want sympathy. Instead, I need confirmation that all this ugliness isn't just in my head.

"Sure," both Leira and Adrienne say. Adrienne runs up ahead, leaving Leira and I to be alone.

Warning signs go off in my head to steer clear of the topic I want to bring up, but I don't listen.

"What did you think of the party?" I ask, gearing up for the big topic.

"It was fun. You seemed to have a good time."

"Yeah, well, probably too much of a good time. I had a few 'don't do as I do' moments. You and Jordan seemed to get to know each other at the party."

"We have a psychology class together." Ooh, that wasn't a friendly tone. I should back off before I even start.

"Listen, Leira, I just want you to be careful."

"Jordan isn't anybody to be afraid of." She says this with a knowing in her eyes and raised eyebrows.

"No, no, that's not what I mean. It's just…"

"I can make my own decisions, Lisa." She walks faster, and it's apparent that I'm losing her.

"Oh, I know! I'm not trying to tell you what to do."

"I'm not looking for more rules. Just like you aren't."

"Tag, you're it!" Adrienne says, touching Leira's side before running off. Leira doesn't hesitate one second to get away from me.

That didn't turn out as I thought it would. It's not quite the same, but now I know how my mom feels when I brush her off.

***

The drive to Eugene is good for me. I've been super tethered to the house for a month and a half now. A calmness overcomes me as I drive, listening to the rain and enjoying the brown and orange leaves dancing in the sky. I can't wait to pelt the psychologist with questions about my mom's controlling ways.

I pride myself on hopping up the stairs without stopping to catch my breath. The backyard walks are paying off! The quaint office foyer offers a view of the city of Eugene. My eyes aren't used to tall buildings beyond the windows. I know some people like this scene, but I prefer the greenery of Garden Valley.

The office is nicely decorated in dark brown and maroon colors. I'm sure the psychologist studied colors to soothe and settle people into spilling their deepest secrets.

"Lisa, come on in." Hal has a friendly face and stands only a few inches taller than me. I pass by him, surprised by his attire of jeans and a sweater with the Eugene College logo. It's Sunday, but still, my dad and sister would never dress down like this in front of a patient.

My anger ramps up with every step I take to the couch. My mother is still telling me what to do. But that's not what is bothering me. It's that I'm obeying.

His office follows the same color scheme as the waiting area. I opt for the brown leather chair instead of its matching sofa, which has undoubtedly seen buckets of tears.

"I'm Hal," he says slowly with his hand on his chest. Oh no, please don't tell me that baby talk will follow. "Your mom set this up for us today to talk to you about your little party last night." Nope, not baby talk, a lecture.

"Yep, I threw myself a birthday party. Apparently, I was supposed to ask my mother how I can behave in my own house." My voice takes on the same tone Leira had just a couple of hours ago when I talked to her about Jordan.

"A party sounds fun!" Hal says, resting his hands on his notepad. I look at him in surprise. "We need that time to loosen up." Wait what? Hal laughs. "I bet you thought I was going to lecture you today." He keeps his round, brown eyes on me until I nod. "Lisa, you're a grown woman. I agreed to have this meeting because I've known your mother for years. I know she can be overbearing, and I was curious how you deal with that."

I stare at him in shock. This has taken an interesting turn, and one I'm going to follow.

"Oh, it's a lot of fun to deal with my mother," I say sarcastically. "She calls me at least twice a week to remind me what I'm failing at. I make it a game as to which part of my life she will tell me I suck most at. Sometimes, I think she has one of those wheels that she spins to pick the topic." I let my angry voice take over. I figure Hal has seen it all in his years as a psychiatrist. Nothing I say will shock him.

"I'm sorry you've had to deal with that." This man is ultra-gentle, sitting before me with his legs crossed. He's someone I wouldn't mind seeing myself if I was into this sort of thing. I laugh at my own thought process. He looks at me in question, giving me the space to explain.

"I wondered if I will continue to see you, and then thought, 'I'm not into that sort of thing.' But I have a degree in psychology myself. Doesn't really make sense, does it?"

"Even I have a therapist," he says with a smile. "We all need an unbiased opinion about the issues we are dealing with.

At least, that's my take on therapy," he laughs. "It sounds like you're in a position to focus on yourself."

"That's a nice way to say I'm unemployed," I laugh, so he knows I'm not offended. It's easy to talk to him. It's easy for me to talk to anyone, but I usually avoid making the topic about my problems. "I was always the child who was never good enough. Yes, that sucked big time, but I'm an adult now who can cope. Well, theoretically. I have my down moments."

"Oh? Tell me about those."

Good going, Lisa.

I sigh and hold my head to the side, indicating that I don't like this topic. "I hate talking about this. So what if some days I have difficulty getting out of bed? I have depressive episodes, but I work through them."

"How do you do that?" He's not prying. I know this is his way, what he's been trained to do.

"I make myself get up. I tell myself I'm important and have important things to do. I slam that negative voice aside and move on the best I can. I go on walks, I crochet, I make a video."

"All excellent techniques. Do they work?"

Once again, he allows me the space to think through this, a technique I also practice with my patients. "Actually, they do. It's funny. I beat myself up for feeling down like I don't have a reason to feel that way. I recognize it, deal with it, and pull myself out."

"It's not bad to feel down. We can't always be in a good mood."

I nod through his point. "It's true. Yes, I get that." I continue to nod this into my existence.

"It doesn't help to put yourself down for your depression. You should give yourself praise for using your techniques and seeing there's a way out."

"True. I don't blame my mom, but it isn't like she helps."

"Does she know you struggle with depression?" Hal asks genuinely.

I reel back in surprise at the question. "Definitely not. I'd like to keep it that way please."

"Your secret is safe with me. Based on what you said earlier, do you think her actions cause your episodes?"

"For sure! I don't want to be like her and I feel like that's what she's trying to do."

"I wonder," he says, resting his pen on his lip, "what your mother would say if you opened up to her about your depression and how her words alter your self-esteem."

"She'd probably recommend I take more vitamins," I respond the second he's done talking. "This has always been her way of dismissing my problems. Lisa you should take this. Lisa you should take that. We talk a lot, but it's very one-dimensional, meaning my mother talks about how my choices in life have affected her."

He nods in understanding. "I can see how that would be difficult. What if you keep doing what you're doing and try not to care what your mother thinks. You're the one living your life, after all."

It's nearly what Leira suggested as well. "I just want her to see that what I'm doing is worthwhile. I've gotten into a good routine, and for the first time, I'm meeting my goals."

"In our busy world, that's quite an accomplishment. What have you been working on?"

I think back on the last few weeks I've been off work. Sure, I've had my ups and downs, but what is life without the challenges that push us to improve?

"I really like to crochet and make videos for my YouTube

channel. I call my community my 'Crochet-iacs.' It sounds like such a simple life when I say it in one sentence. I've been off work, which was hard to deal with initially, but I have time to crochet now. I've been able to spend as much time on my projects as I want. I have other responsibilities with my daughter, house, and husband, but I love it all! I'm selling a ton on Etsy. I never thought my closet full of homemade blankets and scarves was more like a treasure chest. And I think I'm going to raise my prices even more. I know it sounds silly."

He shakes his head as I speak, and for a moment, I think he will tell me this is ridiculous. "You need to realize what your pieces are worth. I don't think anything is silly if it makes you happy, and all of that sounds like fun."

"I should bring my husband in here so you can tell him that," I say with a puff.

"Does he not agree with what you're doing?"

I pause for a moment before I dive into this topic. Upon second thought, Patrick has actually been quite supportive lately. "At first, he didn't, but he's coming around. All he wants is for me to bring in some kind of cash flow, and over the last six weeks, I've made roughly what I did at the clinic."

"That's really good. What else?"

"We have a girl living in the back, and I've enjoyed getting to know her. I think she has some demons in her past, and it feels good to be helping her.

"A word of advice?"

"That's why I'm here, doc?" I say with my hands out wide.

"Don't push her. If you stay a loving constant in her life, she'll come to you on her own. Just be there for her. Once she trusts you, she'll give you more information."

I breathe in a calming breath to let that sink in. "Thank you. Great advice."

"What else? You have a psychology degree. Do you think you'll ever work in the field again?"

"I've been thinking about getting into the life coach area. I don't know much about it or if I'm qualified. It's just something that keeps coming up."

Hal gets off his seat and hurries to his desk. "You're probably more qualified than most of them out there. Pretty much anyone can be a life coach. All you're doing is listening and offering advice. From what your mom said, you did that at the clinic. You'll be surprised to hear this, but your mom talks about you during our sessions."

"Does she now?" I say, raising my left eyebrow.

Hal laughs before responding. "I can't tell you what she says, of course, but I'll just say there's more pride than disappointment in our discussions." I give him a look of shock. I'm literally speechless. "Anyway, back to being a life coach. It's quite the thing these days. You get to pick your hours and means of talking with your clients. You can be in person, on the phone, or on a video chat. I know someone you should contact. His name is Josh, and he even lives in Garden Valley by the lake."

"It sounds like I become a part of someone's entourage, follow them around, and help them make decisions. 'No, no, get the coffee with caramel and creamer, Linda.'"

Hal outright laughs at my explanation and accent. "It's not like that. It's pretty much a new name for this age-old psychiatry practice. In a few years, I might be changing my title."

"I don't know," I say, looking down at my hands. "It seems like a lot to have someone's life in my hands."

He shakes his head, uncrosses his legs, and leans towards me with his elbows on his knees. "I've talked to Josh about what he does. He says he works out of his cabin on the lake. He sets up Zoom calls with his clients, meets with them once a week, and gives them advice on whatever areas of their life they want to share with him."

"Sounds a lot like what I did at the clinic." My voice is hopeful about this possibility for the first time. "Thank you for seeing me today. And I'm sorry you had to come in on a Sunday."

"Hey, my wife is, um, a lot like your mother. It was a great excuse to get out of the house."

My side of our laugh holds a bit of release. I glance at the pamphlet Hal gave me about becoming a life coach. It might just be the ticket to my fourth income stream.

✳✳✳

I treat myself to a coffee in Eugene before heading back to Garden Valley. I rarely allow this sort of uninterrupted alone time away from home. Lately, my calendar has been full of making videos, crocheting, taking Adrienne to ballet and piano lessons, cleaning, and cooking. It's weird to think of this as my job, but *I'm making* money and having fun!

I don't mind sitting alone in the coffee place, cozying up in my jacket while my drink slowly warms me from the inside out. I skim through the life coach pamphlet. The idea has lingered in my mind, much like my other passions.

An employee catches my eye as he tapes up a poster. The big bold lettering reads, 'Help Us Find Her.' It's heartbreaking—parents missing their child. I can't even fathom something like that happening to Adrienne. I glance at the poster again, noticing that the girl looks older than Adrienne. When I take a second look, I freeze.

The goth style throws me off, but beneath the heavy makeup, her small features and striking green eyes are unmistakable. The girl on the poster is Leira.

Chapter 22 Leira

You Hide, We'll Find You

W ho does Lisa think she is giving me advice about my sex life? Wait a minute, I'm a virgin. I don't have a sex life. About my romantic life. There.

I reach for a cigarette on my drive to school and pause. Why am I still catering to this habit that links me to the dads? They were always surrounded by clouds of stale smoke. Why have I kept that memory in my new life?

I roll down the window and, without hesitation, throw my remaining cigarettes out. I don't care how bad the cravings get. This is not going to be me anymore.

I quickly roll up the window, not wanting the wind to mess up my hair. I curled it for the first time ever this morning, wanting to look nice for someone at school today.

What is Jordan to me? Is he a boyfriend? I don't know what will launch us to the boyfriend-girlfriend status. We have yet to kiss or hold hands. I've already decided to let him take the lead, telling myself I'll put on the brakes when my limits have been reached.

I inch into a tiny parking spot, one of the last at school. I keep watch of the cars I'm squeezing between, careful not to get too close to either one when I'm jolted to a stop. I look ahead of me, and, yup, I've hit the light post. Darn. If Lisa knew how bad of a driver I am… then what? Would she take this truck away? 'Grit' already has a hundred dents and scratches on it. I seriously doubt she would do that.

She cares.

As I grab my bag, a thought makes me pause. Lisa is one of the few people who has reached out to me, who has stuck by me day after day. And how have I been responding? I lower my head, thinking about my bratty teenage attitude the other day. Even when I messed up watching Adrienne, Lisa didn't scold me. I've added dents to their pickup, and they don't care. She's had me over for dinner several times, has made me lunches, and is teaching me to cook.

Instead of scolding myself for my moody behavior, I walk into class with a lighter feeling, determined to make it right with Lisa the next time I see her.

I nearly stop when I see Mia draped over Jordan's desk. It's fifty degrees outside, and she's in a crop top and those shorts that barely cover anything. How does no one else think about their ass sitting directly on the chairs? I definitely do.

Mia glances at me and lets out an over-the-top laugh. I sit down, focusing on my notebook and pen, pretending not to notice her. Two can play this game, but she's in a whole different league than I'll ever be.

"I think class is going to start," Jordan says with irritation. Mia falters before peeling herself off Jordan's desk and sashaying to her seat. How do girls learn to wiggle like that? "So," Jordan says, leaning over to my desk, "that was quite a fun party, huh?"

"Yep," I say without looking at him. His expression out of the corner of my eye is one of worry. I glance at Mia with a pang of jealousy that I don't feel bad about. Even with a couple of full meals a day, I don't have half the curves she does.

"Hey, do you want to talk about class after… well, after class?" He laughs slightly at his wording.

"Maybe," I reply. I'm not trying to play hard to get, but I also don't have it on my list to get my heart broken within my first month here. The less attachment, the better, especially when a girl like Mia is around.

Our teacher runs through the door with top-notch energy to start class. He drops his bag on his desk with a loud thud. It's a sudden movement I wasn't expecting, and I flinch with a gasp. He resembles Phil and wears a tweed jacket similar to the one Phil always wore to business meetings. I look down and around in embarrassment. Of course, Jordan is staring right at me.

"Today, we're going over chapters eight through ten. I know you all read them diligently, so these worksheets should be easy to fill out. The topic of today is childhood trauma. It's a hard one to discuss, but something that is very real and much too common for my taste. Since I know you've read the text, I'm curious about your thoughts."

The worksheets make their way around the room and to the back, where my seat is. Great, we're in the childhood years. I've already read these chapters and saw myself all over those pages. The word 'neglect' stares at me from the page. I glance around, wondering if it's also stamped on my forehead. Hey, I have bangs now, so no one will be able to see it. I smirk at my wit, my expression alerting the teacher.

"What do you think?" Silence resides with a couple of looks my way. Oh no, please don't tell me he's calling on me.

"I'm sorry. What was the question?" I ask, my eyes dancing self-consciously around me.

"I want to know your thoughts about childhood trauma. Did anything in particular stand out for you in the text?" I don't want to answer, but at the same time, I *am* the book of knowledge on the topic. Even if I hadn't read the chapters, I'd be well-versed.

"It's not uncommon to see kids raising themselves these days." A glance at Jordan shows he's listening intently. Everyone in class is.

"And what do you think of that?" he asks.

I take a deep breath, wondering which phrase to speak out loud. "It's not the best for society. Kids need guidance and, uh, the care of an adult. But kids do grow up, as you said," I say, raising my chin. "Hopefully, they can grow out of the neglect."

"'Grow out of the neglect?'"

"I mean, they move on, become adults, and have the choice to form their own lives. They can sort of outgrow what happened and make better lives for themselves. Hopefully, they will break the cycle and not neglect their own children." Mr. Strickland nods as I talk. He points his dry-erase pen at me, finalizing my turn.

"Exactly. It's not as easy as this, but I've seen my fair share of people who have turned their lives around. It's been my privilege to help them do so," he says, his eyes boring the statement into mine. "A great spin on this, Ms..." he stays quiet for me to fill in my name.

"Ari..." Shit! "Leira."

"A little dyslexic today, huh, Leira?" he jokes. A few people laugh, and I sink down in my seat. He continues his lecture with me wishing to be invisible.

No! This was the old me. The new me realizes that I can make mistakes. It's not like anyone will remember my flub with my name after a few minutes.

"Let's do an exercise to wake you guys up." Mr. Strickland tosses his pen to a boy in class who is paying attention enough to catch it. "Pair up and talk about why you're in this class. What do you hope to gain? What are your absolute passions for psychology?" He dramatically holds his hand to his chest, gaining laughs from the class.

Before he stops talking, I scoot my chair next to a girl who is also in my culinary class. I move my eyes to Jordan, who is frozen by my actions. He finally moves his desk next to the guy to his left. At least he hasn't paired up with Mia.

"Why do I want to be in this class?" Sarah starts. "Because I don't know what the hell to do with my life yet." I smile at her comment and nod.

"Same," I lie.

"I don't know. You seemed pretty fluent in your response. Do you think you'll be a psychiatrist or something?"

I shrug. This isn't exactly the setting I want to spill my story in. "Maybe." Sarah widens her eyes as if wanting to hear more. "I've thought about it."

"It's funny how we're in this class and the cooking class together. Maybe we'll help our clients deal with their problems with food. A healthy relationship, of course." She laughs, but it's not exactly a bad thought.

"My landlord has a YouTube channel and couples mental health with crocheting," I boast.

"That's a good idea. I guess whatever takes your mind off the problem." I sit with this for a few seconds, thinking this is off base.

"Um, I actually look at it as what helps *deal* with the problem. Something that's not drugs or bad like that." Did I really just bring up drugs?

"That's true. Do you have plans for the holidays? My parents are thinking of having us all go on a cruise. My sister is in high school, and they say this might be their last chance before we all have husbands and stuff."

How am I supposed to respond to this? *Yeah, the dads and I do the same thing with their druggie friends. Vacations are a great way for them to target new clients.* That would make for an exciting discussion. The whole term could be centered around my life.

"Sounds like fun."

Mr. Strickland brings us back to the lecture, saving me from coming up with more conversation. "So, is this a class full of future psychologists? Why are you here?" he asks a guy across the room.

I don't hear the answer. I know why I'm here, even if I cannot fully admit my reason. I think back to the kids on the playground at Adrienne's school. Those kids might have it good with a normal household, but I know thousands don't. I would like a chance to help them and show them how to get out of the tangles their parents have wrapped them in. Just as I have.

Why am I here? I see myself in every topic in the book and know I can help others who are like me.

✳✳✳

Everyone at the college is squeaky clean. It hasn't bothered me until today when I feel out of place again. Knowing they have a weed like me in their flowery garden of a town would surely bring out the spray.

This isn't really what's bothering me. I rush out of class when we're done so I can avoid Jordan. Mia blocks his way, giving me an angry-thankful feeling.

"Hey, Leira, wait up." I turn and see Amber from the Inn. I don't have to fake a smile; seeing her is good.

"Hi, Amber."

"How are your classes going?"

"Pretty good," I say, with a nod, looking around to watch for Jordan. "You?"

"I'm only taking two classes this term, but I like them. Hey, I wanted to let you know that I got a weird call from some guy asking about you the other day." My stomach clenches so hard that I stop walking. I face her and am unable to control the fear from showing. "It was strange; two guys were on the phone pelting me with questions. They described you to a 'T,' or at least what you looked like when you first arrived. I love what you've done with your hair, by the way," she says as if the previous comments wasn't the worst thing I could hear.

"What did you say?" I ask, wanting to grab the collars of her jacket and shake the answer out of her.

She scrunches her mouth up before talking again. "I didn't feel comfortable telling them anything, so I kept my mouth quiet. I'm not the best liar, so they might have seen through my responses."

My eyes wander to the ground. The dads are looking for me. They know I'm gone, and they've somehow tracked me here.

Charlotte.

"Well, thanks. It was probably just a prank call," I say with a forced chuckle. "I've got to get to class." I hug my books and rush off to my algebra class. I search the halls, looking from person to person for any resemblance to Phil or Gary. My confidence flies away, with me resembling more of my old self rather than my fresh new powers taking precedence. Thankfully, everyone here are students my age, including Jordan, who is waiting for me outside the classroom. He pays no mind to the chaos swirling around us, his intense gaze fixed solely on me. So serious.

Seriously sexy.

Stop that!

I don't want to talk to Jordan right now. I am in serious shit here. It's all mine, and I don't want to put anyone else in the path of the danger I know is heading my way.

"Hey," he says with a chin nod. "Let's talk for a minute." He walks away, either knowing I'll follow or taking his chances. I follow, and I can guess what the topic will be about.

We're having luck today with the weather staying dry and not raining or freezing. The shining sun, however, does nothing to brighten the news Amber just gave me.

Jordan slows once we're outside the crowded hallway, allowing me to catch up. He cups my elbow with his hand. He doesn't squeeze. It's more like he's letting me know he's here with me.

"Leira, I don't want to pry into your life. I know you're somewhat private. It looked like you wanted to hide when I saw those cigarettes on the counter the other night." I look down in embarrassment. I hate that he's brought this flaw up. "I'm not trying to make you feel bad. It's just that something seems to be going on. I want to make sure you're safe and let you know you can talk to me."

"Hey, hey, what's up, Jordan!" A boy walks by us with a shout, holding his fist up for Jordan to bump.

He barely looks at the guy he touches his knuckles with, keeping his eyes on me instead, searching my face for an answer. "Are you okay?" he asks with a serious tone and eye contact. "I mean, you were afraid of that guy who was just walking down the street at Lisa's house, and at the beginning of class, I saw you jump when Mr. Strickland came in. Of course, he's going to come in; it was the start of class."

His wide smile is meant to soften the topic, but I don't need this. I can do it on my own. I don't need his help. I'm making it. I'm on my own and doing fine. School, work, and managing my money. I'm here now, and there's no returning to my life that was leading to an empty hole. This time in school and this town… these are all *my* choices.

So is the choice to not wanting to be tied down to someone who is prying into my life. At least, I can't do this now when the risks are increasing.

"You don't need to worry about me, Jordan." I give him a smirk of fake irritation. "Really, you don't."

Another guy walks by and pats Jordan on the back. I use this as the perfect time for my getaway.

"Wait, Leira!" he shouts from behind.

I dig within to remember how good I am at holding back my tears. I had to do this quite often 'back then.' I would love Jordan's help and companionship in seeing me through this mess. I suddenly want the safety that his tall, broad stature could provide. But I can't. I have to get through this on my own.

The part that's scaring me is that I have no idea what 'this' means yet. I don't know what the dads will do if they find me.

I hate that they are looking for me. Deep down, I know the real reason they want to take me out of this existence I've created for myself.

I know too much about their secrets.

Chapter 23 Lisa

The Work-Life Balance

Today I'm meeting with Josh, the local life coach. While I'm thrilled, all I can think about lately is the picture of Leira on the poster. She was younger and decked out in all-black, but I instantly knew it was her. I haven't decided how I'm going to bring it up. Her reaction to my simple conversation with Jordan has thrown question marks and caution tape in the mix.

I can put the topic on the back burner for now. I don't want to press the issue and push her away. Besides, I have plenty of other things going on in my life. With my time limit to get a job almost up, trying to post as many videos as possible, and keeping up with my Etsy orders, my life is as windy as one of my blankets.

I'm not worried that Patrick will lay down the hammer. He probably doesn't remember the date we chose. He can't even remember haircut appointments when he's made them within the same week. I've gotten a few callbacks on jobs, but working at the hospital in Eugene isn't what I'm after.

The clarity settles my spiraling mind as I walk around the fully grown trees in the yard. These walks have done wonders for easing my anxiety about my various priorities.

I'm worth it. I'm worth going for my dream. I've welcomed the repetition of this phrase. I repeat this in my mind when it hits me—I'm actually living this dream. I've been whipping up YouTube videos daily, crocheting creations on demand, and gathering a small but mighty community of loving fans. I'm not swimming in thousands of followers yet, but I'm savoring every step of this wild ride.

I make it back to the house with ten minutes to spare before my first Zoom meeting with Josh, the local life coach. We talked on the phone, and he offered welcomed encouragement about me stepping into the life coaching arena. I grab my binder, a couple of pens, and my triple-C combo and click on the Zoom link as Chuggers settles around my ankles. My nerves are on edge for our meeting. It will be the weirdest interview I've ever had being over my clunky computer.

Josh's blue eyes and blonde hair pop up on the screen, making him look more suited to catching waves than offering advice. "Hello, Lisa!" he shouts, with the enthusiasm of someone who's just discovered how awesome life can be. Someone like me!

Right off the get-go, I'm drawn to his energy. "Hello! It's so nice for you to meet with me. I think we can still say that over the computer." I pick up the current blanket I'm working on. The weaving motion gives my nervous energy an outlet instead of being bottled inside.

"We can! I do at least. And, it's nice of *me* to meet with *you*? I have more clients I know what to do with. It's nice of *you* to offer to take a few from me. So, let's see if we're a good match, shall we?"

I blush slightly at his phrasing. This man is clearly younger than me and very handsome. His clean-shaven face and tousled hair go well with his striking features. He appears to be tall, or at least I'm assuming this is the case. Usually, a broad chest like his goes with long legs.

"Sounds good," I say, keeping my smile on. My intuition already tells me this is a good move on my part.

"I didn't know when I started being a life coach what my maximum number of clients would be. It's thirty," he says with a laugh. "I'm pushing forty clients now, and I'm over my limit. I do my own record-keeping, insurance billing, and keeping up with the state requirements. I've been working sixty-plus hours a week, even on the weekends, to catch up, and I am ready to cut down a bit."

Uh oh, I'm not looking to work that much. Josh starts laughing at what I can see as a scared reflection in my window of the Zoom.

"I'm not looking for someone to work that much. I would like a side-kick to take a half dozen of my lighter cases. I have the people pegged. A few of my lady clients have said they would prefer to talk to women about some of their issues. They also want my side of things to help with the male issues in their lives. So, I'd have you see them once a week or so, and then I'd see them once a month. That is if they want to return to me after seeing you."

We share a laugh, and just like that, I know I'm on the right path.

"I'm guessing it'll be fifteen to twenty hours on your part. It would help me out a ton. How does that sound?"

"That sounds perfect." And it does. This is totally doable with my schedule now!

"Okay, great. We can move on to getting to know you. I want to ensure that this is something you're looking for, not full-time."

"Nope, I have other pots in the fire as well."

"Oh yeah, your YouTube channel. I've checked it out, and I've got to tell you, I took some notes."

"You're kidding?" I ask, getting closer to the screen.

"You have good advice. I think my clients will really like you."

"Well, thank you. I might make you into a fellow 'Crochet-iac."

"My mom crochets. She and my sister tried to teach me one time. It was actually kind of fun. So, some of my clients might make you work for their trust. What do you think about that?"

"Well, I'm not you, so I'd expect a time period of adjustment. I saw clients at the clinic who took a few sessions to realize that I wasn't going to judge them or grill them about their decisions. None of us are perfect. I offer suggestions, sure, but ultimately, I won't tell them what to do. And I don't want them to hold anything back for fear that I'll scold or look down on them."

Josh nods here and there when I talk. With his good ol' boy look and smile, it's no wonder why he's become popular. I don't see a ring on his finger when he talks with his hands, and mentally I think about all of my single friends who I could set him up with.

"What if someone comes to the appointment and complains about their family members. It's not like they can just cut them out, necessarily."

"I think boundaries are a good option," I reply, making a mental note to consider this further with my family situation. "I'm currently working on this with my own family."

"Oh? The other day, a client told me her mom is overbearing, and she's well into her forties," Josh starts.

"You mean it's going to continue into my forties?" We both laugh. "Someone told me the other day that it's not like your family members are going to follow you around all day and night, so you might as well do what you want." It makes me think about Leira again. The picture of her in thick black eyeliner and lipstick will stick in my mind for a while.

"That's good advice. I've had a couple of people threaten to commit suicide. What would you say if someone said they had a gun ready right now? I don't think any of the clients I'm giving you are in this boat, but you never know."

"I've actually had to deal with this. In college, we were required to be in charge of the suicide hotline for a semester. I got quite a few of these calls. They were stressful, let me tell you." I can't help but be animated when I talk. I do this now, using my hands and expressions to help make my point. "But ultimately, people want to be heard. They call because they want a way out. They want options and help, someone to listen to them. I always helped them through it and guided them to a specialized center."

Josh stares at the camera with a serene smile. "Well said, Lisa."

∗∗∗

Josh and I clicked right off the bat, and he set me up with a personal link that I'll give my clients for my meetings with them. It feels so official, professional, and legit. He says he's been set up to have someone under him for years but never thought he'd find anyone who would mesh with his ways. Josh even said he'd replace my dinosaur of a computer if this all works out!

It surprises me that people can get something out of this

way of talking, but it makes sense. There's no driving involved, and they can speak more freely in whatever comfortable setting they choose.

Josh offered a description of a therapist versus a life coach. A life coach helps discover 'how' to work through a problem, while a therapist works on 'why' the problem exists in the first place.

I can do this!

I float throughout my day on cloud nine, loving the dream life I've created. I'm scheduled for my first two appointments today and will have plenty of time to shoot a video and volunteer in Adrienne's class.

I've read the files about the clients Josh sent me and am ready. Now, all I have to do is allow my client, Stephanie, into the Zoom meeting, and I'm set. She lives in Idaho, but it doesn't matter when we use this method to meet.

I click a few buttons, and she's in!

"Well, hello. You must be Stephanie. I'm Lisa."

"Hi Lisa, it's nice to meet you. Josh asked if I'd be up for moving to a woman, and I was like, *yes!* I like him, but there are some things men just don't understand." She waves her arms around for emphasis. I'm instantly drawn to her, but I am always careful to stay professional instead of acting like a friendship is blooming.

"I understand that. I read your file, but tell me about yourself." As much as I like to talk, I'm always respectful of the client's time. After all, these appointments are about them, not me.

Stephanie has no trouble diving into her problems with her husband. "He jokes about everything I say. It's all one big f-ing joke. I can't have any serious conversations with him."

I think about this for a moment. "So, if I paraphrase, you

can't go into anything with a deep meaning. He jokes, making whatever you were talking about meaningless."

"Yes! That's exactly it. It's so frustrating, and I don't know how to get him out of it or take me seriously."

"How about this? What if you say something, and he makes his dumb little joke… oops!" I cover my mouth because of this slip, but Stephanie laughs.

"No, that's okay. They are totally dumb."

"Sorry. Anyway, let him get all that out, and then stay quiet. Just look at him until he's done. Maybe he'll run out of things to say and then be ready to listen to you."

"And maybe he'll finally get the hint! I've tried getting mad and yelling… nothing really works. But I haven't tried to be quiet yet. Can you imagine *me* being quiet?" she laughs at the poke at herself since she has talked non-stop for almost the entire hour.

This appointment has been just as helpful for me as I hope it has been for Stephanie. It's my first appointment in this life-coaching venture, and it has been a great experience. After searching for my true place in this world, with all my new adventures, I've finally found it.

Chapter 24 Lisa

Picnic in the Park

I am more than hyped after my two successful appointments. It's a high that usually worries me since I have the track record of crashing into a depression afterward. This feeling is layered with gratitude, pushing me to ride the wave of excitement. I get to practice my psychology trade! I get my much-needed contact with people and I get to help them. Best yet, I get to stay in the comfort of my home and make my own schedule!

Patrick is more than a little weary about my setup with Josh. "You need a *real* job, Lisa. You know, one that has a steady paycheck? This 'fifty dollars here and twenty dollars there' stuff doesn't give me warm fuzzies." His voice isn't mean, and I allow him to get his opinion out.

I grab a piece of paper to write it out for him, knowing he's a visual person. "I'm going to make sixty dollars per session with Josh's clients he passed to me, and I have seven sessions per week. Josh is adding another hundred dollars weekly for meetings with him and all the notes and filing involved after seeing each client." Patrick's eyes enlarge while his mouth forms a line. "He also said he ordered me a new computer, which will be here next week. He offered and said

I can use it for my personal stuff as well. I've been making between two and three hundred a week on Etsy. Leira pays us three hundred dollars a month, and I'm almost to the benchmark of making money on YouTube."

Patrick stays silent and so do I for a change. I follow use the same advice I gave to Stephanie, hoping to drive the math equation home. He's not the only one who can understand the finances in our house, and I'm tired of him making me feel like I'm not doing my part.

"This is just the start. The sky's the limit here, Pat."

His contemplative look, complete with an open mouth, joins us. I laugh, a sound that dramatically eases our tension.

"What?"

"There's that look I like," I tease.

"You know math isn't my strong suit," he says, poking me in the ribs before counting on his fingers. Patrick excuses himself to clean up. Admitting you're wrong isn't exactly a walk in the park. Not that I think Patrick's wrong here, but I'm willing to give him some solo time to craft the perfect apology.

I can only imagine what my mother would say if she knew I was giving advice over the computer? I'm using my degree, just not in the way she intended. I stop the thought process, relishing in the positive right now. I'm sure Patrick and I will still have issues to work through, but I've cinched this one up tighter than my latest projects.

I laugh slightly at the irony of me being a counselor in the space of my own home. My whole family prides themselves on their exclusive building with marble flooring and high-end waiting room furniture.

I keep my eyes on Patrick when he returns as if awaiting his verdict. "It looks like your plans are working, babe. I think it's great. I've never heard of any of these money-making ideas, but it sounds like you're already an expert. Proceed, my lady," he says, bowing in front of me. His kiss ends our tense discussion. It's hard for most of us to admit when we've said something wrong. Patrick included. I realize that all he's doing is ensuring our family can live comfortably.

"I know we've had a few years where we've been strapped for cash. I'm thrilled I could stay home with Adrienne during that time, but…"

"Lisa, you've already thanked me for that a million times. I'm glad you got to stay home, too. We have a sweet, smart little girl, mostly because of your time with her."

He snuggles in for a hug and a twirl of my hair, something I'll never turn down. It's a long overdue heart-to-heart. I'm glad he's allowed all my irons in the fire to heat up. I'm finally making the money I deserve, and it's just the start!

"Adrienne is back with Leira, isn't she?" he says, kissing that sensitive spot under my left ear.

"Mmm hmm," I answer. I tag him and dart off towards the bedroom. "The last one between the sheets is on top!" Patrick follows for a quick romp before I get dinner ready.

We don't have long to snuggle afterward when I hear the back sliding door open. I get out of bed and throw on my clothes before we get caught, drumming up a conversation like we hadn't just shared a sweaty workout.

"Hey, the weather is supposed to be nice this weekend. It could be the last time for a while. We should go on a picnic or something."

"Sounds good to me," Patrick says, pinching my bottom before heading out to the back garage to tinker with something.

I see Leira head into her apartment out back. The last

time we talked was the day after my birthday party when she gave me sass when I tried to talk to her about Jordan. I walk over to pay her a visit, and to my surprise, she opens the door before I can knock. Her orange and brown shirt only adds to her bright, cheery demeanor. It's a good sign.

"Wow, someone is really getting into the fall season," I compliment.

"I love the weather here. It's like it's snowing but in the form of leaves, if that makes sense."

"Of course, it does. Hey, we're going to have a picnic tomorrow. It'll be a bit chilly, but it's not supposed to rain. Want to join us?"

"Sure," she says in her straightforward way.

"Is this Violet?" I ask. The cat freely comes out to greet me. Leira picks her up in a hurry and frantically looks around outside.

"Sorry, she likes to dart out, and I'm afraid she won't come back."

"Animals are pretty loyal to the person who feeds them."

"Tell me about it," she grumbles. She does something unexpected: she laughs. It's not a small laugh, either. It's a laugh where she throws her head back while keeping hold of the grey tabby.

"I'm not sure what that's about, but seeing you happy is nice. No need to bring anything. I make quite the picnic spread. You just need to bring yourself and a jacket."

***

We leave around noon the next day with Adrienne and Leira in the backseat, acting like school girls. They are both school girls, but you'd never know by listening to them that Leira is

257

a decade older than Adrienne.

"See, you put your hands like this, flip it over, and look what happens." Adrienne wiggles her fingers.

"Cool!" Leira says, copying her. Adrienne keeps them both busy on our fifteen-minute drive, showing Leira her playground tricks. Patrick glances at me with a big smile, showing he's also enjoying the chatter.

We set up at the park next to the lake, bundled in our thick jackets. The sun can only do so much to warm us this time of year. Still, it's not freezing, and the fresh air does wonders for freeing my spirit.

"I like Leira," Patrick states with his hands on his hips as he watches her giving Adrienne a piggyback ride in the field next to the lake.

"Me too."

"You should see if she's free for the holidays. It doesn't seem like she belongs to anyone. You know?"

"Yeah, I get that feeling too." I flash on the sign I saw the other day getting coffee. With Leira being so private, I've put the brakes on telling Patrick. "She's pretty much a closed door."

"She'll come around. You have a way about you that makes people tell you their secrets."

"I've never had to work so hard to get someone to trust me," I say, spreading the blanket. Patrick comes up behind me and circles his arms around my middle.

"So, are we going to celebrate the holidays this year?" he whispers.

I stay quiet for a minute, hating this topic. I used to love Christmas and all that went with it. Nana used to go with it. Still, I no longer want to ruin everyone's holidays. "I think so," I answer quietly.

"I know two little girls who would love it." I follow his gaze. He's right, of course. Leira might help me get rid of my holiday funk.

We aren't the only people admiring the beautiful day and surroundings, but it isn't crowded. A noisy, old car pulls into the lot off to the left of us. Leira freezes and spins her and Adrienne toward the noise. She pauses for a moment and watches a woman and man get out before she continues to play. The sign with her picture has shed light on some of her secrets. I'd be guarded, too, if someone was looking for me.

I pull my blue crochet bag out and adjust Chuggers on my lap to have space for my current project. I continue working on my fourth witch blanket that I started yesterday. I've gotten a lot of praise for these blankets and more orders than I have been able to fill.

"I had to put my 'out of stock' sign up on my Etsy shop for these."

"How much do you charge for those again?" Patrick asks.

"I raised the price to forty-five. And look at these adorable little ghosties. I've made almost fifty of these, raised my price to twenty, and people are still eating them up."

"Wow! That's awesome, Lisa."

"Wait… darn it!" I say when I realize I've messed up. I start yanking the yarn out when Leira and Adrienne join me.

"What's wrong, mommy?"

"Oh, I messed up again." I've been spending every extra minute crocheting my Etsy requests, going faster than I should. I've put a two-week lead time for everything, just in case I get bombarded with orders, which I realize is happening. If I don't get going, some people who put their requests in might get their items after Halloween, which is an unwelcome stressor.

"Hey, that's Darren over there. I'll be right back," Patrick says, hopping up.

"I wish I was an octopus," I say.

"Maybe I can help," Adrienne says. She holds her hands out to take the project from me. I agree and hand it over. Adrienne's fingers are small but move almost the same in the yarn.

"Well, look at you. Those knots are turning out perfectly!" I look at Leira, who is just as surprised as I am. "She gets that from me," I say proudly. Leira laughs and watches as Adrienne works.

"Want to learn?" Adrienne asks.

Leira's face scrunches up. "I've tried and don't think I have the crocheting thumb. Or, whatever you call it."

"I happen to have another couple of hooks in my bag and look, even an extra bowl to keep everything organized," I laugh. "We can all work together." I give a tutorial to the girls, who dote on my tips and soak up my words. Leira fumbles a few times but doesn't give up. Soon, we are all wiggling our fingers and hands into colorful masterpieces.

"What's the bowl for?" Leira asks.

"It keeps the yarn from tangling," Adrienne answers. "My mom likes to wind the skeins into balls, and the bowl helps. Right, mommy?"

I nod with a feeling of pride overcoming me. "I think Adrienne could take over my channel. At this rate, you two might be able to help fill a few of my orders!"

"What's going on here?" Patrick asks when he returns.

"I've multiplied my empire," I reply with a grandiose voice.

"I can see that. You three keep at it, and I'll get lunch ready," Patrick says, digging into our picnic basket. His spirits have considerably increased since our discussion this morning. Or, maybe it was the time between the sheets.

"I made something to go with lunch!" Leira says, popping up and running to the truck. The three of us stay behind and look at one another in surprise. Leira returns quickly and pulls a container out of a black bag. She takes the cover off to reveal chocolate chip cookie bars. "They're fresh from the oven this morning," she says with quiet proudness.

"Yummy!" Adrienne shouts.

"She's a keeper," Patrick says.

"I agree," I say, smiling at the girl blossoming before my eyes.

We enjoy our club sandwiches, homemade potato salad, and a variety of fruits. Leira dishes out her dessert to our oohs and awes of approval.

"This is delicious," Patrick says with his mouth full as he lays back. He twirls a lock of my hair between his fingers, and just like that, after weeks of tension, I know we are okay.

I settle back into my project while the girls wander around the outskirts of our picnic blanket. I'm living my best life, sitting with my project resting on my lap, watching the girls play. I'm piecing together my dreams with every knot of color I add. A cool breeze rustles my hair and the color-changing leaves above us. The sound adds to the waves lapping at the beach nearby. It's all working out better than I had imagined.

Ding! *Lisa, Hal said he met with you but he won't say what you talked about. I hope it wasn't about me. All I want to do is help you get a job.*

My mother is the only thing that's not working out, as always. How am I going to convince her that I am capable of running my own life? Confronting her has never been my strong suit, but I know it's necessary for me to break free from her hold. It means Adrienne won't have her grandma around as much, but maybe we can work something out.

I watch as Adrienne pops up and starts on a quest for bugs. She catches one and throws it into the air. "Fly, buggies!" she exclaims with her arms up.

"Um, honey, those bugs don't have wings," Patrick says. Adrienne covers her mouth in shock before crouching to check if the bugs are okay. Leira and I look at each other, and both start cracking up.

"Uh oh, looks like Chuggers is getting rid of his breakfast," I say, grabbing a baggie. Adrienne and Leira follow, playing tag along the way.

Leira makes it there before us and freezes when she gets to Chuggers. "Oh my gosh! What's happening here? Those bugs are rolling the poop away!"

"Those are dung beetles," Adrienne says with a giggle. "Isn't it gross?"

"I've never seen such a thing. Look at them go!" Leira lowers herself to look at them more closely before backing up quickly. "They're all over! They literally popped out of the ground. They're rolling the poop everywhere!"

"What in the heck are you guys doing over here?" Patrick asks, joining us.

"Dung beetles," I reply.

"Yeah, they're pretty gross. Tyler just sent me a text asking if I can help him with a car project he's working on tonight, and then we might play some poker. Do you mind if I go?"

I look at Adrienne and Leira with a plan for the evening formulating. "Not at all. I have two friends who might be up for a night of movies and crocheting."

Chapter 25 Leira

Dangerous Secrets

It's been a tie for which event has won so far for being the most fun: Lisa's birthday party or the entirety of our picnic day. It's just an hour into our girl's night, and I'm by far having the most fun I've ever had. We start with the music cranked up and the three of us putting together another 'snacky dinner,' as Lisa calls it. We gather our crocheting projects, pick out a movie, and find a spot on the couches.

Lisa has an idea of filming a video for her channel, which flicks my radar to full blast. She doesn't put Adrienne on camera, which I hone in on like bees to honey. "I'm going to be in Adrienne's category and not be in the frame." I bring with this statement an edge like I hate being on camera, which isn't really fake. I don't care how small Lisa's channel is or how much of a long shot it is for the dads to find it. I can't risk being seen.

"No problem. I'll just point it at our hands. Do you mind saying that you're a beginner?"

I hesitate. I still don't favor this compromise but don't want to call attention to my stance. "Sure." The chances of the dads finding this video are slim, but I don't want to take any chances.

"Have I told you how much my channel has grown? I'm up to six hundred and fifty subscribers!"

"Lisa, that's great!"

"It is. I've gotten a lot of orders too from Etsy, but unfortunately a couple of negative reviews," she says, her face dropping. "Some of my threads pulled out. One woman said her son kept pulling on a string."

"I would think that would unravel anything eventually," I comment with an obvious tone.

"True." She sits quietly for a moment, deflated with this topic.

I don't have experience in this area, but I want to help her all the same. "Maybe the bad critique will just make you double check some things. Maybe you need to tug at your knots one more time." I add a shrug to signal that this isn't that big of a deal.

Lisa nods. "I spy a video with that theme." My eyebrows come together in confusion, so she continues. "Most of my videos are about real-life topics, as you know. Hey! Did I tell you? I've started in the life coaching business. It's going really well."

"That's cool. Hey, what are you wearing there, Munchkin?" I ask Adrienne when she comes out of her room.

This is as comfortable as I've ever been around anyone. I don't have to worry about saying anything wrong. I don't have to worry about how I'm sitting or standing or any of that. Lisa and Adrienne genuinely seem to enjoy having me around.

"My fuzzy pajamas match Chuggers." She holds her hands down to the dog, who matches her red and green outfit.

"Getting ready for Christmas, huh?"

"It's quite a big deal around here," Adrienne comments.

Once again, Lisa's posture shrugs for a moment.

"Nana used to decorate when the first leaves would start changing colors. She would start early in September and put out a decoration a day." Her voice is in that far-off place as she remembers. "We'd wake up and dancing Santa would be out or the mini tree."

"That sounds fun. We never did anything for Christmas," I say with a shrug. Lisa's head slants as if she's feeling sorry for me. "You should do that this year; take a decoration out a day." I'm not afraid to say this. Lisa was receptive to my suggestions to keep her traditions going the last time we talked about her grandma.

"It's a good thought," she says with a smile. "No more excuses. If ifs and buts were candies and nuts…"

Adrienne and Lisa look at each other and finish together. "We'd all have a merry Christmas." They laugh, but I have no idea what they're talking about.

"I have no idea what that means," I comment, trying to remember the saying so I can look it up later.

"It means everyone has excuses," Lisa says with certainty. It seems to be the clencher, the comment that gives her sadness the boot. "I have a whole lineup of items I want to crochet this season!" she says with pep.

"My birthday starts the holidays," Adrienne says.

"Oh?" I ask with interest. I remember us sharing the same birthstone, and I'm curious when hers is.

"Yup. It's November nineteenth." I reel back, unsure if I should say something. "What?"

"That's my birthday, too," I say quietly. I've never had anyone I've connected with. Since being in Garden Valley, I've made a couple of friends. Lisa and her family have taken me into their home, and if I'd stop doubting myself, I'd realize how into me Jordan is. This birthday coincidence with Adrienne is a perfect reminder of how in tune I am with this town and the amazing people here.

Lisa and Adrienne erupt in a celebration of hoots and dances. Chuggers joins in, turning in circles in his tutu pajamas. These people are crazy… and I love it.

"We can have our party together!" Adrienne yells.

"No, that's okay," I say, waving it off.

"We'll have some type of party for Adrienne. We can make it a double party. It's okay to come out of that box. Come on, it's fun out here!"

Even without looking at myself, I feel my eyes grow. "Nope, I'm fine in here." We go through another round of laughter before I blurt my next thought. "Don't be expecting me to light my farts on fire." Lisa and Adrienne pause. For a second, I think I've overstepped my boundaries since this caused more problems with Lisa and her mom. Lisa leans back and howls with laughter.

"Oh my gosh, that's hilarious," she says. "Hey, it's your 'golden birthday.'"

"My what?" I ask, looking at her like she's crazy.

"You know when you turn your age on the date of your birthday. Won't you be turning nineteen on the nineteenth?"

"Oh yeah, I guess so," I shrug as if this isn't a big deal. And it isn't. None of my birthdays have ever been on anyone's radar except for the celebration cookie in the lunchroom at school.

Adrienne excuses herself to her room for a toy or something.

"This sure is a nice change from homework," I say, weaving my fingers in my easy scarf project full of soft pastels.

"How's school going?" Lisa asks.

"It's okay. Psychology is very revealing." This statement actually tells more in itself than I've wanted.

"How so?"

I shrug, hoping she'll brush it off. "We're in early childhood development, you know, the kid stuff where our parents screw us up." I laugh this off, hoping she won't dig deeper.

"I had a lot to deal with when I was a kid, too." She could have left that last word out. Since she said it, I know she suspects there's more to my story than a lack of Christmas decorations. "My mother expected perfection, and then she had me." Lisa laughs, the perfect example of how to deal with these issues as an adult. I'm glad she has been telling me about her upbringing. It shows that she's gotten past it. "It was hard growing up, but I'm an adult now. I still have to deal with my family nagging me, but you were right the other day; it's not like they're following me around."

I stay quiet, hoping the dads aren't trying to find me. I'm done with them and that life. I know I'll have to face them one day, but I hope it isn't anytime soon.

"I, too, found myself in the pages of my psychology books. I think that's why I was drawn to it so much. I wanted to help others who had to deal with the same thing but may not have the tools to escape it like I did."

These are the exact words that brought me to the psychology class. "How *did* you get out of it? Mentally, I mean. It's not like you don't see your family anymore."

Lisa thinks for a second before answering. "I knew I would get away one day. We grow up and move away, and then our past gets further away. As the intensity of the memories fade, we can build our own lives. We can make our own decisions and add good memories to our memory bank.

We learn and grow, too. Do we repeat the cycle of dysfunction and, heaven forbid, abuse? Or do we create our own path and make something of ourselves?"

It's more profound than I could have put it. It's not a surprise; I'm only eighteen. "That should be in one of my textbooks."

"Yes, it should," Lisa says with a firm nod.

The crackle of the fire soothes us into silence. Adrienne's faint voice of her playing drifts from her room. It's more than comforting; it's homey and safe, qualities I've never experienced.

"Looks like she got distracted," I say quietly with a smile. It was like that for me, playing by myself in my room. I don't want to dive into it, but I can't help myself. "The dads weren't necessarily mean, but they never played with me, not even once. They were too busy with their business.'" I say with air quotes that hopefully show how loose this term is without me giving it away. "I'd stay in my room with my dolls and toys. I only had a couple, but that's all I needed. I honestly didn't mind playing by myself."

Lisa looks between me and the blanket she is working on. I'm glad she hasn't focused completely on me. It makes it much easier to continue with my talk.

"It would have been nice to have someone care about me. To have someone hold me during a thunderstorm or brush my hair before school." A tear escapes, but I don't care. "But I'm growing up now," I say with a slow nod, reiterating Lisa's advice about moving on.

"It doesn't mean you shouldn't work through your feelings though, Leira. I tried that approach, wanting to forget what my mother put me through with her incessant need for me to be perfect. Or, I'd dwell on the past, hoping it would change. It won't," she says, shaking her head. "We're given our pasts for a reason. We can learn from them, grow as humans, and maybe we're even strong enough to help others in a similar situation. I'll always be here to listen." She reaches across the couch and gives my forearm a squeeze. I don't flinch away from her touch but allow the calming effect to seep into me.

I nod with a defiant smile on my lips.

"Hey, I didn't mean to intrude on your personal life the other day, about you and Jordan. When I was sixteen, I got involved with a guy… and got pregnant." I gasp, and my eyes flicker to Adrienne's room. Doing some quick math would mean Lisa would have another kid about my age. "I don't have the best reproductive organs and lost the baby after a few weeks. But the initial freak-out was enough to shake me straight. Anyway, that's where my advice was coming from. I've known Jordan for a long time, and he's a great guy. I'm happy you're friends."

It makes sense now that she was just looking out for me instead of setting a boyfriend rule. "I'm sorry for my attitude that day. I'm not used to someone looking out for me like that. I'm here and free and… want to create my own rules."

"I'm definitely not trying to set rules for you!" she says. "I just wish someone had told me their own preggo story to knock some sense in me. You know?" I connect my eyes with her and give a nod of understanding. Adrienne saunters into the room with a silly wiggle that we laugh about. "There's my miracle child," Lisa says, wrapping the little girl in a hug.

"Mommy, how do you spell Christmas?"

"C-h-r-i-s-t," Lisa starts.

"No, *Christmas*," Adrienne says with emphasis.

"That is how you spell it, sweetie," Lisa laughs. "The 'h'

is silent."

"Well, I know what I want for Christmas," Adrienne says with a goofy tone while pronouncing the 'ch.' She shows Lisa and me a dollhouse she's brought up on her device.

"A dollhouse, huh? This is a hundred and fifty dollars! It's a good thing you can't buy anything on this device."

Adrienne looks at Lisa with a knowing smile. "Don't worry, if it's from Santa… it's free."

Lisa and I exchange and look, each struggling to keep another laugh.

The doorbell rings out through the house, causing me to stir. Lisa pops up to answer it before I ask her to ignore it.

"Can I help you?" Lisa asks someone beyond the door.

"Have you seen my cat?" It's a voice and demand that sounds familiar. My stomach goes wild with nerves as I await Lisa's response. I hope she will be on my side.

"No, I'm sorry, Ms. Ryland, I haven't seen one around here. Which one are you looking for?"

"She's orange with white stripes," the woman answers.

I look at Adrienne with shock. My tensed shoulders sink in relief. This lady isn't after Violet!

"I'll keep my eye out," Lisa says before shutting the door. She comes back into the living room and looks at Adrienne before giving me a shrug. "It's not even the same cat."

"Thank you anyway. You told her you hadn't seen a cat before getting the description," I say, relief now swimming through me.

"Well, Violet has been neglected. She's in a good place now where she'll get the extra love and attention she needs."

I know she's not referring to the cat. Lisa has just proved she's on my side by standing up for me!

A few minutes later, she prepares her phone for a quick

video of Adrienne and me ticking away at our blanket. Thank goodness she keeps the camera pointed at our hands. It's fun to be on this side of the video. Lisa's a wiz at keeping the commentary interesting during the twenty minutes.

She finishes up and works on uploading the video. My phone dings with a text from Sarah, the girl from my psychology class. She's snapped a picture of her fish dinner and added a happy face. I send her a 'great job, looks delicious' text back. She has sent me a few texts, all happy and light like this. These texts are a big deal to me. I had Charlotte as a friend but kept her at a distance. I haven't given her updates on my life now, purposely wanting to leave her behind.

We laugh, eat, and crochet our way through Luca, an animated movie geared toward kids. I love it. Adrienne falls asleep towards the end, but Lisa and I finish it while working on our projects.

"Look how far I've gotten!" I say, holding my pink, green, and blue scarf up.

"That looks a whole heck of a lot better than my first scarf." I watch her fingers in awe, wondering if I'll ever be as skilled as her.

"Crocheting is your superpower," I say.

Lisa holds up her project with pride. "It's finally paying the bills! I never thought it'd be possible."

"Why not?" I ask, genuinely wanting to hear her answer.

"I guess because it was just a hobby. But now... now I'm building this community and it feels so much better than I thought it would. I'm able to share this love of crocheting with the world and give some advice on the way."

I nod, liking how Lisa's goal isn't just to make money or have a million subscribers. She truly wants to help people.

I watch the last bit of the movie, enjoying the good vibes

from the ending. "I like how Luca's parents ended up being on his side."

Lisa purses her lips in thought. "Like my mother will come around," she says with irritation.

I don't want to break the news to her, but I feel like we can go back and forth with our advice now. "What if she doesn't?" I say with a shrug. "I'm almost nineteen and realized the dads would never come around when I was Adrienne's age. Sorry, that's kind of…"

"No," she says, shaking her head like she did the last time I had something hard to tell her. "You've hit the nail on the head yet again. Maybe if I keep this in mind, I'll keep my hopes grounded instead of letting them take flight."

"Like maybe you shouldn't try so damned hard."

"Bingo!" she says.

Lisa heads off to the bathroom and my phone dings again. I glance at it and become rigid when I see Charlotte's name. She has only sent me one text saying she hopes I'm okay.

I might have messed up, she says. *Your dads came by looking for you today. I told them about dropping you off at the bus station. They wanted to know what day and time you were there, where you went, and asked all kinds of questions. They were really persistent and kind of scary. You don't think they can trace back to that day and find out where you went, do you?*

Crap.

I sink into the couch, keeping my gaze on the fireplace. Lisa's house has become a place of safety for me, much more than my house growing up was. It seems like my little haven of freedom might have come to an end.

Chapter 26 Leira

A Date to Remember

After many texts and a couple of voicemails from Jordan, I finally accepted his invitation for a date. The last time we were together was tense, but you've got to hand it to the guy—he doesn't give up easily.

It's the first date I've been on, and I'm nervous as hell. I can't tell if this is because I feel the dads' presence getting closer or from the date itself. Lisa and Adrienne are at my place, helping me pick out the proper outfit and hairdo to match. It's all fun for them while I've resorted to mulling over everything that can possibly go wrong tonight.

"This is dumb to dress up. Jordan has seen me in jeans and a shirt every day. Why does he need to see me with makeup and a skirt?"

"Because you need the state of mind that it puts you in," Lisa informs. I'm relieved that she's helping me. After our talk the other night about her getting pregnant in her teens, I no longer feel like she's against me seeing Jordan.

"I don't know why Jordan wants to go out with me anyway. I'm so high maintenance."

"Oh, you are not," Lisa says, but I figure she knows this isn't true since I told her more of my story. I don't know if she's figured out that I'm a runaway.

"Listen," I say after ensuring that Adrienne is playing with Violet out of earshot. "Thanks for taking me in. It's meant a lot to me. If something happens to me… just make sure Adrienne knows I really liked her friendship."

"Hey, what's going to happen? Are you okay?" I feel bad for putting my issues on her. I shouldn't have even left home and gotten my hopes up. In my efforts to be independent, I've gotten people to like and even care about me.

I smile, but it's a weak one. "I'm fine. I just wanted to say thank you."

I'm glad she doesn't push, even if her expression is filled with worry. If I go down this road, I'll be late for my date.

I have a date.

With Jordan.

This should be interesting.

∗∗∗

I'm glad it's a slow ushering to our table so I can observe the restaurant. It's all new, from the low lighting to the cloth coverings and perfectly laid out place settings on the tables. I take it all in as a cat does to its new surroundings. Violet didn't even seem this nervous the first time she was in The Hideout. Here I am, formulating an escape plan of how I can hide under the table or behind a plant.

We sit, get our water, and then… what?

"Cloth napkins," I say, trying to be fun by running my hands over the fabric. I pick up a corner of the dark red fabric. I've been to fancy hotels with the dads before when they were at conventions, but I was mainly sequestered to our room, only to order room service.

274

My napkin unravels, releasing my silverware. It clings together as it crashes on the table, sending a few people looking my way. It's not like I haven't seen cloth napkins and nice restaurants in movies before, but watching something and experiencing it firsthand are two completely different things.

Real smooth, Ariel.

I freeze at the thought of my old name, my real name. Why do I keep doing this? I don't care if the dads are searching for me; that person is gone.

A look at Jordan shows him smiling that big, toothy grin. Great, I've amused him with my napkin trick. It makes me wonder if he's brought other girls here on a Friday night. Girls like Mia.

"What looks good?" he asks. My mouth waters at the thought of a complete dinner. I feel like I haven't eaten in months. The only meals that stand out since I've been here are the ones I've had with Lisa, and I've only allowed myself to crash their dinners once or twice a week.

Food has always been plain until I came to Garden Valley. Up until now, I've mainly lived on granola bars and school lunches. A few days in culinary class hasn't prepared me for reading the menu, which seems like it was written in a foreign language.

"You look like you're deep in thought," Jordan says.

"I just don't know what to have." I try not to panic. I don't know the items on the menu. Marsala? What the hell is a caper? Adrienne is probably better versed than I am in the food department.

The waiter comes over, introduces himself as if he will be our best friend forever, and asks for our drink order.

"What kind of pop do you have?" I ask quietly. I

remember why I haven't gone out to dinner: it means certain conversations with others.

"Pop?" the guy who isn't much older than me asks.

"Um, yeah," I say, looking at Jordan for help. "Drinks?"

"Soda?" the waiter asks. I nod, and he finally gets the gist. He takes our orders and eventually goes away. I stick to the most basic thing on the menu, keeping my question of why it takes a whole paragraph to describe chicken and potatoes.

"Jeez, it's like we're on a different planet," I mutter when the waiter leaves after asking me twenty questions about my order. Jordan laughs.

"I don't think our rural area uses that word for soda."

"I hate that word: 'soda.' It's like saying sofa instead of couch, or sneaker instead of tennis shoe." He shakes his head with a chuckle, and I bite my bottom lip.

Jordan does a good job filling in the gaps of silence before they become awkward. Still, self-consciousness is coursing from head to toe as we sit across from each other. I am his focal point. Obviously, I'm his focal point. I'm the only other person at his table!

I find safety with my small bag in my lap. My fingers fiddle with the contents inside, inadvertently gaining Jordan's attention.

"Whatcha got in there?" Jordan asks while leaning forward.

"Nothing," I answer quickly, trying to make my voice aloof enough to shove him off this road.

"Well, there's something in there. Otherwise, you wouldn't have it. Let me guess, there's a book."

"You've got me there," I agree, hoping he'll drop the subject.

"Please don't tell me you have a textbook in your bag?"

he teases.

"I don't have a textbook!" I blurt.

"Then what is it?"

"Oh look, food." I'm saved by the bread basket. I dig in with eagerness, hoping to sway his attention.

It works. Jordan adds a massive hunk of butter before shoving a whole piece in his mouth. I guess I was right about his big mouth being able to handle a lot. My worries fly away with my laughter. Here I am, worried about every step I take, and he's purposely displaying bad manners.

"What?" The words barely come through the bread that's filling his mouth.

"What do you mean, 'what?' That was, like, four of my bites."

"It loosenth ewe up, right?" he sputters. I giggle with my hand in front of my mouth. It takes him forever to chew through the bread with the hard crust. "That was a chore. I won't do that again," he says, massaging his jaw.

"I guess that's what you get for bad manners."

"Don't tell my mom. So, about this book in your bag." I give him a look that says, 'Are we really going back to this?'

"Jordan…"

"I just want to know what's in there."

"Why? Why is it such a big deal?" I pretend to be upset by the whole ordeal. He bumps the table as he reaches for my bag, making everything cling and clang. "Jordan, stop it!" I scold in a whisper, looking around to see if anyone noticed.

"Nope." He does it again, this time gaining looks from the people at the next table.

"Okay, I'll show you! Ugh." I slouch down dramatically. This is going to be the highlight of embarrassing moments for me. I pull the book out, wishing I could hide it under my napkin. On the cover is a woman in a red bra straddling a man. His bare chest lies underneath her. He sits halfway on his elbows, ready to take her open mouth in his.

Jordan snatches it from my fingers the second he's within reach. "Whoa! What's this?" he asks with amusement.

"It's not what I normally read!" He holds the book beside his head with the cover towards me, bobbing his eyebrows up and down.

"Does this guy look like me, or what?" he teases.

"I normally read superhero fiction, but I just snatched whatever was available from the library." It's not entirely true. Fantasy normally scratches my literary itch, but with Jordan's attention, I figured I needed to read about what the birds and bees are up to these days.

His look is full of doubt. "And this is what you came up with? Was it misplaced in the mystery section or something?"

"Ugh, this is awful," I say, lowering my head to rest in my hands.

Our food arrives before I can take the book back and shove it deep into my bag. Jordan raises his eyebrows and places the book face-up next to his water. I purse my lips with a half-smile and shake my head.

"You're awful!" I say, reaching across the table and forcefully taking the book back. "I'm going to throw this away now." Jordan laughs and digs into his food once it arrives. "Please don't tell me that steak is bite-sized."

He shakes his head with a smile that can't get any bigger. It's a vision I always want to remember.

No matter what happens.

This dampens my thoughts, throwing an unwanted kink in the night.

"What?" he asks with concern. "Does it not look good

to you?"

"No, it looks fine," I say, shaking my head.

"Something happened. You don't like it."

"I haven't even had any. It's just…" How do I stall here? These words are usually followed by the truth or bad news. Neither of these I'm going to share with him at this point. "I, uh, usually like my chicken with ketchup."

"It has gravy," Jordan says.

"It does?" I ask, eyeing my food. His laugh rings out again. I glance around our table and am thankful no one else notices his booming voice. It's one signal that shows how much he's enjoying this date.

"You're a kick." He holds his hand up, signaling the waiter to come over.

I hold the glass jar of ketchup over the plate when it comes a moment later. I shake it a few times without any results. I take a peek inside, and nothing is happening. I shift only my eyes to Jordan and lower my voice. "You're kidding, right?"

"Here," he says, putting his napkin on the table and coming to my side, bringing his wonderful masculine scent. "My mom uses this trick." He holds the jar in his right hand while tapping the end on his left index finger. In just a couple of taps, the ketchup is free.

I barely notice the magic trick. Jordan's side brushes against my shoulder the whole time. My entire body tingles in awareness, and I like it. I bask in the softness of his arm, of the sweet aroma of his soap. It's the opposite of the harshness that used to sting the insides of my nostrils from 'back then.' I resist the urge to rest my head on his side, leaning into him for extra comfort.

"Thanks," I say quietly when he sits back down.

"Don't mention it."

I dump a large pile of red condiments on my plate and eye the rest of my food. It looks good, but there's layer upon layer of flavor in a way that I've never seen.

"Now what's wrong?" Jordan asks with his chin resting on interlaced hands.

"Nothing." He gives me a look again like he doesn't believe me. I tell him to prevent a disaster like what happened with the book. "A lot is going on here," I say, waving my hand over my plate. "There's chicken and then some sort of gravy, mushrooms, and these green things. I know this one," I say, pointing to the white stuff. "Mashed potatoes." Jordan laughs and shakes his head.

"I had no idea you were so funny!" I squish my face, figuring I'll give Patrick and Lisa my leftovers. "Just try it. I think you'll like it."

"If you say so." I cut a piece of chicken and give it a lick before putting it in my mouth. The green things burst with a salty flavor of surprise. "Oh!" I chew faster, loving the mixture of chicken and gravy. "This is good!" I say, taking another bite.

"Probably shouldn't have dumped that much ketchup out, huh?"

"Oh, I'll use that for my mashed potatoes."

"What?" he asks flatly.

"It's what fries are dipped in, after all." I go about my business, flattening my potatoes before smearing the ketchup over the top. I trace a pattern over the top, cutting the mashed goodness into small cubes before taking a bite.

Jordan laughs yet again. "Is that something you're learning in culinary school?"

"Yes, every meal calls for a cup of ketchup. So, um, do

you know your major yet?”

“Oh yeah, nursing.”

“What?” I respond as if he’s pulling my leg.

Jordan chuckles while finishing his bite. “Being with Mom has made me realize that I like helping people. I want to work in a nursing home or something similar.”

“The jock wants to push wheelchairs. That would be very sweet.”

“Who says I’m a jock?” he asks, with that ever-present look of amusement. I look from left to right in embarrassment as I search for an answer. “I just like to play with the guys on the weekends. Our school is too small to have a formal team.”

“Oh,” I mumble. I should have noticed that. “I haven’t seen a nursing program at the school.”

“There isn’t one,” he sighs. “I’ll have to go to Eugene for my core classes, but I can still take my electives here. It’s only a forty-five-minute drive, so it’s not that big of a deal, but still, all that time in the car…”

“Maybe your textbooks will be on audio or something.”

“That’s a good tip,” he says, pointing his fork at me.

It’s the best date I’ve ever had. True, it’s the only date I’ve ever had. And, with any luck, it won’t be my last.

Chapter 27 Lisa

Stitching it Together

My mom sends me a text first thing with her daily reminder to get my shit together and go for more jobs. "I'm a life coach now, Mom," I say smugly to my phone. I don't dare tell her. I will eventually, but I want to sit with this successful transition for a while.

My first of two appointments today start in fifteen minutes. It's a Tuesday, and I'm snuggled in with my crochet project, listening to the rain, with Chuggers on my lap. My client from yesterday said she enjoyed talking with me and booked another appointment for Thursday. I asked Josh if this was okay, and he was thrilled.

I'm in the flow, and it feels great! I have clients, I'm getting three to six Etsy orders a day, and Patrick is off my back about nailing down a 'real' job. I've gotten two negative reviews, but I'm shrugging them off with a promise to double-check my work.

The only thing that feels off is Leira. Seeing her face on the poster only added to her mystery. She turned away when I was filming the video the other day as if she was scared. She has cracked herself open about as much as a book with a padlock. I don't know the true source of her worries. I feel a sense of urgency with this while at the same time having no idea how to help her more than I already am without scaring her away.

I take a crocheting break and check my subscriber count, which I've deemed my guilty pleasure.

"Almost nine hundred!" I throw my arms in the air in excitement. I check my 'watch time' for my channel, and it's over three thousand hours. "I'm almost there." I'm almost to the monetization mark, where they'll pay me for the views watched. I hold the phone to my chest, close my eyes, and say a prayer of thanks. I click on Zoom and see that my patient is already waiting.

"Hi," the woman named Alexandra says. I take note of the irritation in her voice. "You're late." I glance at the clock, and it's still five minutes until our appointment. I always wonder if I should point this out to people when they are in the wrong.

"Hello. Shall we start early?" I don't want to start our session on a negative note, but I also want to make sure she knows that I wasn't late. "I'm Lisa. It's nice to…"

"I thought I got one more meeting with Josh before he passed me on to you."

Uh oh. "Well, Josh added you to my appointment list this week. Can we give it a try?"

She slouches in her seat and sighs. "Here's the thing, I'm not good with change, and Josh knows that."

"How about this: if it doesn't work, we can talk to Josh." I'm using my serious voice now. I hate when people try to sugarcoat things, even when the topic isn't comfortable or in my favor.

"I guess."

"I don't blame you for not wanting to change. My life

turned upside-down a few weeks ago, and I did not take it well." I cross my hands like an umpire does when a player makes it safe to a base.

"What happened?" Alexandra asks. Her engagement with this question is good news. At least she didn't say, 'I don't care,' or bulldoze over me with more complaints.

"I got canned!" I shout. Alexandra's eyebrows shoot up in surprise, and I laugh in response. "At first, I was totally freaked out, but that eased. Like anything else, the more we get used to something, the less intense it gets. I started to love the extra time around the house. That quickly faded, and I had a hard time getting out of bed more than I'd like to admit. I let myself cry and get angry."

Alexandra is nodding now with eyes that show understanding. "That happens to me! I put all this energy into something, and then I crash. I hate it. I literally can't get out of bed. My doctor says I need more vitamin D, but really, how much can that help?"

"Actually, I was adding a couple of drops to my coffee in the morning, and then my doctor said, 'Lisa, you need to add ten to fifteen drops.'"

"Whoa, really? I think I'm in the same boat. I throw a pill in my mouth every now and then, but that's it."

"Seasonal Affective Disorder is real. I see you live north of me and probably get less sun than we do."

"As evidenced by…" Alexandra moves her computer camera to show a view of rain amongst a plethora of green grass and trees.

"Wow, that's beautiful outside."

"I hate the rain."

"And you live in Seattle?" I laugh and hope she doesn't take offense to my words.

"Yeah," she laughs back. "This is where my kids have landed with their spouses. My husband and I moved here from L.A. a couple months ago to be closer to them. I haven't settled in yet." I nod in understanding but stay quiet to give her the floor. She talks about her love for being outdoors and hiking, but since she moved to this area, she hasn't been able to enjoy any of those things. "I work remotely, so I'm kind of cooped up."

"Maybe there's something special you can do when it rains, like brew your favorite cup of coffee or tea and have a snuggly blanket on your lap. Here's the one I'm in the middle of now." I hold up my latest creation before plopping it square on my legs.

"That's beautiful! Are you making that?"

"It's my side gig, what gets me all excited to do in a day. What is something you have that's similar? You seem athletic, so maybe you can meet people at a gym." She sticks her tongue out in dislike of this suggestion. "Or maybe not," I say quickly in joking. "You're in a big city, so I'm sure there are rock climbing groups, there's swimming or…"

"I haven't gotten back into swimming, but I should." I nod to her comment. "It's funny, I've been meaning to."

"Sometimes, even us adults need someone to tell us to do what we know we should be doing. Unless it's my mother telling me. I'll just do the opposite of what she says." Alexandra laughs, and I know I've won her over.

Overall, the appointment is successful, with Alexandra agreeing to meet with me again next week. Her file shows she feels trapped by her husband's house rules. I plan to dive into that with her, having experience with this.

I stretch my legs on a walk before deciding to make another batch of Halloween videos. I've relinquished to the calling of ideas when they come to me like this, sometimes doing five at a time. I've figured out how to schedule my videos, which has helped my daily flow. I'm going to open with live rain noises and footage outside and then have talking points similar to the ones I gave Alexandra. I hit upload thirty minutes later and still have a few minutes before my next appointment.

I sit with the ease of what my life has become. Even if my mother and family aren't proud of my accomplishments, I am. Still, as much as I hate to admit it, I crave their acceptance. I don't know how or if I'll ever get it, but I want to at least try.

With a few minutes to spare, I hit record yet again for a short for YouTube that I will upload. "You know, sometimes we become something other than our family intended. Or something entirely different than we expected. All that matters is if *you* are happy at this moment. If you like where you are, but it's a hundred miles from where you thought you'd be… in my book, that's a success."

I'm good with this video, believing my words as the truth. I'm settling into these new roles I've created for myself and am happy.

After my next appointment, I pick Adrienne up with a sense of fulfillment today. I surprise her with a trip to the fabric store to gather supplies for her Halloween costume. We've sketched out her fairy princess dress and need to get started since the clock is ticking down with only a week and a half until Halloween.

"Leira!" Adrienne sprints across the store and practically launches herself into Leira's arms. "We're getting my costume fabric today and will start on it tonight. Want to come help?"

"Sure, Munchkin," Leira answers. It's a simple answer,

and one that brightens our day.

***

I'm a total fan of all things creeping and crawling during this season. This year, I've shared my joy for this holiday with my community of fans, who have commented like crazy on my channel. The night of Halloween is rainy, so we opt for driving to a few places before going downtown to beg for treats.

Downtown is like a party. A new Top Gun movie just came out, and Ted in town came up with the cleverest costume of the night. He sits on a motorized skateboard with a painted cardboard around him to look like a jet plane. The soundtrack from the movie blares from unseen speakers. He makes his rounds and we hear the music before we see him come around the block. The people on the street hoot and holler in praise when he 'flies' by. It's all fun and connects everyone who is here tonight.

We are in the crowd when we run into Leira, who is out with friends.

"Come with us, Leira!" Adrienne begs her new friend.

"You don't have to if you're having fun with your friends."

"I want to come with you!" Leira's expression borders terror, one I haven't seen on her before.

"Are you okay?" Leira clutches my arm, which is entirely off for her. She looks around us wildly. "I don't like crowds; this one is spooky. Everyone is dressed as something different." A kid dressed in a simple skeleton costume walks our way, and she grips my arm harder.

"Haven't you ever been out for Trick-or-Treating

before?" I ask.

"Hey, Leira, there you are," Jordan says from behind us. Leira once again leans in closer to me, a clear indication of my role.

"Hey, Jordan. We're kidnapping Leira for the rest of the night if you don't mind," I say, stepping in to defend her. Jordan's face falls, but he graciously accepts the change of plans.

"That's fine. I should check on my mom. She loves passing out candy but doesn't know when to stop. I'll send you a text, okay?" Jordan says, looking worriedly at Leira.

She nods and pulls on my arm to get us to walk again. "Adrienne is up there! We need to catch up to her!" she says with urgency.

"Okay, she's fine. I've kept my eye on her."

"There are so many people around her. She could get lost!"

It's not a voice to argue with. I quicken my pace, and within five seconds, we are right behind Adrienne and her crowd of friends. "Are you okay? Did Jordan do something?"

"No." She shakes her head with enough conviction for me to believe her. "I thought tonight would be fun, but I don't like this. Everyone looks like they could be… it's just scary."

"That's fair. Adrienne usually poops out after two hours, and we're almost to that mark."

"Good," she says, keeping her eyes on the people walking by.

"We have Adrienne's birthday party planned for the weekend after next. Would you like to invite a couple of friends?" I ask to try and distract her. "It's going to be cake and ice cream at the house, maybe a couple of games."

It doesn't do the trick to ease Leira's grip. "Okay, fine,"

she says with a tense nod.

We get to our last shop at the end of the street, with Adrienne luckily slowing down. This store always has signs out front, but one I get a glimpse of has me doing a double-take. It's the same as the one I saw in Eugene with Leira's picture plastered on the front.

It's unmistakable, mainly because I've seen it before, Leira in dark shades and black lipstick. Leira may have a right to fear the monsters. It seems hers have made it to our town.

***

I've vowed to enjoy the holidays this year and start with the red and green decorations the day after Halloween. I'm here for Adrienne, smiling and excited with her, but my mind is focused on Leira.

The face of the missing person poster has been seared into my memory. There she was, jet-black hair, gobs of black makeup, and not a hint of a smile. What had she gone through to make her so unhappy to run away? I've already concluded that she's a runaway. Why would she run to Garden Valley?

The picture only fueled more questions. I figured she was a runaway. I suspect I've played a part in her leaving wherever she was. She's said a couple of times that she is grateful she found my channel and found me.

"What's going on here?" Leira asks, freely coming in through the sliding door. This morning, I texted her that our house was about to explode with red, green, silver, and gold, and she should join us.

"It's our weird family tradition. The day after Halloween is sort of a holiday for us. Want to join in?"

"What are you doing?" she asks in complete confusion.

"We're decorating for Christmas, Leira. Come on!" Adrienne pulls her into the guest room, overflowing with our Christmas boxes.

"Lisa, did you make these trees?" Leira asks, her voice full of amazement.

"Mommy made everything in here," Adrienne answers.

"What can I say? It's a yarny Christmas," I joke.

I study Leira's face, trying to click the final pieces of her scattered story puzzle. Who put those pictures up? Are they in town now? Is she in danger of these people? It makes me wonder if the cash she had when she first got here was stolen. I toy with the idea of telling Patrick, wondering if he should be on guard for any trouble coming our way. I've listened to my gut, allowing it to lie dormant until now. I've put my intuition on speed dial, awaiting the slightest tingles to throw me into action.

Leira is completely flabbergasted by the number of decorations we have staged in the guest room. "You put *all* this around the house?" she asks again.

"And even more outside. That hedge that runs the length of the long driveway gets filled with lights, and we decorate everything out there to the hilt." My grandma's memory is all around me. I focus on making this a memorable event for them, wondering what kind of advice Nana would give me about Leira. What if she comes from a good family? What if her mom and dad are frantically searching for their little girl?

Wait a minute, what am I talking about? Didn't Nana take me in when I had enough of living with my parents? I didn't have a bad upbringing, per se, and I still needed someone to rescue me. Nana was there for me, telling my mom to back off and give me space. My parents came for me one night, thinking I would give up and willingly go with them. If Leira had a good home life, someone would have already come for her. Is that sort of stand-off going to happen with Leira and whoever put the posters up? I think about the other night when I freely opened the front door to the neighborhood cat lady, wondering if I'll get a surprise visit from Leira's parents.

I remember that night when Nana stood between my parents and me. She wouldn't let them in the house. She wouldn't even let them talk to me.

Lisa is not going home with you. She's going to college here. She's safe and happy. She's an adult now, and it's time you let her live her life.

I'm more than willing to repeat this lecture to defend Leira. I decide to stand by her if it comes to that.

Leira examines every decoration as if this is the first time she's ever decorated for the holidays. For all I know, it is. My heart breaks when thinking about what she's gone through, nixing the idea of her two successful parents leaving their house with the white picket fence to look for her. Something tells me that picture is far from the one she's running from.

Watching Leira with Adrienne gives me pure joy. She laughs and smiles more than any other time I've seen her. In my book, Leira will stay, and I'll fight whatever bullies are out there for her.

Chapter 28 Leira

You Can Only Run So Much

I run to my next class with my bag over my head, shielding me from the blanket of rain crashing on the town. I've never seen as much rain as I have in Garden Valley. I'm kicking myself for not buying an umbrella the last time I worked. I shake my wet jacket off and plop my bag down when I get to the culinary class. So far, we haven't cooked much, mainly learning the theory of cooking with a splash of actual cooking and tasting here and there. I've loved all of it, the recipes and mixing and tasting new flavors. Even if I don't go into this as a career, the lessons I've learned have been invaluable.

I have a couple of minutes before class, so I scan a few lines of my new adventure book.

"Has the rain got you down?" Sarah asks with her sweet, round cheeks. I hadn't noticed that she had sat down next to me. It's why I read, to tune everything else out.

I sigh. "I have bangs!" I say with irritation, pointing to my forehead, which now shows a matted-down mess of hair. "I look like a drowned rat." Sarah's laugh fuels my point, but I back down. It's not like it's her fault it's raining.

"You should keep a clip in your bag or a headband to pull

your bangs back. Here's I think I have one," she says, rummaging in her bag. "Yup! Here you go."

"Good idea," I say, clipping my bangs back. "Does it always rain here this much?"

"This time of year, it does. You can't complain about the green if you don't want to pay for it with some wetness. That's what my mom says."

So far, our friendship consists of these moments before class when we chat, coupled with a few texts here and there. It's enough to realize that I like Sarah.

I've made friends in the short time I've been in Garden Valley. It's only a handful, but much more than I had before. I didn't have to use smoke and mirrors or twenty-dollar bills either. I was myself, and that was enough.

"So, I'm having a small birthday party. Lisa's having one for Adrienne, and since hers is the same day as mine, I'm piggybacking. You don't have to come. I just..."

"Sure. When is it?" Sarah asks like it's no big deal.

"Saturday," I reply in surprise. "It's going to be a little girlish."

"Oh, I hope so! My best parties were from when I was younger than thirteen. Once my friends grew up, all they wanted to do was those creepy Ouija board things."

"Oh, okay, good!" I go through the rest of the class feeling elated.

Jordan is waiting by my truck when I'm done with class. I can't prevent the big smile that takes over my face as I approach him. "At least the sky isn't dumping buckets of water on us anymore." He laughs, and I must mentally keep my head from tilting to the side while I swoon inwardly.

"You look different without bangs. If you were Superwoman, you could use them as your disguise."

Little does he know this was exactly my plan. "I'll keep that in mind," I say. "Hey, um, Lisa's throwing a party for Adrienne and me on Saturday."

"I want to come!" he says, inviting himself.

"Sure. I've invited Sarah from my culinary class, too, just so you know."

"Yeah, she's okay." He looks at his watch dramatically before shifting just his eyes to me. My heart nearly stops. "I was going to see if you had time for a coffee, but now, it seems, I have birthday presents to buy." He's said these words about needing to leave, yet he steps closer to me.

Oh no, he wants a kiss! Except, he doesn't bend down to my level. He lifts his arms slowly, looking down at my face as if gauging my reaction. I shift my body toward him, allowing the right side of my face to rest on his chest.

I can't help but inhale to my fullest. He smells of soap and perhaps a spray of cologne or scented deodorant. My eyes close, allowing the goodness of this memory to warm me from the inside out. His arms weigh heavy on my shoulders, bringing a sense of the comfort I've wanted from him. I could get used to this. With the feeling that the dads will be here any minute, I don't think I'll be given that chance.

***

Luckily, no one at work knows it's my special day of the year. I certainly haven't told anyone. This day has never been special, which is why I can't wait for my first party.

On my way in to work I pass the post office, which sits to the right of the fabric store. A picture in the window stops me dead in my tracks. It takes only the blink of an eye to recognize my own face.

"No!" I say upon seeing the paper haphazardly taped to the window. I look around, expecting a crowd to form, connecting the girl in the picture to me. I pull on the door, but the post office is closed on the weekends. I resist the urge to tape a blank piece of paper over the missing person sign on the outside. This would more than likely bring even more attention to it. I'm forced to go to work, or else I'll be late.

I go through my shift in a daze. I glance at the door every few seconds to see if anyone is studying the picture. *My* picture. Does anyone pay attention to these signs? Would anyone recognize me anyway?

I look over my shoulder and jump at every loud sound. Even a man taking his keys out of his pocket makes me flinch. After my bathroom break, I wash my hands and study myself in the mirror. I breathe a little easier when I don't recognize the reflection as the same girl in the picture. It's an old one from when I was a sophomore in high school. My hair was dark, I didn't have bangs, and it was during a phase when I caked black makeup on.

This was part of my ultimate plan. I wore that look for years, hoping to change it to what stares back at me now. I wanted people 'back then' to get used to how I looked so they wouldn't recognize me when I switched to how I look now. My life is entirely different, not just my look.

I throw the damp paper towel away with defiance that even if the dads do find me, I'll fight for this life I've created for myself.

I finish my shift and walk past the picture with unease. I cannot shake all the worry that has come to my day. Even with the determination to stay in Garden Valley, I still need to be on guard. I'm quite puny, without enhanced muscles or the power to run as fast as lightning. I don't think the dads will hurt me, but they'll continue their search until they get what they want, and right now, that's me being back home.

My eyes dart around the road on my drive home with the feeling that one of them will jump out of the bushes or drive by in their dirty Plymouth. I allow the safety of Lisa's place to overcome me when I pull in. Adrienne rushes out to greet me with a hug.

"Hey there, birthday girl!" I say, looking around the yard. I usher her inside, hoping that I haven't brought harm to this little girl who has been a savior in my life. I walk through the door and jump at the yelling of 'happy birthday' shouted at me.

Lisa smiles and rushes to me. "I'm sorry. I know we were supposed to have the party in an hour. Jordan, Sarah, and Adrienne insisted on making it a 'surprise.' Are you okay?"

She looks at me with an expression of worry that matches how I feel inside. She's on to me and my secret. Lisa has been texting me a few times daily, asking mundane questions requiring a response. I know it's to check on me, and I'm grateful for this. At least someone will know when I go missing.

I look around the room, forcing a smile and a thank you from my lips. I'm relieved Patrick and Jordan are here, but their innocence is probably not a match for Phil and Gary. I take my coat off by the front door and nonchalantly lock it before joining the party.

"What do we do first?" I ask Adrienne, who is glued to my side.

It's a mix of being thrilled to have my party with the worries of the dads lurking in the background. I constantly check the backyard, expecting to see them prowling amongst the trees. I keep an eye on the doors, partly expecting them to creak open on their own, mimicking every spooky movie I've ever seen.

Despite my worries, the party is pretty fun, with three of Adrienne's friends running around with her. Of course, I've been to a birthday party, but I can count how many times on one hand. And those were mostly at school. Lisa has the whole thing orchestrated with snacks and games like pinning the tail on the donkey and even a piñata outside for us. When it's my turn, I don't imagine hitting the dads. I pretend that I'm batting my old self out of existence. She's gone, with this version of me here to stay.

After three swings, I finally hit the mark squarely with force. I take my blindfold off to see Adrienne's friends dashing around the wet grass for the candy. I laugh at seeing Jordan and Sarah join them.

The party goes as perfectly as I could imagine, even though my expectations weren't extreme. Sarah gave me a plant for The Hideout and a cookbook. Lisa, Patrick, and Adrienne gave me a gift card to go shopping. Adrienne also gave me a stuffed animal kitty that looks like Violet. I genuinely love it and hug it affectionately for the rest of the party.

"Hey, do you mind if we go to your place for me to give you your gift?" Jordan asks. It's after things have died down and Adrienne's friends have been picked up. The spotlight isn't on us one bit. Sarah stayed a reasonable amount of time and left for work after giving me a hug that I happily accepted.

"Sure."

We run through the rain that appears to have settled over our area for the night. Violet greets us with a meow while dancing between our legs.

Jordan stays by the door with his hands in his pants

pockets after he hands me a small gift. It's the first time I've seen him fidget. "I hope you enjoy it."

"Enjoy?" I say in a teasing voice. "Yes, sir, I'm sure I'll enjoy it," I say in a goofy deep voice.

I take the small blue box with sweaty hands, unsure what he's gotten me. I open the box and suck in a breath of air. Inside is a pair of dangly earrings with my birthstone swinging from what looks like a gold chain.

"How pretty!" I've had my ears pierced several times over the years but have kept the one regular piercing since I've been here. "I'll definitely *enjoy* these."

He laughs and looks at my lips. "There's something else. This might be lame and old-fashioned. I don't even know if we're supposed to say this out loud these days. I'm just going to ask: will you be my girlfriend?"

Hearing the words out loud sends a rush of happiness through me. It shouldn't be a shock, but it is. I've never been anyone's girlfriend. I've kissed a guy, but that was more like, hey, I've never been kissed, let's take care of that.

"Wow," I say with a nod before looking down.

"I know you're not big on talking, which is fine. I'm not saying that's bad. But does that mean yes?"

I nod again, but he stays quiet, keeping his intense stare on me. "It means yes."

He claps his hands together once in triumph. "Yes! She said yes." He gives me the mega-smile, inching forward for a kiss. A million things run through my mind, and not all of them are regarding what's about to happen. Does Jordan know the real me since he doesn't know about my past? Would he still like me if he knew what I've been involved in?

And yet, I allow him to close the distance between us. I welcome it and what he's offering me.

I purse my lips, hoping I don't let the sudden laugh that has joined me out. Jordan stops, obviously seeing my problem. "What?"

"It's nothing," I say, shaking my head.

"You're about to laugh. What is it?" His head is tilting down with his hair flopping forward in the most adorable way.

"It's just I pictured you eating that huge bite of bread the other night, and for a second thought, I hope he doesn't do that to my mouth." I finally let myself laugh it out, hoping this weird thought process will stop.

Jordan chuckles and reaches his hands out to rest on my hips. His touch does wonders in putting a stop to my joke. Now, with just the task at hand, nothing else clutters my mind.

His mouth certainly does not engulf mine. He barely parts his lips, much to my agreement. It's a sweet, gentle kiss as if he knows I need more of a connection with someone instead of the sexual side of our relationship. I'm sure that will come if we stay together, but for now, it feels good to know that I have friends on my side.

Chapter 29 Lisa

An Unexpected Intervention

I am deep in a session with Josh, discussing my last patient's appointment, when I hear a car pull into my driveway. At first, I think it's the delivery guy or someone turning around. A glance through my front windows shows my mom and sister getting out of the car!

"Uh, Josh, I'm sorry, but I need to go." I pop out of my seat with a near-panicked feeling setting in. "My mother and sister are here for some reason. Probably to tell me how horrible I've been at navigating my life."

"Why would they do that?" he asks with sudden irritation.

"Oh, because that's their way." I look between Josh and my mom, and my sister, who are approaching my front door. I've been putting it off, telling them about the changes in my life. It's not a secret why. I can detect their sneers of judgment as they look around my front yard.

There isn't enough time for me to ask if we can continue our meeting later. "You've touched on this before like it's the norm, and it shouldn't be."

I rush to the door, squeeze myself through the crack, and slam it behind me. "Hey, what are you guys doing here?" I ask in a high voice.

My mother jumps back in surprise. "Lisa, how is that a way to greet company? It's no wonder why you don't have any house guests."

"Who says I don't have house guests?" I say in automatic defense. "I had my birthday par-" On second thought, this is a terrible example. My mother purses her lips in anger.

"That's right, I heard about your farty party," Diane says. "Wish you would have invited me to that one, sis. Have you lost weight?" she asks, grabbing my sides.

I wiggle around, feeling ticklish. "Stop that! You guys, I'm kind of busy right now. Can you come back later?"

"Lisa, this is absurd. You need to let us in!" my mother demands, pushing past me. "For crying out loud, it's raining."

"We know you aren't busy," Diane sings, coming within an inch of my face as she pushes by me. "You don't even have a job yet."

"So that's the only reason a person can be busy?" I ask with my hand on my hip as they scoot by me. Maybe this is a good thing. I've needed to confront them for years, and, ready or not, here they are. Chuggers jumps on my mom and Diane. I let him. Maybe it'll help them decide to leave.

I think of Leira and the monsters she's up against. Sometimes, those monsters are from the outside world. Sometimes, they are the inner demons of negative self-talk. And other times, they are your own flesh and blood.

"Lisa, can you put your dog in your bedroom?" my mother chides.

"He lives here and has a right to be out. It might be a shock, but I'm actually quite busy. Next time, please call or otherwise let me know you're coming over."

"You should be at job interviews," my mom says.

"What makes you think I'm not working?" I throw back.

"Oh, Lisa, stop. Here it is in the middle of the day on Wednesday, and you're home," my sister throws back.

"You're not working right now!" I say. My mom sets a basket on the table and takes a wine bottle out. "Did you want to have a picnic?" I ask in confusion.

"It's an intervention, sis."

"With wine?" I ask with a disbelieving tone.

Josh laughs from the computer, startling my mom and sister to turn in his direction. "I'm sorry; I'm not meaning to mettle, but here we are." Josh turns to a more serious tone that shows he's unafraid of this confrontation. I love the anticipation of a match between these three. "Do you mind me asking what this intervention with Lisa is for?"

"Do you mind me asking who the hell you are?" my sister asks in her snotty voice.

"Diane, rude much?" I scold.

"Well, who is this guy?"

My mom has always huffed and puffed to blow my house down with Diane as her sidekick. She's succeeded time and time again. But not anymore. What have I been doing these last couple of months if it hasn't been to rebuild my foundation with a hefty layer of bricks? I smile, picturing how I've been figuratively rebuilding my house, looping one stitch at a time.

"This guy is my boss," I say, rounding the kitchen table to stand behind my laptop. My mom and sister look at me with the most confused and blank stares I've ever seen. I laugh in response, the sound of my own voice jump-starting my rebuttal. "You two have no idea what I've been up to. You haven't even asked! If anyone needs an intervention here, it's you. Neither of you has had a regular conversation with me aside from telling me how horrible I am for losing my job, for dressing the way I do, for not wearing lipstick... for every decision I make," I snap at them. "Why can't you be more accepting of me, like Dad is?" I've been dreading this very moment for years. Now that I'm here, I'm standing strong, defending myself as only I can. "I am plenty successful without a traditional job, and no, that might not be in the same definition as your idea of success, but it fits mine."

"Lisa, you can't exactly call fifty subscribers on a YouTube channel success."

"I'm almost to one thousand subscribers, and I am growing every day, thank you very much. I have thousands of hours of my content watched. Over the last month, I've filled over a hundred Etsy orders for my blankets and crocheted critters. And Josh here has given me some of his clients to work with. I'm a life coach now."

"A life coach?" my mother snickers.

"Yes, mother, I'm a life coach. I have clients, and I'm helping them. I'm talking through their problems and suggesting how they can help better their lives because that's what I am good at." I hold my hand to my chest, feeling my heart race behind it. I've never talked to my mom or my sister this way. I'm not yelling or being rude, but I am getting my point across.

"Lisa..."

"I'm tired of being the family's black sheep," I say quietly. "Dad has accepted me. I don't know why you two can't. I can't help it if I didn't get the fair skin and lighter hair."

My mother looks at me with a set of confused eyes. It's not her 'feel sorry for me' look, either. This is real.

"Is that what you think, Lisa? That I've been hard on you because you look more like your dad's side of the family?"

"Yup. That and not going into the family business," I answer bluntly. The two give each other a look before I delve deeper. "I have my own life, you guys. It's more than just the numbers. I'm following my heart, my passions, and… I'm happy." I let that percolate for a few moments before putting in my request. "I don't see why that is so bad. I need both of you to stop bossing me around and start being my friend."

"Friend?" my mom asks. I analyze her tone. It's uncertain as if it had never occurred to her to be friends with me.

"Yes, Mom, I want to be friends. With both of you," I say, looking at my sister to include her. "I don't need someone to tell me what to do anymore."

"Lisa, I've always been proud of your Indian heritage. I've never said anything along those lines," my mother starts softly.

"I know," I say with tears clouding my vision. "It was the only thing I could think of why you don't like me."

"That's not true at all," my mom says, regretfully looking me up and down. "I'm sorry I made you feel that way. I just want you to be happy, and work is what makes us happy." The three of us stare at each other in silence, no one knowing what to say. "I guess I have been hard on you."

"I'm not in the family business," I shrug.

"But I am, and that should be good enough. Right, mom?" Diane says, her tone changing to softness.

"Gosh, it doesn't bother me that you aren't a physician, Lisa." She looks down and wipes a tear. "I'm sorry you haven't felt accepted. I don't know how to make it up to you."

"There's no better way to make friends than over a picnic," Josh suggests from behind the computer.

I curl my lips in to stifle a laugh. I keep quiet, waiting for one of them to make their move on the offer. After a moment, with the two staring each other down, my mother sets the wine bottle down and lays her hands on the picnic basket. It could go either way. She could push off and leave my house for good, or agree to my suggestion of easing up enough to be my friend.

She takes her sweet ass time thinking it over! I look at Josh with my eyes big and my hand up as if to say, 'What gives.'

"Well, this soup and bread are best served warm," she says, sitting. I look at Diane, who gives me a wink, picks up my latest crocheted blanket, and holds it to her stomach as she sits down. *Finally*, they're on my side. For the first time, I've won them over.

***

I can barely describe my elation after a day of appointments, filming and uploading a video, answering comments, filling my Etsy orders, and *reconciling with my mom and sister!* I even got dinner ready, and the house is relatively clean.

It's everything I've wanted, and yet, something is missing.

Amy asked to pick Adrienne up so our kids could have a play date. I agreed and am using this time to finish my Etsy orders and drop them off at the post office. My phone dings with Amy's picture showing our kids happily playing together.

I'm fiddling with the back of my van, sorting orders, when two men in dirty clothes catch my eye, loitering outside the post office. They're standing close enough for me to notice them eyeing the same missing poster of Leira I've seen around town. I don't claim to know every face in Garden Valley, but I've got a knack for reading people, and these two are worse than a group of boys with a bucket of tomatoes.

My instincts scream at me as I cautiously approach the building, keeping one eye on them the whole time. I instinctively know why they're here more than I know how to do a v-stitch. These are the guys looking for Leira.

Taking the long way around, I enter the post office and handle my business quickly, but they're still lurking when I step back outside. A chill runs down my spine. I know without a doubt that their presence spells trouble—for Leira and probably me too.

"Excuse me?" It's one of the men. I turn and see that both of them are looking at me from only a few feet away.

"Yes?"

"Have you seen this girl?" The man points to the poster on the window. They both start walking, quickly closing the distance between us.

"Nope. I saw that poster earlier but haven't seen anyone who looks like her. I know everyone in town and would know that face." As I talk, I start to edge away, the urge to bolt overpowering the intuition I've kept dialed up to high alert.

I'm talking too fast to be believable. It's more than bold of me to speak to them; it's downright stupid! At the same time, I want to defend Leira and steer them away.

They look me up and down as they continue to walk my way. The cloud of smoke surrounding them has soaked into their skin in layers, giving them a rugged, greasy look.

I turn to walk faster to my car. I can feel their presence behind me. I put the keys squarely in between my knuckles to give them a jab if it comes to that. Their quickened footsteps indicate that it just might. One of the men has peeled off to go to their car while I can see the other gaining on my left. Regret replaces the boldness I felt just thirty seconds ago. Why didn't I ignore them and run? The police station isn't even a mile away.

I unlock my van but don't make it in time before one of the guys wraps his hand around my elbow.

"Hey, let go of me!" I wiggle with all my might, but I'm no match for this man who's at least a foot taller than me.

He comes within an inch of my face. His gravely voice alone scares me silly. "Since you know everyone in town, maybe you can tell us who Amber at the inn is."

Chapter 30 Leira

A Fly in the Web

My mind is miles away while my body is here at school. I fear a black cloud heading my way. Something is wrong, and I don't think it's my imagination this time. I rush out of class when our instructor dismisses us, not even thinking about walking with Sarah. I was just in one of the afternoon culinary labs. We were supposed to make a master recipe, but I mostly sat in a worried daze. Luckily, we had partners, and Sarah didn't seem to notice.

"Hey, there." It's Jordan, waiting for me outside of class. The campus is mostly empty. I wonder why our teacher chose Friday afternoon to schedule our lab sessions. "I just got off work at the registrar's office. Ready for dinner?"

"Oh, Jordan, I forgot. I can't go," I say bluntly. My instincts tell me I should be home with Lisa and her family tonight, not to be out and about where I'll be an easy target. I've decided I need to open up to them about my past, ready for their healing words and shields of whatever protection they can provide. "I'm not feeling very good. I'd rather just go home." I don't care if this is too blunt for him. I start to scan the darkened campus, but he stops me with a hand on my shoulder and a furrowed brow.

"Hey, what's wrong?"

I spin around, not wanting his touch to confine me. "Nothing."

"You can tell me. It's okay."

I've wanted to tell him, but I don't think his innocence can handle it. My phone rings with a number I don't recognize. Do I dare answer it? Even if it is one of the dads, don't I want this to be over? Don't I need to confront them and tell them that their adult daughter isn't coming back home?

"Hello?"

"Leira, is that you?"

"Patrick? What's wrong?" I ask in a rushed voice.

"Nothing's wrong. Well, I don't think so. Is Lisa with you? She didn't pick Adrienne up from Amy's. That's not like her, so I figured maybe the two of you were at the fabric store or something. She gave me your number a week ago and was all serious. I'm sure it's nothing."

Oh, if it were that easy. I pause when my eyes land on a figure in front of me stepping from behind a tree. "Leira, what's wrong?" Jordan asks, focusing his attention on me. I don't answer.

I've seen his false outline several times in town, but it's for real now. This time, the figure is standing in the rain about a hundred feet from me. A few feet back, Gary is holding Lisa by the arm.

"Patrick," I whisper into the phone. I'm nearly frozen. I'm surprised I even have my voice. "You need to come to the college. *Now.*"

"The college. Is Lisa there?" he asks in confusion.

"Yes, and it's not good. *Come now.*"

"Okay, let me get Adrienne first."

"NO! Leave her where she is. Do you understand me? *Do not* bring her with you. She's safer that way."

"Safer? Are you okay? Leira, what's going on?"

I don't have the capacity to answer him. I hang up, hoping this will drive the urgency home for Patrick.

"Leira, who are those guys?" Jordan asks in an unsure voice. I've almost forgotten that he's next to me. I finally break my staring contest with the dads and flicker my eyes at him.

"Nothing good is going to come of this. Jordan, you need to leave. Go get campus security."

"I'm not going to leave you," Jordan says with certainty, understanding a glimmer about what's going on.

It's my worst nightmare, having them show up at school seeming to hold Lisa hostage. Upon first glance she appears to be unharmed. Having them show up at all is awful, let alone in public like this. And on my turf! I roll my shoulders back, ready for the bitching session I'm about to give these two. It'll resemble a Chiwawa bawling out a Doberman Pincher, but still, I've got to try to stand up for myself.

I walk to them, fully aware that I don't have the ability to fly or have superhuman strength. Still, I conjure all the fake confidence I can muster. Jordan walks with me, ignoring my advice to leave.

"You don't have to be here. This could get ugly. It's not a side of me that you've seen before."

"Like I'm going to leave you alone with these guys. Who are they?" He doesn't know all the facts, but I have a feeling the pieces are connecting for him. My flinches and false visions aren't fake.

"You found me," I say with irritation and a cock of my head. "And it looks like you have Lisa. *Let her go.*" I glance at

'Grit' in the parking lot, wishing I could hop in the mini-sized truck and flee. *Superheroes don't flee, they face their fights.* The thought adds a snarl to my lip, readying me to stand firm.

"It's not that easy, Ariel," Gary says through clenched teeth. Jordan quickly turns to me at the mention of my real name. "Do you know what we had to go through to find you? How many sales we've lost?"

"Hey, I didn't ask you to come after me. You don't need me! Just get a frickin' maid!" I boldly yell. Phil steps forward to grab me, but Jordan steps between us.

"You don't know what you're dealing with here, hick boy." The muscles in his neck are flexed as he continues to approach me.

"We don't need to do this!" I yell, stepping back with my hands up for emphasis. "I'm not coming home with you, so just go away and forget about me!"

Phil takes a swing at Jordan while he's looking at me. It's a cheap shot, but nonetheless, it does the trick. Jordan falls to the ground, holding his chin. I bend to help him, but Phil pulls me back.

"That was shitty!" I yell. "Your filth doesn't belong in this town!"

Phil hoists me up and holds me close enough that I can smell the weed and alcohol on his breath. "It doesn't matter what you've done with your hair or clothes, Ariel. We know what our little girl looks like." It feels odd to have him handling me like this. This is one of the only times he has ever touched me.

I struggle against his force with as much strength as a feather against a hurricane. "You can't just yank me out of town!"

"I can when you've run away from us. You don't belong

here, Ariel."

"That's not my name anymore! That's not who I am." I plow my free elbow into Phil's gut, turn, and give a swift kick right between his legs. I want to flee from these two monsters of my past, but Gary still has Lisa. One look her way shows her struggling to free herself.

I advance on Gary, aiming to help her. He keeps me away with his one free hand for a few seconds, but these feet want to connect with more balls. I kick my foot, but he deflects my violence. I swing again, and Gary grabs onto my foot. He lets go of Lisa now that he has me.

"Leira!" The voice rings over the sound of the rain, alerting me that Jordan has come after me like a fool.

"No!" I don't want him to mingle in this mess. He's too young and innocent to be up against the years of harshness that are Phil and Gary. I'm hoping around like an idiot since Gary has my foot. Lisa stands from the ground with blood running out of her nose. It all enrages me further. I wish I had more weight and muscle to push around and defend us all.

"Leave me alone! I don't want to be with you!" I scream in Gary's face. "Do your dirty work yourselves. I swear I won't tell anyone." A few people have gathered around to watch. It's embarrassing to be kicking and screaming against him. Lisa jumps on Gary's back, pushing him forward and loosening his grip on me. "Jordan, run!"

But he doesn't. He comes for me as the rain smears blood down his face. Phil tackles him from behind, and the two fall to the ground in a heap. Jordan holds his own at first as they tumble through puddles and mud. He sits atop Phil and gets a good punch directly at his nose. His victory, unfortunately, doesn't last long.

Phil isn't in the dominant position, but it doesn't matter.

He lifts his upper body, giving him the power to punch Jordan. It hits him in the jaw again with a crack that makes me cringe. It throws him off guard enough to allow Phil to toss him on the ground and gain the upper hand. Phil swings wildly at him with punch after punch.

"No, Jordan," I whimper. My voice has the sound of someone who has given up. It's hopeless to fight them. Everything happening is the opposite of what I've been building for the last two months.

I look back in time to see Gary throw Lisa off his back. She falls to the ground with an 'umph' sound. She bounces back up, screaming and coming at Gary with her nails out. He deflects her again, easily pushing her back to the wet ground.

Phil has grown tired from beating Jordan's face and stands to join our dysfunctional threesome. Lisa comes back for more, still willing to fight for me. Phil and Gary each take a step before me, unwilling to give up.

"Enough!" I scream, wiggling between them and turning to face them. I throw my arms in the air and give Lisa a look that makes her stop. "I'll come with you. Just stop this!" I glance at Jordan, knowing he's badly hurt, but at least he's moving to wipe his face. "I give up," I say in defeat, knowing I've lost.

I'll return with them for now, but it doesn't mean I'm giving up. Right now, my friends are worth more than their sacrifice for me. They've stood up to these goons more than I ever could.

"Just leave them alone. I'll come back home with you."

"Like hell, you will." The voice through the rain is unmistakably Patrick's. This fight, it seems, isn't over. "Lisa, come here, babe." Lisa looks at me as she trots sideways to her husband. He wraps an arm around her and stands firm.

He holds a fierce stare with water dripping down his face. For such a nice man, Patrick has quite a presence when angry.

A guy I recognize helps Jordan off the ground, his cell phone up to his ear. Several people keep their distance, all with their phones either recording the scene or holding it up to their ears, no doubt reporting the disturbance. My psychology professor starts our way, but thankfully, something more powerful stops the dads. Sirens approach from the distance, snapping both Gary and Phil straight.

"Guess who knows the sheriff in town?" Patrick says with a grin. "Come here. I want to make sure you stay still for the police." Patrick stomps to them as faint red police lights bounce off his face.

"Let's go!" Phil says, sprinting away.

"You think you've seen the last of me?" Gary growls out.

"Yes, we do," Lisa snarls. "Because everyone in town loves your daughter, and we'll *all* fight for her."

Gary backs away slowly with his eyes on me as if he's still toying with the idea of taking me with him. Phil pulls up and shouts from the driver's side of the Plymouth. Gary jumps in, and the whole ordeal is over in what seems like two seconds.

The rusty car screeches around the corner. I fall in a heap to the ground, the letdown from the adrenaline rush having drained me. Lisa rushes to me, falling on her knees to stretch her arms around me.

"It's over. They're gone," she says, hugging me to her chest. For the first time, I believe her words to be true.

I'm finally free.

Chapter 31

The Final Thread

I thought it would take a while to get over the ordeal of seeing the dads. Lisa's family took me in like a momma bird snuggling her baby under her wing. They've done this already, but I can fully allow the comfort of their safety this time.

It's a cozy December evening at Lisa's house. Snow drifts silently outside as we sit by the fire. I could sit here for days, enjoying her decorations and beautiful blinking tree.

Every day this month has been a special event that I've been involved in. We decorated the tree, drank hot chocolate, and have eaten more than a few platefuls of goodies. My pants are noticeably tighter, which Lisa says looks good on me.

"Cinnamon rolls are rising in the oven, and Jordan and Beatrice should be here soon," Lisa says. Before she finishes her sentence, the doorbell rings. But it's not just any ring; it's in the tune of 'Jingle Bells.'

Jordan's face has healed nicely from his many bruises and a gash above his eye that needed stitches. Now that it's several weeks later, he finally looks back to his old self.

"Hi," I say, standing close and looking into the face of

the person who fought for me. I'll never forget how these people didn't second guess the fight for my freedom.

"Merry Christmas, Leira," Jordan says with a tiny kiss on my nose. Adrienne comes up and stands by us. "Yes?" Jordan asks, looking down at her.

She holds up four fingers. "Four bites," is all she says.

"Oh yeah? Three," Jordan answers.

"What's going on?" I ask.

"You'll see," Lisa answers, getting themed paper plates out.

I dig into a gooey, warm cinnamon roll, and I've never tasted anything like it. "These cinnamon rolls are amazing." I admire Lisa's crocheted snowflakes and tree decorations. Mine aren't too bad if I say so myself, but she's the master.

There was no stopping her from making Christmas ornaments and decorations once she fully immersed herself in the season. She has shared the joy of family traditions with me, seeming to get through the grief of not having her Nana here.

Jordan plays a game with Patrick and Adrienne to see if the huge cinnamon rolls can be bite-sized. I guess I'm not the only one who has teased Jordan for having a big mouth. I pretend to join them, loving the howls of their laughter as I do the opposite of their rules and take the tiniest bite my teeth can pinch off.

"Don't choke on it now," Beatrice warns.

It's yet another activity that includes me. It doesn't matter if I'm sometimes blunt or quiet during others. They've accepted me and like me for who I am.

I took pride in helping Lisa with the family cinnamon roll recipe. I help her with a few dinners throughout the week, learning about different flavors and techniques firsthand. I've decided to stay in the culinary class, even though I've found my passion with psychology . It's fun to dream up crazy connections between a career in food and psychology. Sarah and I do this in between classes. We keep Lisa in mind with her combination of yarn and mental health coping techniques.

We sit by the fire in Lisa's living room after our tummies are full of sweet bread. It's a picturesque scene with snow falling outside and stockings on the mantel. It's one that I could never have dreamed of.

We take turns handing out presents to each other. I hold the ones I have for others tightly to my stomach. It sounds weird, but I'm self-conscious about my wrapping and worried if they'll like the gifts I bought. I've wrapped maybe two or three presents in my life. Violet helped me in this area, showing her adventure side by hiding under the paper and throwing her paws underneath.

Patrick has already shown Lisa the new office desk he made for the guest room. It's her space to make videos and be on Zoom calls with her clients. Her happy squeals were so loud I'm sure their neighbors down the street heard.

"One other gift," Patrick says, handing over a long cylinder.

"What the heck is this?" Lisa asks with a huge smile. Inside is a huge piece of paper with sketches she eyes with confusion.

"These are some plans to remodel the office. I thought since you're going to be working in there so much, maybe you'd like to open it up with some French doors," Patrick says. Lisa sits with her mouth open, now studying the sketches with a sense of knowledge on her face. "Do you like it?" Patrick finally asks.

"Like it? You bet you cute little tushy I like it!" She leans over and throws her arms around her husband, smacking a big kiss on his cheek.

"Phew," Patrick says, sinking down and pretending to wipe sweat from his forehead. "Since I'm off for a couple of weeks this month, I thought I'd get started. Darren said he'd come over tomorrow and help me out."

"Patrick, I... I just don't even know what to say," Lisa stumbles.

"Well, there's a first for everything." The rest of us chuckle, taking our time to enjoy this special moment.

Lisa hands Patrick an envelope as one of his presents. Her smile is so broad it can barely fit on her face. "My turn. Go ahead, open it. Open it, open it, open it!"

"Okay, okay," Patrick says, working his fingers in the envelope. He pulls out a check, and his face is enough of a surprise to satisfy Lisa. I can see the 'giver's satisfaction' on her face from the other person liking the present. I'm after this, too, especially with the Swiss Army knife I got for Jordan.

"It's from YouTube! I'm monetized!" I glance over and see the check for $217. "It's not a ton, but I have almost two thousand subscribers now! They've said once you reach the one thousand subscriber mark it's a straight line up, and it's true in my case. Every video posted adds to my backlist of what can be watched. The more videos and subscribers I have, the more income I make."

"That's great, hon."

"That's not all." Lisa hands him another envelope, this time with a picture of a spa inside.

"You didn't!" Patrick asks with a grin.

"A spa!" Adrienne exclaims, jumping up and doing a

twirl.

"You've been sore for far too many years, my dear." She leans over and plants a peck on his cheek.

I look on with inspiration. Here is this woman who had a wrench thrown in her life when she got fired, and she used it to build something she loves and is proud of. I can use these words to describe myself, too. What can I say? I learn from the best.

"Now, where is that one present for Leira?" Lisa asks, looking under the wrapping paper piled on the floor before finding it under Chuggers. "Let me have that, sir," she says, pulling it from under him. Lisa hands me a large brown envelope. I have no idea what this means, and I open it in front of everyone. I pull the papers out and study the top that says 'official adoption papers.'

"Do you want me to adopt a child?" I ask, confused. Lisa and Patrick smile and look at each other.

"Leira, I know you're nineteen, but we were wondering if you would like to join our family," Lisa says softly.

"Does that mean Leira would be my sister?" Adrienne yells as she hops to her feet again.

"That's exactly what that would mean," Lisa confirms with a teary nod. "It's a surprise for both of you."

"I don't know what to say." And I don't.

"You're not just a tenant in the back. You're family," Patrick adds.

Yes, I want this, but I don't want to bring any more drama to these people who have already put up with enough from me. "It's in the past," Lisa says as if reading my mind. "Your dads are in jail now. Busted for all their wrong-doings."

"I have a feeling that they will be there for a while,"

Beatrice says. It's more than a relief to be rid of them and the cigarettes that linked me to my past. I look at Jordan with expectant eyes. He nods with a smile that matches how I feel inside. I smile back fully without a bite of my lip in sight.

For the first time, I can finally let go of my door wedge. I don't need to shut people out anymore.

I nod, my eyes filling with tears that I hope show just how much this moment means to me. This family has been with me throughout my journey in Garden Valley, helping me piece my life back together in ways I never thought possible.

I pinch myself, half-expecting to wake up from this perfect dream.

"What's that for?" Beatrice laughs.

"It's just... everything's so perfect. Thank you all. I'd love to be your adopted daughter and your sister, little Munchkin." I bend down, pulling Adrienne into a hug. Before I know it, Lisa and Patrick join in, their arms wrapping around us both, and I allow the warmth of the embrace to fully seep into me.

At nineteen, most of my life has felt like an uphill battle, and I didn't really believe I could make it through.

But here I am, taking Lisa's advice from her videos to go after what I want, even when it seemed impossible. It hasn't been easy, but I didn't give up. I'm finally embracing my true superpower: finding peace with my past, looking forward to the future, and, for the first time, trusting the loved ones who stand beside me.

Thank you for reading Coping With Yarn! I would sincerely appreciate if you would give me a review.

Ready to dive deeper into the charm of Garden Valley? Meet Joanie in *Welcome to Garden Valley* as she shakes things up in the heartwarming town everyone's talking about! Plus, if you love freebies (who doesn't?), sign up for my newsletter at www.jeanshelbybooks.com and get a FREE copy of *Winter in July*. Cozy up with these delightful stories today!

Stay tuned for my next release, From A to Z, coming out in January, 2025.

Want to officially become a 'Jeanie?' Join my private Facebook club, 'The Jeanie Book Club!'

Jean Shelby writes heartwarming, witty Women's Fiction that leaves readers laughing, tearing up, and always wanting more. Nestled in the scenic beauty of Southern Oregon, Jean balances life as an author, wife, and a proud mother of two lively girls. Her stories are inspired by the chaos and charm of motherhood, aiming to inspire and entertain with relatable characters and uplifting themes. When not crafting her next novel, she's either making memories with her family, playing the piano, or swimming laps. Get cozy—you just might find a piece of yourself in her books!

Connect with Jean:

Website: https://jeanshelbybooks.com